D1561366

The Uneven Road

Linda Cardillo

BOOK TWO OF
First Light

BELLASTORIA PRESS
Books that nurture the soul

ISBN: 978-1-942209-23-2

The Uneven Road

Cover photo by Stephan J. W. Platzer

BELLASTORIA PRESS
P.O. Box 60341
Longmeadow, Massachusetts 01116

For Stephan

An old man cocked his ear upon a bridge;
He and his friend, their faces to the South,
Had trod the uneven road. Their boots were soiled,
Their Connemara cloth worn out of shape;
They had kept a steady pace as though their beds,
Despite a dwindling and late risen moon,
Were distant. An old man cocked his ear.

William Butler Yeats, "The Phases of the Moon"

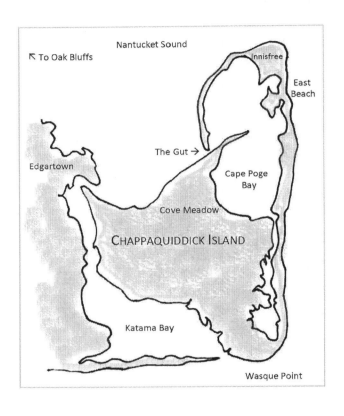

Nantucket Sound

↖ To Oak Bluffs

Innisfree

East Beach

The Gut →

Edgartown

Cape Poge Bay

Cove Meadow

CHAPPAQUIDDICK ISLAND

Katama Bay

Wasque Point

1955
Cape Poge
Chappaquiddick Island
Martha's Vineyard

Chapter 1

"On the grey sand beside the shallow stream"
Josiah

"Izzy, come on! Mom's waiting for these last buckets of quahogs for the chowder. It's almost lunch time and I can see boats heading over to the dock already."

Josiah called to his sister from the base of the rough-hewn steps that led up from the clam flat to the promontory where his family's house perched overlooking Poge Bay. Beyond the house were Betty's cottage and then his family's Boat House Café itself, where his mother and Betty were busy in the kitchen preparing for the lunch crowd. It was late June, a week before the Fourth of July, and summer people had begun arriving, swelling not only the population of Chappaquiddick but also the number of bowls of chowder his mother needed to fill every day.

It was hot, with not even a light breeze to lift the Stars-and-Stripes. It was his job to raise the flag every morning, the signal that the café was open. He wiped the sweat running down his forehead. He and Izzy had been out in the shallows raking for clams since the tide had run out a few hours ago.

Although she was only seven, Izzy could wield a rake pretty well and usually filled her bucket almost as fast as he could. Her bucket was smaller, of course, suspended like his in the middle of an old inner tube that floated as she moved over her patch of the bed. They each had their own territory. Their dad, Tobias, had settled their squabbling one day last summer when Josiah had thrown up his hands in frustration that he couldn't do his job right when Izzy was close. He worried that he'd accidentally run the rake over her foot or knock her over as he pulled the rake through the sand.

Josiah worried about Izzy a lot. She was five years younger than he was. His parents sometimes called her their miracle baby, a child they never expected to have because his mom had been so sick. He worried because Izzy was a dreamer, her mind often someplace else instead of paying attention—like the day when a monster wave rolling in on East Beach was about to swallow both her and the sand castle she was building. He had raced to pull her away just in time.

He called to her again. She was kneeling at the edge of the shallow pool of stagnant water that filled a dip in the sand along the shore of Shear Pen Pond. She was braced on her hands, staring at something in the water. It made him think of the myth his English teacher had made the class read. Narcissus had admired his reflection so much that he fell in love with it and drowned. Josiah shook off the creepy feeling that came over him. Izzy couldn't drown in that shallow water. Besides, she knew how to swim. His dad had said island children learned to swim almost before they could walk. It was stupid to think Izzy would come to harm watching whatever it was that had so captured her attention.

He stalked over to the water and picked up Izzy's bucket.

"I'm not going to wait for you another minute. Mom needs the clams. Don't be late for lunch."

He shrugged, realizing that she probably hadn't heard him. He knew it would mean that he'd have to come back to get her, but he wasn't going to drag her away. He trudged up the steps with both buckets, the clams knocking together as he swung his arms. It was too hot for chowder, he decided. Instead, he'd eat his clams raw.

He remembered the first time he'd tasted a raw clam. He'd been down on that same beach with his dad, younger than Izzy was now. Tobias had raked up a full bucket and set it on the sand, beckoning Josiah to pick out one clam. Josiah had studied them for a long time and finally pulled one out of the pile, the coarse white and gray striations of its shell swirling with precision from its hinge. Tobias took the clam and slipped a short blade between the two halves, prying them apart to reveal the flesh. He rinsed off the morsel in the sea and handed it to Josiah. He tipped it into his mouth, tasting the brine and feeling the different textures—the soft, tender belly and the tougher foot—against his mouth. He wiped his mouth with the back of his hand and grinned at his father. Tobias grinned back and then they made their way back up to the house. When Josiah was older, Tobias had taught him how to wield the knife and Josiah had offered his first shucked clam to Izzy, right here on this beach.

Now, when Josiah got to the top of the steps he looked back at his sister, still crouched over the water, oblivious to the heat and the bugs. He turned reluctantly toward the café with his laden buckets, knowing his mother was waiting for him but feeling uneasy about leaving Izzy. His eyes didn't detect any danger—no storm clouds were gathering over East Beach, no brush fires were smoldering on the edge of the woods. But he sensed something hovering over his sister, unseen and menacing, and it made his skin prickle.

Chapter 2

"I have walked and prayed for this young child"
Mae

Mae was shucking quahogs on the wooden table behind the Boat House Café when she saw the tall, athletic woman shepherding three children along the path that led from East Beach. The children, two boys and a girl, looked to be around Jo and Izzy's ages; and like her own children, they were bursting with pent-up energy after being cooped up inside after three days of unrelenting rain.

The sun had finally broken through this morning, heralding what Mae anticipated would be a busy day at the café as other mothers, driven to distraction trying to contain and entertain their children, would join her.

Most of Mae's customers arrived at the café by boat, but a cottage had been built just west of the lighthouse. Mae guessed that the family making its way along the meadow were the people Frank Bennett had told her were renting the new place.

"Yoo-hoo! Is this the Boat House Café?" The woman strode up to Mae, one hand clasping the hand of the little girl, the youngest of the three children, while the boys ran ahead to the dock.

"Boys, stay away from the edge!"

Mae put down her knife, wiped her hands and stuck one out in greeting.

"This is indeed the café. Welcome! I'm Mae Monroe, the proprietor."

"I'm Lydia Hammond. This is my daughter, Susan, and the hellions are Richard and Louis. Do you know if there are any other children out here?"

Mae smiled. "There are—my own. I have a twelve-year-old son, Josiah—we call him Jo—and a seven-year-old daughter, Isabella, who answers to Izzy. From what I can guess, around your children's ages."

"Oh, thank God! Frank mentioned there were children nearby, but with all the rain, we haven't seen another soul—child or adult—since we arrived."

"Well, come on into the café and we can acquaint the children with one another when mine get back from clamming. Where are you folks from?"

Mae picked up the bowl of shucked clams and led Lydia through the back door and into the kitchen.

Betty, Mae's best friend and the heart of the Boat House Café, was at the counter, peeling potatoes.

"Mae, have you got some clams ready for the chowder?"

"Here you are. Betty, this is Lydia. She's renting that new cottage beyond the lighthouse."

"Welcome, Lydia! How long will you be staying?"

"We've rented the cottage for the whole summer. My husband is a cardiologist in Philadelphia and will probably come up on weekends. But I'll be here with the kids till the end of August. Speaking of which, I better go round up the boys and get them settled at a table before they wind up in the water."

She moved purposefully through the swinging door into the dining room.

"She seems down-to-earth for a city doctor's wife," said Betty, watching her go.

"It will be different, having another family within walking distance of Innisfree," Mae mused. When she had first returned to Chappaquiddick in 1941, Mae had purchased an abandoned fishing camp on a remote patch of meadow and woods on Cape Poge, not far from the lighthouse at the northern tip of the island. She had named her land "Innisfree" after the Yeats poem beloved by her Irish mother and as a memento of the cottage across the bay where Mae had grown up, which her mother had also called Innisfree.

"Different good or bad?" Betty never missed an opportunity to zero in on Mae's concerns.

Mae shrugged. "I'm not sure. I know the kids are lonely sometimes, especially Jo. Having a seven-year-old sister as your only playmate can get boring really fast. I was surrounded by siblings and neighborhood kids growing up and loved it. I can't expect Jo and Izzy to appreciate the solitude the way Tobias and I do now. I guess I knew this part of the island would change eventually, with more people wanting to stay for longer than a day trip to the beach. I just don't know if I'm ready for it."

"Well, one family is not exactly an onslaught. And she seems decent."

Mae peered through the glass in the door as Lydia corralled her boys at a table near the front of the dining room overlooking the dock. Lydia struck Mae as a woman who had everything effortlessly under control. Despite the rain, she already had a glowing tan and her long-limbed, graceful body looked less like that of a mother of three and more like an Olympic athlete. The figure skater Sonja Henie popped into Mae's head, an odd image in the midst of this steamy late June morning. But there was definitely something Nordic about Lydia.

Mae shook off the creeping insecurities Lydia's arrival had unleashed. Betty was right. It would be great for Jo and Izzy to have playmates this summer.

At that moment, Jo pushed open the screen door into the kitchen.

"I brought up the last of the quahogs and left them on the table outside."

"There you are, Jo." Mae looked past him. "Where's Izzy?"

"She's lost in one of her other worlds at the tidal pool. I think she's watching a crab. I brought her bucket up."

"We've already got customers. Please wash up and then take the orders of the family who just arrived. After that, I need you to shuck the clams. Betty and I are going to be too busy between the dining room and the kitchen."

He nodded. She knew he'd be pleased to be trusted with the shucking, less so with working the front of the house. A little too much like her when it came to strangers.

She turned to Betty.

"I'm going to fetch Izzy. If I don't, she'll be there all afternoon."

Mae covered the ground between the café and the steps down to the sand flats on Shear Pen Pond quickly. The lunch crowd was arriving. She could see a couple of boats approaching the dock, and she knew Betty would have her hands full in the kitchen.

She called out to Izzy as she approached the steps, but didn't hear a reply. She was less worried than exasperated. She knew Izzy was a dawdler and a daydreamer. She checked her impatience as she headed down the steps. Just as Jo had described, Izzy was crouched on the sand intently studying a tiny crab inching its way toward the water.

"Izzy, lunch time. Let's get these rakes put away and you washed up."

Izzy looked up at Mae, slightly dazed as she was pulled out of her reverie.

Mae was used to seeing her daughter's attention somewhere other than the present moment, but the expression on Izzy's face was disturbing. She saw pain, confusion, disorientation. Her little girl was lost somewhere inside herself.

Mae reached out and stroked Izzy's face. Her skin was hot, more than expected after a morning in the sun.

"Honey, do you feel OK?"

"I feel funny, Mama. All wobbly. That's why I sat down. I think I'm going to throw up." And she did, onto the poor crab.

Mae wiped Izzy's face with the edge of her apron and scooped her up in her arms. She was a lightweight, their hummingbird, Tobias had called her. She flitted from one absorption to another, drinking in the world around her.

Izzy moaned softly in Mae's arms, where Mae was even more aware of the heat emanating from her daughter's body. She climbed swiftly up the stairs and into the cottage, where she settled Izzy on her bed.

"I'll be right back, Hummingbird. I'm just going to run over to the Boat House to let Betty know I'll be staying with you."

Mae ran to the café unencumbered by the weight of her daughter. She burst into the kitchen from the back door, out of breath.

Betty wheeled around.

"What's happened? Something with Izzy?" Betty rushed to Mae's side.

"She's sick. Feels like a fever and she just upchucked her breakfast. I'm sorry. You're going to have to handle lunch alone while I figure out what's going on. Give my apologies to the new neighbor."

"I'll manage. Jo's taking orders. I think he's trying to make up for the fact that he left his sister. I'll check in on you as soon as it quiets down after lunch."

Mae was sponging Izzy with lukewarm water to cool her when she heard a knock at the door and the voice of Lydia Hammond. She tucked a sheet around Izzy and went to the door.

"I heard from Betty that your little girl is sick. I'm not trying to intrude, but I thought I'd offer my help. I'm a nurse."

"Thanks. I wouldn't want to expose your kids if she has something contagious . . ." Mae looked beyond Lydia, but her children were nowhere in sight.

"I've left them at the café. Betty apparently has things under control with some homemade donuts. Is there somewhere I can wash my hands?"

Mae led her through the house to the kitchen and then to Izzy's room.

Lydia was gentle with Izzy, asking her a few questions before turning to Mae.

"Why don't we let Izzy rest? You and I can talk about what will help her feel better."

Lydia took Mae by the elbow and guided her out to the front porch.

"I'm not going to sugarcoat this. It has all the marks of the early stage of polio. I saw several cases during the '52 epidemic. My recommendation would be to get her to the hospital today. I don't suppose Chappy has an ambulance that could make it out here."

Mae froze as she listened to the words coming out of Lydia's mouth. A part of her resisted what this woman who had swooped so emphatically into their lives was saying. Why should she trust her or even believe she was a nurse? But if Lydia was right, Izzy was gravely ill. Mae had no choice but to follow her advice. She shook herself out of her numbness.

"There's a firetruck, but it'd be faster to take her by boat."

"What can I do to help?"

"Please go back to the café and tell Betty to close up for the rest of the day, and ask Jo to get the boat ready. You probably want to get your children away from here."

"They were vaccinated this spring. What about yours?"

"The island had a clinic in May. Both kids got shots. I thought the vaccine was supposed to protect them?"

"It should. But no vaccine is 100% effective. At the very least, it may reduce the severity of the infection for your daughter. I'll get things going while you get her ready to transport. We have a ham radio at our cottage. I can call ahead to the hospital to let them know you're coming. I'll see if I can get an ambulance to meet you at the dock."

Mae nodded. "I'm grateful to you."

Lydia left for the café while Mae wrapped Izzy in a cotton blanket. She was still burning up as she carried her to the dock.

Jo was waiting at the wheel of the boat and Betty stood ready to cast off as soon as Mae and Izzy were settled in the stern.

"Do you want me to come with? The café is locked up."

Mae squeezed her hand. "You always know what I need before I do. Yes, come."

Jo pulled away from the dock as Betty clambered aboard. Within minutes they were slipping through the Gut, the narrow mouth of the bay, and speeding across the water to Oak Bluffs.

"We need to get word to Tobias," Mae mouthed to Betty over the drone of the engine.

"I'll take care of it when we get to shore. Let's hope Lydia got through and an ambulance is waiting for you."

As Jo skimmed into the harbor they could see the flashing lights. He maneuvered the boat into a slip and arms were reaching out for Izzy before he had killed the engine.

Mae climbed up to follow.

"I'll stay behind with Jo to get the boat secured. We'll meet you at the hospital." Betty gave Mae a hug.

The ride to the hospital was a blur of activity and questions as the rescue squad took Izzy's vital signs, inserted an IV and asked Mae about Izzy's symptoms. As she answered, she sought reassurance that the situation was not as dire as she feared from Lydia's diagnosis.

"My neighbor, a nurse, thought it might be polio," she whispered, turning away briefly from Izzy's frightened face.

The two technicians looked at one another across Izzy.

"We had another case a couple of days ago. A child from the elementary school, a second-grader."

"Izzy is in second grade." Mae rubbed her forehead. She didn't want this other piece of information, this accumulating evidence that Lydia might, after all, be right.

"Mama, it hurts," Izzy whimpered.

"I know, Hummingbird. I'm sorry. We'll be there soon and the doctor will help make you better."

Mae wanted to believe that Izzy would be made better, but everything she knew about polio offered little hope.

Izzy was Tobias and Mae's miracle child, born against challenging odds. When Mae had given birth to Josiah in 1943, she and Tobias were together, but not married. Because of tribal issues stirred up by Tobias' cousin Sadie, Mae did not want to stand in the way of Tobias' leadership of the tribe. But then Mae had been diagnosed with cancer. It was during her treatment that her older sister, Kathleen, attempted to gain custody of Jo and remove him from Mae's care. The crisis rallied support for Mae and Tobias from islanders and tribal members, and Mae agreed to marry Tobias to strengthen their legal standing as Josiah's parents. Mae had already lost a child—a daughter—to stillbirth, when she had been very young and alone, before returning to Chappy. To have another child snatched from her was more than she could bear. But Mae and Tobias prevailed in court, Mae's cancer went into remission, and the marriage Mae had feared would hold Tobias back had instead flourished. Tobias was elected sachem, or chief, taking on the mantle his father had borne before him.

One shadow hovered over them, however. Mae's doctors informed her that because of the side effects of her chemotherapy, she'd most likely not have any more children. She and Tobias had accepted the news. She was alive. Josiah was safe with them. They were grateful for all they *did* have and did not dwell on what might have been.

And then Mae had become pregnant. Her doctors cautioned her to expect a difficult pregnancy that might end in miscarriage or stillbirth. Every day she held onto the baby was a gift. The fear of delivering another dead baby, like her first child so many years before, was never far from her thoughts.

Izzy had been born a month early, a tiny, squalling bundle who spent her first weeks in an incubator. But she lived and went on to thrive. Watching her daughter now in the ambulance, tethered to an IV and in pain, Mae had visions both of Izzy's past in the incubator and possible future in an iron lung. She tried futilely to push that image out of her mind.

You cannot dwell on what might be, she screamed to herself, *or it will steal the energy you need to deal with what is here and now*.

The ambulance came to a halt at the emergency entrance of the hospital and the doors were pulled open by staff waiting for them. Mae scrambled out as they lifted Izzy's stretcher and placed her on a gurney. She did not let go of Izzy's hand as she was rushed through corridors Mae knew only too well.

Their destination was an empty room at the end of a hall that was closed off from the rest of the hospital.

"We're putting your daughter in isolation as a precaution, Mrs. Monroe. If she does have polio, we don't want her near other children."

"The ambulance workers told me there was another child on the island diagnosed with polio. Where is he?"

"He's been sent to Boston. He needed an iron lung and we weren't equipped to treat him here."

"Will my daughter also be sent away?" Mae gripped Izzy's hand tighter.

"Doctor will decide. First we need to get her settled and confirm what we're dealing with. I'm going to ask you to leave now, Mrs. Monroe. We shouldn't have let you come this far in the first place."

"I don't want to leave her. She's only a baby. You can see how frightened she is and how much she's hurting."

"That's out of the question, Mrs. Monroe. The protocol for polio is strict quarantine, even from parents. You can wait in the family lounge on the pediatric ward. Someone will come to you when we have more information. I have to insist."

The nurse was rigid and implacable.

Mae gathered Izzy in her arms.

"I won't be far away, little bird. Be as brave as I know you are."

Izzy bit her lip and her eyes filled with tears. She clung to Mae.

"Please don't leave me. I'm scared."

"Have courage, Izzy. Even when we are afraid we can be brave."

Mae reluctantly extracted herself from Izzy's fragile hold before the nurse pulled her away.

With leaden feet she located the pediatric lounge and then burst into tears.

Chapter 3

"The key is turned on our uncertainty"
Mae

Betty and Josiah joined Mae an hour later.

"We've been on a wild goose chase trying to find you. Where's Izzy? How's Izzy? Do they know for sure yet what she's got?"

Mae shook her head. "I don't know anything yet and they're keeping her isolated, in quarantine. Did you reach Tobias?"

"I managed to get the Coast Guard to raise him by radio and alert him, but it could be several hours before he makes it back from the fishing grounds."

"Mom, is Izzy going to be all right?" Jo had been a rock getting them from Innisfree to Oak Bluffs. His maturity and calmness were so much a reflection of Tobias. But he was only twelve. Mae put her arm around him. She knew he was too old to hug, especially in public (although the lounge was blessedly empty at the moment).

But she could read the strain on his face. Now that he no longer had the concrete task of getting his sister safely and quickly to Oak Bluffs, his sense of helplessness was bubbling to the surface. She recognized it because she felt it herself. To be forced to do nothing but sit and wait was excruciating.

"The doctors and nurses are taking good care of her, Jo." She had to believe that. But she ached for her children—for her daughter suffering from what could be a devastating disease; for her son flailing in worry for his baby sister.

"Do you remember how tiny Izzy was when she was born, but how feisty she was? Bawling with lungs that were too small to be making that much noise? Your sister is a survivor. She'll come through this. I know she will."

It was late afternoon before a doctor appeared in the lounge. Mae jumped to her feet.

"Mrs. Monroe? I'm Dr. Davenport, the pediatric resident. I've examined your daughter and run some tests. I'm sorry, but we've confirmed it is polio."

Betty held onto Mae.

"What now? Will she be paralyzed? Will she be able to breathe on her own?"

"It's too early to tell. The disease is progressive and it may take some time before we know how severe it will be. In some cases the disease is very mild, but I don't want to raise your expectations. Isabella isn't a robust child; it's not clear if she has the resources to fight the infection."

"What are you doing for her? When can I see her?"

"There's no cure, Mrs. Monroe. We are giving her medication for the pain and she's in an oxygen tent. But I'm afraid you can't be with her. She has to remain in quarantine."

"For how long? Surely I can see her through a glass, even if I can't touch her."

"Once she's stable, we can move her to a room with a glass partition. But tonight that would be too disruptive. I suggest you go home and get some rest. Isabella is facing a long hospital stay before she'll be able to come home."

And then he left.

Mae turned to Betty and collapsed in her arms, sobbing. Josiah turned to the couch and drove his fist into the pillow.

"I don't want to leave, even though I can't be with her. I want to be nearby if anything changes."

"We should stay at least until Tobias gets here. The hospital won't let you spend the night, but the season is still early. We can probably find a couple of rooms in town to get some sleep and be back early in the morning. Why don't I go hunt around to see what I can turn up?" Betty hugged Mae and wiped her tears.

"Can I go with Betty, Ma? This place is giving me the creeps."

Mae nodded. He needed another job to quell the frustration. "Go on, help Betty. I'll wait for Dad."

After they left, Mae paced the room, wondering how many hours, days, and weeks she'd be wearing out the floor beneath her feet with her steps. Her back was to the door when Tobias arrived, but she could smell him, the familiar tang of sea and fish that marked him and announced his arrival home each night.

She turned and ran into his embrace. He bent to her and held her wordlessly, each of them imparting what strength they had to the other; each of them drawing from one another what they needed.

"I turned and headed to port as soon as the Coast Guard reached me. Tell me everything. All I knew was that she'd been brought here, but not why. Was it an accident?"

Mae took him and sat him down and then recounted every piercing moment of this harrowing day. When she had finished he pulled her into his lap and rocked with her as he sobbed.

By the time Betty and Jo returned they were spent. Mae came awake from her exhausted doze, raising her head from Tobias's embrace.

"We found a couple of rooms at a boarding house not far from East Chop. We can walk from here. The woman who runs it has some cold chicken and potato salad set aside for us. Let's get some rest. Tomorrow will be a long day."

The four of them moved together down the hall, arms entwined, heads bowed.

Mae slept fitfully, even wrapped in Tobias' arms. At four in the morning she slipped from the unfamiliar bed and stood at the window. A street lamp across the way cast a hazy puddle of yellow light on the road. A dog barked in the distance. A milk truck rumbled past the house, most likely on its way to meet the early ferry. Mae pressed her forehead against the window frame and closed her eyes, longing for the silence and darkness of Innisfree, for the peace of the moment before she found Izzy on the clam flat.

It had been less than twenty-four hours since Lydia Hammond's arrival with her children had signaled a change in the environment at Cape Poge. How trivial that change now appeared to Mae, and how selfish. Despite the thirteen years she had been with Tobias, her giving birth and mothering two children and her deep and abiding friendship with Betty, a hidden part of her still clung to the independent, isolated young woman who had first set foot on Cape Poge in 1941 and made it her own.

Izzy's horrific diagnosis had smacked her in the gut, stealing from her all the self-assurance and fierceness that had sustained her in her long climb back to wholeness.

The early morning breeze was unusually chilly and Mae rubbed her arms as she shivered by the open window. But she knew she was trembling from more than the brisk air. She was frightened and helpless and overwhelmed by the chasm that had split her soul in two. She lashed out for the second time in her life at a God who was once again taking a daughter from her.

By the time Tobias woke up at six Mae was dressed and sitting at a small table crammed into a corner of the room.

"When did you get up?" he asked, swinging his long legs over the side of the bed and moving across the room to her side. "I didn't sense you leave. I'm sorry."

He put his arms around her and kissed the top of her head.

She stroked his hand.

"It's OK. You were exhausted. I didn't want to wake you. I couldn't sleep."

"You're making a list." He tapped the scrap of paper on the table. "Good."

"I want to go to the hospital. Even if they won't let us see her, I need to be there."

"Give me five minutes to wash up and dress. I'll walk with you."

When they arrived at the hospital the front door was locked and the entry hall looked dim and empty through the glass.

"Let's try the emergency entrance. Someone has to be there."

When they pushed open the door into the ER a single nurse was on duty at the desk. From her posture and the dark circles under her eyes, it appeared she'd been there all night. But despite her obvious fatigue, she greeted them with recognition and concern.

"Mae, Tobias! What brings you here? Are you having a breathing problem?"

Tess Boudreau had cared for Mae during her cancer treatment and often stopped at the café for lunch on her day off.

"It's not me. It's Izzy."

Tess looked behind them, searching for Izzy.

"Where is she? What's wrong?"

"She's upstairs in isolation with polio. An ambulance brought her in yesterday around noon. Tess, they won't let us see her. Something about quarantine. She's all alone."

Tess came out from behind the desk and hugged Mae.

"My shift ends in about ten minutes. As soon as the day nurse arrives and I brief her, I'll go up and see what I can learn."

"Why are you here and not on the cancer floor?"

She shrugged. "Paul got laid off. I'm trying to work additional shifts to help out. Night duty pays extra. The cafeteria is open if you want to grab a cup of coffee while you wait for me. At this hour, it'll be a fresh pot. I'll come get you there."

They turned toward the breakfast aromas seeping through the corridor.

"I wish Tess had been on duty yesterday. Izzy needed someone she knows and trusts, not some officious bitch lecturing me about disease protocol."

Tobias took two steaming cups from the server behind the counter and placed them on a tray.

"Are you hungry?" he asked. But he didn't push her to eat something.

They found a table where Tess would be able to spot them quickly. The cafeteria had been empty when they arrived, but was beginning to fill up with nurses and doctors drifting in at the end of the night shift.

Mae sipped the hot coffee absentmindedly, keeping her eyes on the door. Her foot tapped impatiently on the floor. Tobias reached a hand under the table and placed it on her knee to still her.

"She'll be here soon. Tess will help us."

"Can I get you a cup of coffee?" Tobias offered Tess when she arrived.

"No, thanks. I need to go home and sleep. Here's what I learned: She had a quiet night. They gave her a mild analgesic for the pain, which is mostly in her legs, and her fever is dropping. They are keeping her in the oxygen tent, but so far her breathing is normal. The paralysis seems to be limited to her legs."

"Paralysis?" Mae's voice was barely above a whisper.

"That's what polio does, Mae."

"I know. I know. I just wanted to hold out hope that it might be something else. When can we see her?"

"Even I couldn't see her. I only got to read her chart. The government has set out strict guidelines since the epidemic in '52. I'm afraid it will be weeks before they lift the quarantine."

"The nurse last night said they would move her to a room with a glass wall. I need to see her, Tess."

"And she needs to see you, too. My advice is to go up there now and talk to the physician on duty. I heard from the nurse leaving her shift they've called in an infectious disease specialist from Hyannis. He's supposed to arrive on the first ferry."

"Thank you, Tess."

"Least I could do. She'll get good care, Mae. She has a long road ahead of her, but if anyone can handle a situation like this, it's you and Tobias. I gotta go get some sleep."

She slid her chair from the table, gave each of them a squeeze of her hand and left quietly on her white, rubber-soled shoes.

Mae's coffee was cold and she pushed it away.

"Let's go find the doctor."

The formerly dim and empty hospital lobby was now lit and bustling. Mae and Tobias approached the front desk, staffed by a member of the hospital's women's auxiliary.

"Our daughter was admitted to the children's ward yesterday and we'd like to speak to the specialist who's been called in to treat her."

Mae hoped the gray-haired woman in the volunteer smock would not prove to be as overbearing and obstructionist as the nurse yesterday, and forced herself to remain quiet while the woman checked the patient list and made a call to the ward.

"They tell me the doctor is seeing your daughter now. Please go to the parents' lounge. He'll meet you there."

They made their way to the ward. The day before, Mae had been so focused on Izzy that she had barely been aware of her surroundings. But this morning the smells and sounds of the hospital assaulted her, ripping open the wounds of her cancer treatment eight years before. By all accounts, Mae knew that no one who had cared for her then imagined she would be walking these hallways now.

Tobias seemed to be reading her thoughts.

"You have survived for a reason and this is it. To see our daughter through this so she can be her own survivor."

They waited over an hour in the lounge. Betty and Josiah joined them—Jo as anxious as his parents; Betty a dynamo, ready to fix whatever was broken in this shattered family.

"I've already started making calls, pulling in favors to get help to keep the Boat House open."

Mae smiled at Betty's take-charge action. When Mae had first arrived back on Martha's Vineyard and established the Boat House Café at Innisfree, she had, by choice, led an isolated life. The women in Edgartown had found her strange, an object of derisive gossip or simply someone to be ignored because she wasn't like them, married and safe in their snug houses in town. It was Betty, a waitress at the Vineyard Haven Inn Mae had met her first night back on the island, who had offered Mae a friendship she didn't know she needed. It had begun with Betty's straightforward honesty and humor, followed by the offer of an extra pair of hands in the kitchen as the Boat House began to succeed. They had been friends for fourteen years—years marked by both harsh challenges and deep joy. Mae knew that Betty was ready to stand by her this time, as she always had in the past. The café was vital to the Monroes' financial security. They were moving into high summer and their peak business. Closing while Izzy was hospitalized was out of the question.

"Jo and I will go back to Innisfree this afternoon and get the place ready for business tomorrow. He understands he can be more help to you there than pacing the floor here. Let me worry about him so you don't have to."

"Is that OK, Ma and Dad? I'll only go if you say so."

Tobias took him by the shoulders. At twelve, he was already almost as tall as Tobias.

"Betty's right, Jo. You can be an enormous help at the Boat House."

When the doctor finally arrived, they clustered around him. Tobias took Mae's hand; Betty circled Jo with a comforting arm.

"Mr. and Mrs. Monroe, Isabella came through the night with no additional paralysis beyond her left leg. It's still early, but I think the prognosis is good that this will be a mild case of polio. There's no sign that her chest muscles are involved and she's breathing normally."

Mae leaned into Tobias, relief spreading across her face.

"I'm going to be blunt, however. She still has a long way to go in her recovery, and there is always the possibility that the virus will spread to other muscles. But with rest and pain medication and isolation, she has a very good chance."

"Of walking again?" Tobias asked hopefully.

"With braces, most likely yes. But you need to understand, there is no cure for polio. I meant, she has a good chance of *surviving*. My first impression of her was that she is a frail child, but I've revised that assessment. She's stronger than she looks. Your daughter is quite a fighter."

"When can we see her?"

"Apparently the hospital needs a few days to prepare a quarantine ward with interior window walls. But she's in a first-floor isolation room right now. I can lead you outside and you'll be able to look in on her. But I have to caution you, we can't open the window. You'll be able to see her, but not touch her."

34

They trooped out behind the doctor to a room in the rear of the hospital. The window the doctor indicated was small and multi-paned, but Mae and Tobias could stand together and see within to a dim interior with a single hospital bed enveloped in an oxygen tent. Through its rippled and not quite clear surface, they saw Izzy. A nurse got Izzy's attention and pointed to the window. Izzy turned her head. Mae and Tobias waved. A smile spread across Izzy's pale face as Mae touched her fingers to her lips and then blew the kiss to her daughter.

"Is there a chair I could have? I'd like to sit here for a while to let Izzy know that I'm near."

"I'll find one, Ma." Jo dashed inside and returned with a folding chair. Mae didn't ask where he'd found it, but simply settled into it.

"Thanks, Jo. Now, I think it's time for everyone to get back to work. For the time being, this is my job, being the face at the window for Izzy."

Betty nodded and gently led Jo away. "Come on, buddy. We've got a restaurant to run."

Tobias stood behind Mae and kneaded her shoulders.

"I'm not going to cry as long as I'm in front of this window," she said.

"I know. Stay as long as you can. I'll bring you some lunch. Is there anything else you need or want?"

"I want to go back to the day before yesterday. Since I can't, please go to the library and find everything you can about polio. I need to understand this enemy that has attacked our daughter if I'm to be any help to her."

"I will. We'll fight this, Mae." He kissed her, which brought another smile to Izzy's face, and waved to his daughter.

Mae stayed until sunset and returned the next day and the next, until Izzy was moved to the newly created quarantine ward, where there was a small lounge for parents overlooking three patient rooms.

"Are you expecting more cases?" Mae asked the nurse.

She nodded. "We've already had a third case diagnosed. Another second grader. For a community this size, it feels like an epidemic. We're preparing for the worst."

Mae settled in, coming day after day to watch over her daughter and struggling with her own sense of helplessness. She devoured everything she could on polio. She cooked Izzy's favorite foods, read out loud to her through the intercom and brought her beloved doll and coloring books when she was well enough to enjoy them.

She knew that her vigil with Izzy as well as the care the nurses and doctors were providing only offered her daughter comfort, not a cure. The medical staff eased her pain; Mae eased her loneliness. But none of them could unlock the paralysis in her leg. Izzy was "lucky," the nurses told her. They reminded her the first child diagnosed, the little boy, was in an iron lung in Boston.

As she sat on the other side of the window, unable to hold her child, Mae felt her own paralysis. A spirit that had once soared, like the ospreys at Innisfree, was now stilled, confined within the glass-walled prison of the hospital.

Chapter 4

"Walking with slow steps"
Mae

Izzy spent four months in quarantine. By the time she was released from the hospital it was the end of October. The Boat House Café was shuttered for the season and the family had moved back to their winter home at Cove Meadow. Ever since Josiah turned five years old they had spent the school year there, at the house Tobias had built and lived in before he met Mae. It was on a winding lane not far from Chappaquiddick's one paved road, and the school bus stopped at the foot of the lane for the Monroe children. But this fall, Josiah was taking the bus alone.

Although Izzy was out of the hospital, she wasn't cleared to go back to school. She had only been fitted with her leg braces a week before her hospital release and she was going to need time to learn how to manipulate her crutches and adapt to the metal braces that kept her upright.

The doctors advised Mae and Tobias to keep her at home for the fall while she gained strength.

"Children's classrooms are Petri dishes of infection, especially in the fall," said the specialist. "It's best for Izzy to wait until January to return to school."

The months at home were a balm for both Izzy and Mae, finally able to touch. But they were also an ordeal, as Izzy stumbled and crashed and collapsed in a tangle of metal and cramped muscle learning to move again.

"This isn't walking, Mama. It's lurching and falling down and not wanting to get up again."

"When did you learn the word 'lurching'?" Mae asked, trying not to call out or even wince every time Izzy fell.

"You don't remember when you were a toddler and just learning to walk," Mae told her one particularly discouraging morning. "But you tumbled down all the time and then scrambled up again, determined not to be defeated by your legs, which simply hadn't quite caught up to where your brain wanted them to go. You can do it again, Izzy."

"It hurts. And it's scary that my leg can't move at all. I don't think I was scared when I was a baby."

"No, you were fearless. And you still are, even though you may feel scared. Your brave spirit doesn't live in your legs, Izzy. It lives in your heart. Now, give me your hand and I'll help you up. Try again."

Every day she walked a little farther before she fell; and each time she fell it was a little easier to get up again.

Those months away from school also taught Izzy to be a voracious reader. Mae became her teacher, following the lessons the school had sent home. But Izzy whizzed through the third-grade curriculum, devouring knowledge and covering intellectual ground in ways she wasn't able to cover the physical ground of her world. Mae turned to the library to keep up with Izzy's hunger to learn and discovered a new-found source of happiness for her daughter. By the time Izzy returned to school in January, she was an inquisitive and engaged student who had found in stories the courage she needed to learn to walk again.

In early spring, Tobias hauled a load of lumber out to Innisfree and constructed a series of wooden walkways and ramps to create a smooth thoroughfare connecting all the buildings on the compound—their own house, Betty's cottage, the shed and the Boat House Café. The walkways provided Izzy with an even surface that would allow her to move freely around Innisfree. She had been confined so long within the solid walls of the hospital, and Mae and Tobias wanted to give her as much freedom as Innisfree could offer her.

Naomi, Tobias's mother, moved with them, allowing Mae to return to running the Boat House. In the evenings, when Tobias arrived home from fishing, he unbuckled Izzy's braces and carried her down to the water. He cradled her in the gentle waves of the pond and allowed her to float, buoyed by the tide and unhampered by the metal that kept her legs upright. She closed her eyes and basked in the warmth of the setting sun.

The Hammonds rented the cottage up by the lighthouse again. Lydia and Mae found common ground in their children, their independent natures, and their love of Cape Poge. On rainy days Lydia arrived with a canvas tote bag filled with board games and her daughter, Susan, a year younger than Izzy. She was content to play Candy Land and Chutes and Ladders at the dining table with Izzy while her brothers roamed the dunes. As the summers passed, the games advanced to Monopoly and Parcheesi. Tobias taught Izzy and Susan to sail on a

Sunfish after improvising a seat that allowed Izzy slide from one side of the boat to the other. With her braces off and bundled in a bright orange life jacket, Izzy spent hours zigzagging across the shallow pond with Susan as Lydia watched from the beach and shouted encouragement.

In the evenings, Lydia, Mae and Betty sat on the back porch, drinks in hand. The two families often ate together at the dining table that could accommodate ten people; the boys wandered off after supper to play catch or Tobias loaded them into his truck to take them fishing out at the Gut; Naomi retired to her room to crochet; the girls drew or cut out photos from magazine to make collages.

It was a time to catch the sunset, put up aching feet that been on the go all day—either running the Boat House or supervising very active kids—and enjoy the company of women. It was in those quiet moments that Mae and Lydia became friends, despite Mae's early misgivings. But like Izzy's learning to walk again, their friendship would falter, crashing into obstacles they hadn't anticipated. The bond between them, forged in their love of Cape Poge's wildness and isolation, would also be fraught with pain.

1957
Wampanoag Burial Ground
Chappaquiddick Island

Chapter 5

"You tread on my dreams"
Josiah

He hadn't meant to eavesdrop. His grandmother had sent him to the cluster of trees behind the trestle tables where some of the women from the tribe were putting out the food everyone had contributed to the Pow-Wow, the annual summer gathering.

"Jo, this sun is too much for me. Please go find my umbrella. I left it with the picnic basket under the trees."

As he raced past the heavily laden tables, he saw loaves of corn and cranberry bread; platters of chicken and burgers and corn on the cob; pots of sobaheg, the turkey stew Naomi had made the day before, simmering it for hours till the meat fell off the bones. His mother's pies, blueberry, apple and strawberry rhubarb, were at the far end, already sliced and waiting.

When he got to the trees he groaned. The Monroes had been among the first to arrive at the Burial Ground earlier, delivering tables and tents as well as his mother's and grandmother's food. Tobias, as sachem, had been busy all morning—not only directing the set up for the gathering but also meeting individually with various members of the tribal council. Cove Meadow wasn't far from the Burial Ground—Josiah had ridden his bike over—but most of the tribe came to the Pow-Wow from off-island. This was their main opportunity to air issues with Tobias as well as to socialize with friends.

The combination of the Monroe's early arrival and the number of Wampanoag who had followed had a negative effect on Josiah's task. What had once been a few easily identified baskets under the trees was now a jumble of coolers and straw bags and baskets woven and decorated just like Naomi's. He knelt before the pile and started sifting, searching for his grandmother's umbrella, probably buried at the bottom.

It was then that he heard the voices. They were on the other side of the trees, not far from the water's edge. He recognized them immediately—his father's deeply resonant tone that had reassured and taught and influenced Josiah with few words but always with clear meaning; and the jarring, agitated speech of Tobias' cousin Sadie, whose voice often reminded Josiah of a red-tailed hawk about to dive in the hunt. He knew Sadie and his mother barely tolerated one another, but he didn't know why. The Pow-Wow was the only time they were in the same place, and they kept their distance. Josiah tried to focus on finding the umbrella, but his curiosity finally stilled his search. He stopped moving baskets, sat back on his heels and listened, wishing only later that he hadn't.

"I told you fifteen years ago this was a mistake, but you didn't listen. You married her, you brought those children into the tribe, and yet they cannot carry on your legacy and your father's legacy. In my eyes and in a lot of other people's eyes—people who care about the future of the Wampanoag—they will never lead us because their mother is a white woman. You can dress your children in deerskin and eagle feathers, teach your son to drum and to chant, but as long as I have a voice, Josiah will never be sachem of this tribe."

"Yours is not the only voice, Sadie." Tobias spoke quietly, but with a power Josiah recognized.

"You know, Tobias, you're very isolated here on Chappy. Most of us are out in a world where we understand that the Wampanoag can disappear if we aren't careful."

"Being Wampanoag isn't only about blood."

"Tell that to the Federal government. How will we gain recognition if we continue to dilute ourselves? And tell that to our ancestors, who lost their land, their birthright, to the white man."

"Sadie, do you think I don't grieve for what we've lost, when I walk these meadows and beaches every day? Do you think I'm not fighting in every way I can to regain our heritage? But winning back Chappaquiddick isn't about pure bloodlines. It's about passing on our culture, our language and our traditions to our children. They are the ones who will keep the Wampanoag from disappearing."

"You're a fool, Tobias. Your children may think of themselves as Wampanoag right now, while they are still young and still enchanted by playing dress-up. But wait a few years, especially with Josiah, when he gets swept up in a culture that favors the white man. See how fast he embraces his Wampanoag roots then. Mark my words, he'll call himself an Irishman."

The voices went silent then.

Josiah was too stunned and confused to see Sadie stalking past the trees. He only felt the ripple of air disturbed by the flapping of her deerskin skirt and heard the gentle rustle of her beads. He reached for the wampum necklace around his own neck and stroked it like the talisman his grandmother had told him it was. How could Sadie say he wasn't Wampanoag?

He found the umbrella and returned without a word to his grandmother.

1960
Innisfree
Chappaquiddick Island

Chapter 6

"The cold wet winds ever blowing"
Mae

Mae and Tobias had come through more than one hurricane in their lives together on Chappy, but none was more devastating nor had a greater impact on their lives than Hurricane Donna. As soon as the winds abated and the storm surge was past, they made their way to Innisfree, anxious to assess what they feared might be overwhelming losses. They had spent the duration of the storm at the Martha's Vineyard high school, evacuated with the rest of Chappaquiddick. No one had slept well. The entire island remembered all too well the ravages of back-to-back hurricanes in 1954. Sixty people on Cape Cod had died during Carol, the damage as severe as the historic Great New England hurricane in 1938. So they were apprehensive, after a disturbing night of howling wind and lashing rain, of what they would find.

They went to Cove Meadow first. The boat had survived and the mooring had held. The house was battered and they'd lost some trees, but none had landed on the roof. They were hopeful that Innisfree had fared as well, but as they approached Shear Pen Pond the reality was far worse than any of them had imagined. The dock to the Boat House had torn free, fragments of it poking up in the middle of the bay. Every shutter had been ripped off the café, windows were shattered, debris was strewn halfway to East Beach. The house and Betty's cottage were missing a few shingles, but the plywood boards protecting the windows had withstood the wind.

Without the dock, Tobias moored the boat away from shore and they took the rubber dinghy to get to land. They climbed up from the sand flats, Tobias carrying Izzy because some of the wooden stair treads were missing. Picking their way carefully across the yard, they passed splintered tree limbs, broken shutters and shattered glass.

Tears welled up in Mae's eyes as she peered through one of the broken windows into the café's dining room. Tobias unlocked the door and they stepped inside. Mae collapsed into one of the still-intact chairs, numb with grief. Tobias stood behind her, his hands on her shoulders.

"The last time the Boat House looked like this was when Marcus trashed it." Marcus Gardner had tried to intimidate her when she had defended Tobias nineteen years before. Her testimony that Tobias had spent the night with her had saved him from a murder charge. Marcus, an island judge, had a vendetta against Tobias at the time and had tried to hurt him through Mae by destroying the Boat House. But the island had rallied around them and a flotilla of fishermen and neighbors joined together to help them repair the damage and get the Boat House back up and running.

"No one's coming to our rescue this time, are they? They all have their own messes to deal with." Mae shook herself free of her initial dismay. "We better get started. Izzy, we'll get a couple of tables cleaned off and you can start organizing what we collect. Sort out what can be saved, what needs to be trashed. Jo and Dad and I will do the heavy lifting."

Josiah spent the morning rounding up the shutters and then he and Tobias reattached them to prevent any more damage than had already occurred from wind and rain. Izzy started an inventory and a list of the structural repairs that were going to be necessary. After culling the salvageable furniture, Mae swept the debris—sand, branches, quahog shells, even dead birds—that the forceful wind had driven through the broken windows. Tobias went up on the roof later in the day and come down with a grim assessment.

"The entire thing needs to be replaced. It's a miracle it's lasted as long as it has."

At the end of the day, aching and exhausted, they headed back to Cove Meadow just as the sun broke through the grayness and then dropped below the horizon, its reflection bouncing off the low clouds to unravel a ribbon of deep-hued color that accompanied them across the water to home.

Later that night, reviewing Izzy's inventory and the repair list, Mae started calculating. But she knew that no matter how many times she added up the numbers, the money simply wasn't there to rebuild. She pushed her estimates across the dining table to Tobias. Izzy and Jo were already asleep.

"I don't know how we can reopen next spring. New roof, new dock, replacing the entire kitchen—that's the big stuff. But windows, furniture, dishes—it all adds up to money we don't have. With Izzy's medical bills, we won't be able to save the Boat House."

She thought back to all the obstacles they had overcome in the years since she had returned to Chappy—creating the Boat House from an abandoned fishing camp, beating back a ravaging fire, surviving her cancer, winning the custody battle for Jo against Kathleen, raising their children and then coping with Izzy's polio. Had they not been tested enough? Was it time now to move on? She didn't want to give up or admit she was tired. But she was. When she first entered the Boat House that morning, the weight of what faced them had nearly crushed her. She had forced herself to get up and attack the mess because it was something tangible. Cleaning up the debris had a purpose and a recognizable end.

But as far as she could see, rebuilding the Boat House was a limitless task, rife with risks—both economic and natural. Life on Chappaquiddick Island, especially the life Mae and Tobias had known in the early years of their relationship, had altered over the past years. The fishermen and families who had sailed across Poge Bay for a bite to eat at the Boat House Café were spending less time and money than in the past. Now that more of the barrier beach was accessible by Jeeps, people were heading to isolated coves for picnics and a full day at the beach. This past summer Mae had seen business fall off drastically.

The five years since Izzy's polio summer had drained Mae, but they had also refocused her. Hurricane Donna's shrieking winds had carried a message that she already knew in her heart.

She hadn't been ready, that first night after Donna, to speak aloud what the wind was telling her. But that is the night the idea had taken root, to let go not only of the Boat House, but of Innisfree itself.

It was more than the expense of repairs and the realization the café was no longer the island destination it had been in the early years. Earlier in the evening Mae had watched Izzy's determined back as she moved with awkwardness down the hall to her room, painfully aware of the limitations of Izzy's affected leg. Mae had never given up hope. She had accepted that there was no cure, but every fiber of her being clung with tenacity to the belief that science would find a way to correct the damage done to Izzy's muscles. Surely, if Jack Kennedy thought we could put a man on the moon within the next ten years, couldn't we also find a way to give crippled children the ability to walk?

When she learned that surgeons had indeed developed an experimental corrective surgery for polio patients, that discovery was the tipping point in her decision about Innisfree. It was Lydia who sent clippings to Mae about the surgery and who had alerted her to the procedure being perfected at Boston Children's Hospital.

When Mae and Tobias came to the excruciating realization that selling Innisfree was the only way they could afford the surgery that could change Izzy's life, they decided to turn to Lydia first.

"We're going to put Innisfree up for sale. It's the only way."

"Innisfree is your life."

"It's worth nothing to me if I can't help Izzy."

"How will you let it go, after all these years, all that you've put into it?"

"If I can let it go to someone I trust, I think I can bear it. That's why I'm telling you first. Will you consider buying it?"

Lydia was speechless. Then she wrapped her arms around Mae. "I'll talk to Lou tonight. If he agrees, I promise you we will care for and love it as you have."

Mae knew it was going to be heartbreaking, but the day she signed over the deed to the Hammonds became one of those markers in her life by which she measured "before" and "after." It ranked right up there with the day Izzy was diagnosed with polio and her first daughter, Catriona, was stillborn. Days of darkness, filled with anguish and loss and a deep sense that she was being punished.

Selling Innisfree also meant that Izzy might once more walk unaided.

1961
Cove Meadow
Chappaquiddick Island

Chapter 7

"A fire was in my head"
Mae

They were late. Mae stood at the dining room table, trying to still her anxiety with anything at hand—the pile of laundry she was attempting to fold, the tumbler of whisky resting on the oilcloth-covered table, the rhythmic cadences of Izzy's typing in her room at the end of the hall. They had given her a portable Smith-Corona on her thirteenth birthday in the winter and she had attacked learning to type with her usual intensity.

None of the distractions dispelled Mae's memories of the disruption at supper before Tobias and Josiah had left.

"I don't want to go play Indian," Jo had spit out when Tobias had asked him if he'd checked the tension on his drum.

"It's not a game," Tobias had answered. "You, of all people, should understand that. It's a sacred tradition."

"If your traditions are so sacred, why did you sell Innisfree? You've told me since I could walk across the meadow that Innisfree was Wampanoag homeland. Why did you give it up? You're such hypocrites. Both of you." He turned and included Mae in his accusation.

His words felt like a slap in the face. Now, even three hours later, she flinched at the memory.

Tobias had said nothing in response. He had set his face into the mask Mae recognized, an impenetrable barrier that contained his anger. Jo knew that face as well, and Mae saw reflected in her son the mirror image of his father.

Mae had no shield to protect her. The decision to sell the land had originated with her. Tobias had ultimately, reluctantly, painfully agreed. But it was, after all, Mae who owned the decision—who owned the land in the eyes of the town.

She spoke, breaking the silence that simmered over the table.

"You know full well why we sold. Sometimes we have to sacrifice what we hold precious for a greater good. The good of our family."

"I'm part of this family. Don't I count?"

"You're no longer a child, Jo. Old enough to know that life is often not fair. And old enough to understand that who you are does not depend on what you own."

"You're right about one thing, Ma. I'm no longer a child."

Jo had risen from the table then and retreated to his room.

Izzy had watched and listened, about to collapse from the strain of holding back her tears.

"I hate it when you all fight, especially because it's my fault."

"You're not to blame, Hummingbird. Never think that. Ever." Tobias' voice was emphatic.

"Polio is a vicious disease, but nothing you did or didn't do caused it. And helping you get what you need, protecting you, is far more important than protecting the land," Mae reassured her.

"Before you were born, your mother fought ferociously to save Innisfree from a devastating fire. Now she's fighting just as ferociously for you. And though he doesn't recognize it just now, she's also fighting for Jo."

"I already miss Innisfree."

"It will always be here," Mae touched her heart. "Our memories are not something we are selling."

Tobias left for the drum circle without Jo. While Mae and Izzy were cleaning up the supper dishes, Mae heard Jo go out.

Chapter 8

"A frenzied drum"
Josiah

The drums throbbed in the clearing, a circle of six men, their faces lit by the crackling flames of the bonfire and their sticks pounding in unison as they chanted.

Josiah stood on the periphery in the dark, his eyes closed, listening to the high-pitched keening of his father's voice and feeling the reverberation within his chest of the insistent rhythm. The rhythm of blood, of wind, of the waves crashing below the Burial Ground on the wet sand.

He had made his own hand drum when he was eight, guided by the long, scarred fingers of his father's hands. His father had no thumb on his left hand—a fishing accident—and yet he could weave a net, gut a rabbit and stretch a piece of hide across a frame as deftly as anyone else in the tribe. He had adored his father then. Imitated him. Listened to him.

But he was no longer eight. And the boy he had thought himself to be—Blue Turtle of the Chappaquiddick Wampanoag, the son of the sachem—had been lost in the intervening years. Years when he had careened between the labels of "Indian" and "Irish," when he found himself more often than not on the outside, accepted by neither.

His own drum hung silent at his side. He fingered the wampum beads hanging around his neck, disks of quahog shell polished and strung by his grandmother.

Then he broke the drum over his knee, ripped the wampum from his neck and flung it to the ground, and turned away from the circle.

He left the island that night.

Chapter 9

"I have nothing but the embittered sun"
Mae

Now it was nearly eleven and neither of her warriors had returned home.

The wind was picking up, and she turned on the radio for the weather report. It was still hurricane season, and the Cape and Islands had gotten walloped the year before by Hurricane Donna. The memories of its destruction had heightened the watchfulness this season.

Beneath the monotonous voice of the weather service announcer Mae heard the uneven drag and tap of Izzy's footsteps. She hadn't noticed when the typing stopped. Mae turned her head toward Izzy, who had reached the dining room and was listening to the report, her arms leaning into her crutches.

"The wind gauge is rising. I just checked. Shouldn't Dad and Jo be back by now?"

"I'm sure they'll walk in the door any minute. Why don't you get ready for bed? The storm is still a long way off and I don't think school will be canceled tomorrow."

Mae spun her daughter around toward her room as if this were a perfectly normal September school night. Izzy's radar for life gone amiss was particularly sensitive, and she had unsurprisingly picked up on Mae's anxiety. Mae was less worried about stormy weather than the storm churning through her angry, alienated son.

Jo's outburst at dinner had been no surprise. His reaction to the decision to sell Innisfree had been festering for weeks, ever since Mae and Tobias had announced to the children that their summer neighbors the Hammonds were buying the compound that had been both summer home and livelihood for the family since World War II.

It was nearly midnight when Mae heard the truck in the driveway. She didn't wait, but went immediately to the back porch, her arms wrapped tightly around her, not only protecting herself from the biting wind but also holding herself together in anticipation of what she feared.

She peered into the darkness, straining to hear the voices of Tobias and Josiah beneath the keening squall. But the only sound accompanying the wind was the crunch of footsteps on the gravel.

Tobias emerged into the circle of yellow light cast by the porch lamp. He was alone.

"Where's Josiah?" The words caught in her throat as if she were choking, the knot of worry that had been lodged deep in her chest all night now rising, escaping in the cramped question she already knew the answer to.

Tobias shook his head. "He left the burial ground hours ago without joining the drum circle. I found these on the edge of the clearing."

Then Mae saw what Tobias carried. The shattered drum, its frame splintered and its cover tattered; six polished disks of loose wampum, no longer tethered on their strip of leather—cradled in Tobias' arms. His face was as broken as if *he* had been crushed and not the objects he held.

Mae reached out and drew him into the house. As she did so, a gust of wind rose up from the water. The porch light went out along with the other lights Mae had kept on during her vigil. She felt along the kitchen counter for the lantern she kept by the stove, found the match box lying next to it and struck a light.

Tobias let the broken drum and beads slide from his arms onto the kitchen table, the clatter of wood and seashell echoing through the darkened house.

Another gust slammed against the house.

Mae looked out the window once again, as she had been all evening.

"He's out there in this. We have to find him."

"He's gone, Mae. He doesn't want to be found."

"How do you know? How can you be so sure?"

"Because I've already looked for him. I checked with the Chappy ferry. He went over to Edgartown, left his bike at the shed."

"Maybe he's just hanging out with Gary and Dale…"

Tobias shook his head. "I went over myself, drove to Oak Bluffs and checked at the steamship office. He took the last boat to the mainland."

"I knew he was angry tonight, but for him to leave so abruptly, without a word . . . How could I have missed the depth of his feelings? Have I been so blind to what he wanted?"

"He wanted what we couldn't give him, Mae."

"The land."

"Not just the land."

"Isn't that what the harsh words were all about tonight? My decision to abandon what he saw as his birthright? I've failed him."

"I think it's more than that, and although it's something you and I created, we can't solve it for him."

"What then? Is it because so much of me went to Izzy—my energy, my fears, my search for a cure? It's not just the land I abandoned, is it? I abandoned Jo when Izzy got sick."

"You did what any mother does, Mae. You protected your child as fiercely as a bear defending her cub. Jo was hardly a child when Izzy got sick. No. I don't think he left because of anything you or I did or didn't do for him— other than bringing him into the world. He's struggling with who he is right now, the way anyone who is thoughtful does as he leaves childhood behind. You and I both did; why should we expect Jo to sail through this stage of life without questioning how and where he fits, what he truly wants?"

"When I left home I felt I had no choice, that all I could expect if I stayed was shame and disgrace. I left in despair, not anger."

"Anger can be a form of despair. I've watched Jo over the past months and started to see a burden I know neither you nor I anticipated when we welcomed him into the world as our son. We lived in a cocoon at Innisfree, a world where the rules were ours and the judgment of the outside world was blessedly absent."

"But sooner or later, the outside world encroaches."

Tobias nodded.

"I want to get on the boat right now and go to the mainland. I want to rescue my boy."

Tobias put his arms around her.

"The only one who can rescue Jo is himself. No offense, Mae, but the last people he needs right now are his parents."

"But to go without saying goodbye . . . not even to Izzy. This is going to crush her."

Even with Tobias holding her, enveloping her in his strength and calm, Mae remained rigid instead of softening, alert to the crash of the storm churning outside the home that no longer sheltered her son. She searched her memory for the moments when she had ignored him, believing him to be the sturdy, resourceful and oh-so-smart boy who did not need her in the way fragile, sensitive Izzy did.

"Come to bed, Mae. We can't bring him back."

"I won't be able to sleep. I've been frantic all evening waiting for you and now that I know for sure that he's out there on his own, it gives me no peace."

"Do you want me to sit up with you?"

She looked up at Tobias, grateful for his offer but seeing the fatigue etched on his face. He had been out all day fishing on the Sound as always before the drum circle, and then had spent at least two hours tracking Josiah's movements. She knew he was exhausted, not just from the physical exertion of this long day, but from the emotional loss. She reminded herself that Jo had left Tobias, too. All she had to do was look at the destroyed drum to understand the deep sadness hovering beneath his understanding of Josiah's need to leave.

"No, I'll be fine. You get some rest. I'd only toss and turn, disturbing what little peace there is tonight."

As if hearing her, the wind gusted again, rattling the windows and causing the branches of the cedars close to the house to scrape against the glass like fingernails scrabbling to get inside.

Tobias kissed the top of her head.

"We'll hear from him."

He seemed to be reassuring himself as well as Mae. Then he let her go and found his way in the dark to their bedroom like a blind man whose other senses are heightened.

After he left, Mae pulled one of her mother-in-law's baskets from the top of the cabinet and gently placed the shattered drum and scattered wampum inside. She didn't want Tobias or, especially, Izzy, to wake up to the painful message the brokenness conveyed so starkly.

She held the basket as if she were holding Josiah, these fragments of defiance all she had left. Finally, alone in the darkened kitchen and accompanied by the storm, she wept.

1961
Boston

Chapter 10

"I only ask what way my journey lies"
Josiah

The shudder of the ferry as the captain reversed engines pulling into the harbor at Woods Hole woke Josiah. He hadn't expected to fall asleep, but the dull murmur of the motor as the boat crossed the Sound had eased his agitation, and the exhaustion from his anger with his parents had pushed him into the temporary respite of sleep.

He stretched his limbs and shook off the confusion of waking to the peeling paint and dim lights of the ferry cabin instead of his own bedroom at Cove Meadow. He shook off as well the regret that he would not be waking up in that bed again.

The cabin was nearly empty. Not many people left the island in September on the late boat. He grabbed the knapsack he had packed in anger and thrown into the basket on his bike when he'd left the house for the Burial Ground earlier in the evening. As he made his way down the stairs and onto the dock he could see that the terminal was dark. When he tried the door it was locked. He had thought he might spend the rest of the night on one of the wooden benches inside before catching the first bus to Boston in the morning, but it looked like that wasn't going to happen.

Despite his dismissal of his parents and their inexplicable hypocrisy, he grudgingly admitted to himself that they had taught him to be resourceful and persistent. If one door was closed to him, there were others that would be open.

Zipping up his jacket against the chill wet air moving in off the water, he made a circuit of the dock. The last of the ferry crew was coming off the boat. Josiah slipped behind some stacked crates, but not soon enough.

"Son, was someone supposed to meet you and hasn't shown up?"

The voice was gruff but kind.

"You're Tobias and Mae's son, aren't you? Was someone due to meet you here?"

"No, sir. I planned to take the bus to Boston, but it looks like I missed it."

"Last bus left over an hour ago. They switched to the winter schedule last week. Have you got anyone in Falmouth you can spend the night with?"

Josiah struggled to mask his resentment at the questioning. He wasn't a kid who needed coddling, and even with the prospect of a long, damp night spent in the open, he didn't want to accept help from someone who knew who he was.

And so he told his first lie. "Yes, sir. One of my friends lives just down the road. I was planning to go there."

"I can give you a lift."

"That's okay. It's just a short walk. Thanks for the offer, though."

He swung the knapsack over his shoulder and strode purposefully up the hill to the road heading toward Falmouth. As soon as he reached an intersection he turned off to the right to avoid being stopped again but also to double back to the harbor.

He found a hollow below the road where he could curl up for a few hours. It wasn't the first time he'd slept rough. He molded his pack into a lumpy pillow and closed his eyes against the fear and loss gnawing at his decision to leave. As he fell into a fitful sleep he heard Izzy's voice.

"You're such a hothead! Everything is always so intense with you. Sometimes I envy how worked up you get, but jeez, Jo, you're exhausting. Take it easy now and then. With us, but mostly with yourself."

His little sister, his wise little sister. But it was too late. He couldn't—wouldn't—take the words back. And he didn't think either of his parents understood. Innisfree was the one place, the only place, where he felt he belonged. And now that was gone.

That door that had always been open, always welcoming, had been shut in his face. And now, he had to seek another.

It was the boom of the six o'clock ferry's horn that woke him. He stood and brushed the pine needles from his jeans and climbed down the hill to the bus station. He had a few minutes before the Boston departure and washed up in the terminal.

He studied the face staring out at him in the mirror as if it belonged to a stranger. He saw burdens in the dark eyes. The guilt he carried for the responsibility he felt for Izzy's crippling disease and the isolation that had shaped her. The sense of being split in two—not fully Wampanoag and not fully white. If he'd had a scissors with him at that moment, he'd have lopped off his hair. When he got to Boston, the first thing he'd do would be to find a barber. He had no idea what the second thing would be.

When he left the barber he ran his hand over the back of his head. He thought he'd feel free, that he had cut off not only the weight of his hair but also the weight of his tribal identity. No one could immediately place him into a box marked "Indian" now, the way everyone in the barber shop had looked warily at him when he walked in. He might as well have been wearing fringed deerskin and a headdress.

But instead of feeling free he simply felt naked. Maybe that was what was necessary, before he found what he truly wanted to put on.

He was hungry. He'd left the table the night before without finishing his meal, another hurt he'd inflicted on his mother. He'd find a diner and then figure out what to do next. He had only thought about getting away, getting out. He had no idea what he was going toward.

Not far from the barber he saw what looked like a decent place. When you grow up in a restaurant, you know what to look for. He opened the door into the familiar bustle of early morning, the aromas of fresh-brewed coffee and bacon welcoming him.

He took a stool at the counter and ran his finger along the menu. He didn't know how long the money he'd earned from his off-season job at Cronig's Market would have to last, so he tempered his desire to fill his empty belly and chose a couple of fried eggs, bacon, and toast. No blueberry pancakes.

Despite his hunger, he ate slowly, half-listening to the conversations around him as he once again confronted the consequences of his decision. He knew he wouldn't be able to sleep out in the open as he had at Falmouth, so he needed to find a cheap bed. Then a job. He could probably find another grocery store like Cronig's where he could unload crates and stock shelves until he figured out what to do next.

The anonymity of the diner was a revelation to him. There hadn't been many places in his life where no one knew who he was, where no one labeled him immediately—as Tobias and Mae's son or a loner or "that Indian boy."

He could be anyone now. He had a clean slate, wiped of all the preconceptions people had formed, all the history he carried around like another backpack. He was free.

He paid his bill, eased himself off the stool and headed out into the city.

The hotels around South Station were grim, dark-halled places stinking of despair and indifference. He turned away from the dull eyes and muttered ramblings of the old men crouched over card games on grimy, tattered chairs. The smell of the sea, just a few blocks away, was masked by the clouds of cigarette smoke and the rancid odor of sour beer and sour bodies.

He threaded his way through crooked streets, crossed under the Expressway, and eventually found himself at the intersection of the bastions of Boston commerce— the flagship department stores of Filene's and Jordan Marsh. His mother had worked at Jordan Marsh when she had been his age, a shop girl selling blueberry muffins in the bakery.

He pushed open the heavy brass doors, telling himself it was curiosity and not longing that was driving him to find what had shaped his mother's life in Boston.

Like many things in Boston, thirty years had made little difference in the bakery. Pretty, smiling girls filled cardboard boxes with the muffins for a waiting line of customers. He watched from the periphery, the tantalizing aroma of the fresh-baked muffins pulling him back unwillingly to his mother's kitchen. He tried to imagine her as she might have been as a girl, her honey-colored hair confined to a hairnet, her smooth hands— not yet scarred and roughened by years of chopping and kneading and scrubbing—swiftly grabbing the sugar-encrusted treats.

He knew she had come to Boston unwillingly, forced there with her family by the loss of her parents' jobs on the island during the Depression. She had barely spoken of her life in Boston or her family.

"You are my family," she had said one Christmas years before, embracing Josiah and Izzy and Tobias, and then widening her arms to the others in the room—Betty and Naomi and Naomi's brother George. They were the people who had been ever present in his life, from his earliest memories.

He had never questioned that there might be others, except for a fragment of memory from his childhood when he was about four years old. It was a hot day, his father knotting Josiah's tie behind the courthouse in Edgartown, Betty taking his hand, and hurrying him quietly up a back staircase, her finger placed gently over his lips when he asked where they were going. He remembered his legs dangling over the edge of a chair in a room filled with thick old books, sunlight through a narrow window casting slants of light filled with dust motes. A man in a black robe came and sat next to him.

That was all he could recall, although the beginning and end of the memory felt very different because of his parents' faces. At the start, Mae's had been stiff, like she was trying to hold herself from flying apart. He had seen that face again only once more, after that long-ago morning when they had been waiting at the hospital not knowing if Izzy was going to live or die. His father's face had also been rigid, but with anger, not fear. It had been Betty's reassuring hand and soft murmurs that had cushioned him from his own fear.

"We'll get an ice cream when Mama and Daddy's meeting is over," she had promised. That's what they had all called it, a meeting. But the expression on his parents' faces later had been far sweeter than the chocolate ice cream dripping down his chin and melting all over his hand.

It was only years later, when he was fifteen, that he had finally understood the impact of the blistering morning. The weather had suddenly turned cold at Innisfree and his mother had sent him up to the loft to retrieve some blankets stored in a trunk. He had opened the wrong trunk and would have moved on to the other one if not for the packages with his first and middle names printed on the outside—"Josiah Liam." His mother was calling him, so he let the lid drop carefully. The next day, when she had gone to Edgartown to do the marketing, he had slipped up the stairs and opened the mysterious trunk again. He discovered a treasure trove of "little boy" toys—a Lionel train set, Lincoln Logs, even a cowboy outfit at the very bottom. Underneath the holster and hat and miniature leather chaps was an envelope with the return address of the Dukes County Courthouse. Inside was the explanation for his fragmented memory.

He had sat for more than an hour in the dim light of the loft reading the court's decision to deny the petition of a woman named Kathleen Bradley to take custody of Josiah. The secrets shrouding that day came tumbling off the page—the severity of his mother's illness; the claims of wealth and privilege that Kathleen Bradley offered as justification for taking him from his parents; Kathleen's identity as his aunt, his mother's older sister; the existence of another aunt and uncles in Boston—names that had never been uttered in the Monroe house in all the years since the hearing. There was even a report about him, Josiah, from a social worker. The language was formal and stilted, as the whole document had been, but he recognized his four-year-old self in the description of "a bright, engaging child with a surprisingly large vocabulary. He also can read."

In the midst of the turmoil and confusion at his discovery, Josiah had to smile at the social worker's "surprise." It was a word that had continued to cling to him, for good or ill. He always seemed to be surprising people.

When he heard the voices approaching the house from the dock he hurriedly stuffed the court papers back in their envelope and placed it under the toys where it had been hidden.

He hadn't understood why the court's decision had been hidden in the first place, never spoken of after that joyful moment when his parents had come out of their meeting and embraced him, Tobias swinging him up in his arms.

He wanted to understand the reason for the secrecy, but didn't believe he could ask his parents. At fifteen, he was already chafing against his parents' belief that he was still a kid—especially with his father.

But he waited until the right moment when he was alone with Betty, harvesting the last of the pumpkins and squash in the garden at Innisfree. Betty was never "surprised" by Josiah and had often been his buffer, especially after Izzy had gotten sick and his mother had been so consumed with her care. In his brain he knew that Izzy needed Mae more than he did, but Betty saw into his heart that he sometimes felt abandoned and adrift. Without making him feel like a whiny baby who wanted his mama, Betty had shown up at his Little League game or paid attention to the music he listened to and bought him an LP of the Everly Brothers for his birthday when Mae had been in Boston with Izzy for another of the treatments that didn't seem to be making any difference in her ability to walk. He had hated his resentment of Izzy at the same time that he felt bleakly guilty for allowing her to stay at the tidal pool that fateful day when everything changed in their lives. Betty seemed to get that, without trying to dismiss his feelings as stupid or wrong. She never said the meaningless platitudes that other adults repeated endlessly. She had once told him, "I don't put up with bullshit and I don't spout it, either."

So it was natural for him to turn to her for answers about the secrecy of the custody hearing and his mother's family.

Betty sat back on her heels and looked at him for a long minute, shading her eyes from the sun.

"Your mom's sister Kathleen was a very disturbed woman. Even after the judge's decision, your parents worried that she might still try to take you away. To protect you, they believed it best to cut off any contact with your mom's family. Even though her other sister and brothers were no danger to you, Kathleen could have gotten to you through them."

"Is she still crazy?"

"I don't know, honey. Once your mom and dad recognized how reckless and troubled she was, they never looked back, never tried to find out whether she had gotten help or not. And now, with Izzy so sick, they don't have the energy or time, even if they wanted to know. Which they don't."

"Do I have cousins? It feels really weird to find out there's a whole group of people I'm related to that I never met."

Betty studied him for a while, as if making up her mind whether to tell him something, something maybe his parents wouldn't want him to know.

"I'm not going to tell you to leave this alone, forget about it and go on with your life as you have before. I've lived long enough to know that's a fool's errand, especially at your age when you are just beginning to figure out who you are and who you want to be. But I am going to offer you some advice. Let it rest for a couple of years. Your Boston roots will still be there when you are old enough to handle whatever you find— disappointment or rejection or maybe even a warm welcome. But don't count on anything and be prepared for slammed doors.

"When I was young and scared and not all that happy with my folks, I wished I had some long-lost relatives who would welcome me with open arms. It was a fantasy, and I realized pretty quickly that no one was going to rescue me. I had to do it myself. You just found out that you do have another family. But it's a family your mom and dad very rightfully kept away from you. Trust their judgment until you can protect yourself. You know I've always talked straight with you, Jo. I'm not talking down to you. You're not a little kid, but you're not yet a man. When you are a man, no one is going to stop you from finding out who your aunts and uncles are. Certainly not me, and I don't think your mom and dad will either. All I'm saying is wait."

He had struggled with what he wanted desperately to know and his trust in Betty. But he had listened to her and had indeed waited. He had only asked her that she not tell his parents what he had found in the loft.

"It will worry my mom, don't you think? She's got so much on her mind with Izzy. I don't want her to think I'm going to run off to Boston. I promise to wait if you promise not to tell them."

In the end, Betty agreed.

And now, he was a man. And although he had left the island the night before without a plan, without any intention of seeking out his mother's family, he knew as he stood there in the Jordan Marsh bakery that he was there for a reason. He would start his journey where his mother had begun hers.

He was next in line, bought a blueberry muffin and asked where he might find a phone booth.

In a quiet corridor near the restrooms he riffled through the densely printed pages of the Boston metropolitan phone directory. He started not with the name Bradley, the crazy aunt who might or might not still be obsessed with her sister's son, but with Keaney. Mae had two brothers, according to Betty. Patrick and Daniel.

It hadn't occurred to Josiah that he would find twenty-three men named Patrick or Daniel Keaney within the city limits. But he emptied his pockets of small change and lined up his dimes and nickels on the shelf below the phone and began calling. The first six numbers yielded nothing but unanswered rings. With a stubby pencil he ticked off each one. On the seventh call, a woman with a frail, barely audible voice answered. When he asked for Patrick Keaney he was met with silence and then a sob.

"My Patsy is only three days in his grave. Can you not leave a mother in peace!"

Josiah apologized for the intrusion and crossed off the name. He knew that Mae's mother—his Irish grandmother—had died before he was born. He made it through three more calls—one number was out of service and the two he reached were definitely not the Patrick Keaney he was seeking. He was running low on coins and an impatient line of people was waiting outside the door of the booth. With his back to the glass, he carefully tore the Keaney pages from the directory, folded them and slipped them into his pocket.

He ducked out of the booth and found his way through the labyrinthine store to a street entrance. Once out in the brisk air he stopped to reassess what to do next. It was nearly noon and the sidewalks at this crossroads were teeming with women who appeared to be on a mission. Most of them looked like office workers rushing during their lunch break to do errands, their feet in pumps flying down the crowded block and their gloved hands clasping laden shopping bags. His mother had worked his entire life, but her uniform had been a crisp white apron over a sleeveless cotton dress comfortable enough for the heat of a kitchen at the height of summer. She'd always been partial to the colors of the flowers in her garden for her dresses—lavender, sunflowers, beach roses, and Indian paintbrushes. Not the somber navy blues and grays of the women here in Boston. He had to press himself up against the side of the building after one shopping bag too many slapped against him in the swirling mass of purposeful women. Not even the tumult of the Fourth of July weekend in Edgartown compared to the intensity of downtown Boston.

He looked out over the heads of the crowd for an escape route and saw a sign labeled "Boston Common" pointing away from the stores. He'd been there once during one of Izzy's Boston hospital stays, when Tobias had taken him on the Green Line trolley to Park Street and they had emerged from the underground terminal, with its screeching wheels and barely recognizable announcements, to a swath of green lawn and shade trees. It had reminded him then of Ocean Park in Oak Bluffs. For an island boy used to the expansive vistas along the cliffs at Aquinnah or room to run along the isolated sands of East Beach, the Boston Common wasn't much, but at this moment, trapped in a crowd of urban shoppers, it was a goal worth pursuing.

When the light changed he moved into the crowd and let it carry him across the street and up into the canyon that led to Tremont Street and the Common. Once there he found an unoccupied bench in the sun and dug into his knapsack for the blueberry muffin, which had managed to survive his escape from the department store crush with a still intact, crisp and sugar-crusted crown. He washed it down with a Coke from a hot dog vendor nearby and then pulled out the pages torn from the phone book. The number of calls he'd made where no one had answered was frustrating. It was going to take him days to get through the list. He hadn't thought ahead before he left Chappy to find out more about his mother's family—but he hadn't thought ahead about anything at all. He'd just left. Although the decision to go had risen up from his belly like the flash of phosphorus his chemistry teacher had demonstrated one day in class, the reasons pushing him to go had simmered for months. As wide as the sea that he loved and the woods that had been both his playground and his classroom as a boy, he had felt a growing sense of confinement on the island, with its small minds and ever-encroaching "civilization" from off-islanders, whose money was scarfing up what little land the Wampanoag had managed to claim. Once his parents sold Innisfree, there was nothing to hold him, to enfold him, to give him a place where he knew in the deepest core of his heart that he belonged.

He didn't think he belonged in Boston, either. Only half a day in the city and he was already seeking the open space of the Common, however bounded by stone and brick and iron railings on its edges. As much as he wanted to stay longer on there and not plunge back into the city, he knew he needed to find a cheap bed as much as he needed to find his uncles. He saw a tourist shop across from the entrance to the Park Street MTA and asked for a map of the city. He figured he'd plot the addresses of the Keaneys and try to find a hotel or a Y nearby. It was nearly five when he folded up the map. The hot dog vendor was packing up to leave the park and Josiah approached him. Unlike the men in suits emerging from the State House and law offices and publishing houses on the periphery of the Common, the vendor looked like a man who knew the kind of neighborhood where Josiah might find a boarding house or hostel. He'd resume the search for his uncles tomorrow.

The vendor eyed him warily as he walked up to the cart.

"I'm closing up now, son. The franks are all gone. I can open another Coke for you, but that's all. I've got to wheel this back to the garage."

"No thanks, sir. I was just wondering if you knew someplace where I can get a room."

"Where you from? You one of those Cape Verdeans from New Bedford?"

Josiah masked his face. It was not the first time his darker skin had elicited curiosity about his origins. He clenched his fists to keep from reaching for the hair he'd cut off earlier in the day.

"I'm from the Vineyard. My dad is a Monroe and my mom's a Keaney," he answered evenly.

"How old are you?"

"Eighteen." He wanted to say "old enough," but kept his mouth shut.

"You look older. You look like you can handle yourself. If it's a cheap place you want, there's a couple of Single Room Occupancy rooming houses down Washington Street toward the Combat Zone. You know the neighborhood? Place is full of bars and strip joints attracting sailors in port on leave. But if you keep to yourself and lock your door you'll be fine. One more thing, don't take any booze if somebody offers you. More'n likely it's spiked and once you're knocked out they'll grab whatever you've got in that bag of yours. Of course, if you can afford it, there's the Parker House, just a block from here. Or are you a college kid? In that case, get on the Red Line and take your chances of finding a room in Harvard Square. Those are your choices. It's up to you."

And with that, he heaved on the cart and started pushing it down the path toward Boylston Street.

Josiah watched him disappear into the crowd. He knew enough about Harvard from the summer people on the island who frequented the Boat House as if it were some adventure in "slumming." They acted as if they were bestowing some favor on Mae by eating her sandwiches and pies instead of the tasteless fare at the white-tablecloth places in Edgartown. He'd stay away from Cambridge, thank you very much. And from what he'd seen of the Parker House when he'd passed it earlier in the day, he'd spend his entire savings on one night in one of their beds.

He grabbed his knapsack and resigned himself to the Combat Zone. Some of the older guys on the island had brought back wild stories of bars and strip joints frequented mostly by sailors in port, college kids out for a thrill that they could easily drive away from at the end of the night, or bored salesmen traveling around the region and not likely to run into anyone they knew from church.

The hotdog vendor had been right in his assessment that Josiah could handle whatever he might encounter there. He knew how to use his fists; he knew how to use the knife sheathed and buried in the bottom of his pack. The crowds of workers heading home in the deepening twilight thinned out considerably the closer he got to his destination. As he approached the neon-lit, garbage-strewn streets that provided shelter to Boston's transient population, his stomach reminded him that he'd only had that blueberry muffin to eat since breakfast.

After the vendor's warning he was wary of eating anything at one of the joints where he was heading and glanced around for a more likely—and safer—establishment. His map indicated that Boston's Chinatown was not far from downtown and he struck out in that direction, letting his nose lead him to dinner.

He found a small neighborhood place and settled in, relieved at the cheap prices and large quantity of food. Well-fortified, he made his way back to the dim, lonely streets of the Combat Zone.

The man behind the grill at the first place he stopped didn't care about anything except Josiah's cash. He paid for one night only, not willing to commit to anything more, and followed the manager up the narrow staircase to a room in the back. The mattress was lumpy and had no sheets, but Josiah spread his pea coat and stretched out. It was a bed with a roof over it. It was enough.

Under the light over the bed he studied the map and the phone list, hoping to find a cluster of Keaneys who might lead him to his uncles. There were several Keaneys in Jamaica Plain, a neighborhood on the southern fringe of the city. In the morning, he'd start there, knocking on doors rather than calling.

He had rarely spent a night off-island. He thought that a room in the back would spare him the raucous sounds of the street, the throb and hiss of the flashing neon sign announcing "Nude Girls" next door. But he discovered that the alley behind the building was as teeming with urban life as the street. Some of the sounds were familiar to him. The slithering of a feral cat on the hunt, its prey rustling through the weeds and trash until it succumbed. Other sounds were at least identifiable—the insistent wail of sirens, the piercing intrusion of shattering glass, the trickle of someone relieving himself against the rotting fence. Even the voices, words muted beyond understanding, held a tone all too expressive of conspiracy or anger or despair.

He wasn't afraid. The forces of nature he had known on the island were to be feared—wind, fire, water. But men, even hyped up on booze or weed or drugs, were just men. He had locked his door, as the vendor had cautioned him. And when he heard the raised voices and thwack of fists meeting flesh in the hall outside his room, he pushed the dresser against the door.

But later in the evening he heard another voice, a girl's voice. Not the tough, smoky voices of the women coaxing him from alleyways on his way back from Chinatown, commenting to one another about his handsome face, his youth, what they assumed was his virginity. They teased him, pretended to be fighting over him. Despite his understanding that they were prostitutes, as predatory as those who would steal from him; despite his perception of them as immensely unattractive, with worn-out bodies, too much makeup and bruised arms; he found himself getting hard, as if they were actually stroking his dick instead of his ego.

He had turned away from them, from the ripple of laughter as soon as they realized he was aroused.

"Better go home to Mama before you get yourself in trouble," they cackled, and then moved on to the next potential customer.

The voice he heard from the relative safety of his room was not one of those jaded, teasing voices. It was a voice tinged with fear, a voice begging, a voice in trouble.

He moved from the bed to the door, leaning over the barricade of the dresser to press his ear and listen. He heard the smack of a hand, accompanied by a man's voice screaming profanities, the girl now whimpering, her voice coming closer to the floor than earlier, as if she had slipped from the force of the blow.

Without caution, ignoring the words of the hot dog vendor, Josiah shoved the dresser away from the door and threw it open. The man, well-dressed for this part of town, was kicking the girl, who was cowering against the wall, her arms raised to protect her head. Blood trickled from her mouth.

She looked not much older than Izzy, her thin limbs barely covered by a purple satin miniskirt. One of the straps on her high heels had broken.

Josiah took in the scene, saw it once again as he had earlier in the evening through the prism of predator and prey. But this was not some hungry cat following its survival instinct. It was a creep beating up on a kid less than half his size.

He rushed the guy, pushing him away from the girl and slamming him against the wall.

"Get in my room and shut the door," he shouted to the girl as the creep recovered from the surprise of being hit and came after Josiah with his fists. Josiah saw the flash of a ring on his finger that must have cut the girl when he hit her. It was a wedding ring.

The girl scrambled across the hall into Josiah's room.

The guy was big and angry, but slowed by both Josiah's initial shove and booze Josiah could smell when he got up in Josiah's face. Josiah was also angry, but he had learned how to fight on the wrestling team in high school. He finished off the older, softer man quickly. When the guy finally slumped against the wall at the top of the staircase, Josiah fought back the impulse to push him down the steps.

You don't want to kill him, a voice warned him inside his head.

He left him, but not before hearing the guy mutter, "You'll be sorry, you punk."

Josiah thought the girl might have locked the door, but when he tried it, it gave easily. He found her curled up on the bed, her face already swelling and a black eye blooming around her left eye.

She flinched as he approached her and he realized she was as frightened of him as she had been of the man who had beaten her.

He went to the sink and soaked an end of the threadbare towel with cold water.

"I'm not going to hurt you," he said softly. "Will you let me wash away the blood or do you want to do it yourself?"

She reached out her hand and he gave her the towel. While she wiped her face he took a step back and leaned against the door. If the guy came back he wanted to be ready. His breath was coming more easily now, and with it, thought.

A part of him wanted to grab his knapsack and get as far away as possible from the rooming house, the girl and whatever trouble was circling her. He watched her, his arms folded across his chest. Her skin was paler than he had ever seen. Even the white girls on the island, the blondest ones who arrived every summer to sail on their father's boats, play tennis in Edgartown and eat ice cream on Circuit Avenue, had skin with more color than this ashen-faced creature huddled on his bed. The hands that had taken the towel were scabbed and almost gray—filmed, he realized, with a layer of dirt. She was just a kid, her breasts barely discernible under the flimsy camisole that was as filthy as her skin.

"What's your name?" He asked gently.

"Cheryl." She thrust the sodden towel back at him, its surface now blotched with blood and grime. Her face, beneath the swelling and the bruises, had a look he recognized—defiance, bravado. Like an animal puffing itself up to frighten away an attacker. If she had been a skunk, he'd have been sprayed by now.

"I suppose you think I owe you something for 'saving' me." Her voice threw out a challenge. "Well, think again. You get nothing from me unless you pay like all the others."

He held up his hands.

"I don't want anything from you, except for you to be safe. You can stay the night here and I'll sleep on the floor."

"Yeah, right. And then Mick'll come looking for me in the morning and put his hand out for all the cash I should have earned while you slept on the floor."

"Who's Mick?" And then he understood.

"Well, where the hell was Mick when the creep was kicking you in the hall?"

"He's got more than one girl to watch out for. He was busy." But Josiah could see that his comment had hit its mark. He wasn't happy he had upset her, but he was torn between protecting her and getting her out of his room, out of his life.

"You can go if you want to. I can't pay to make it worth your while to stay."

Her eyes swept over him and his things—his L.L. Bean knapsack; his pea coat; his watch, a high school graduation present from his parents, on the dresser.

"Where did you come from? Some quiet town in New Hampshire that doesn't have any whores? Did you hear about the Combat Zone and decide to have a little fun? You're not a sailor, and you're not a pervert. I know you're thinking, how did this girl wind up in a hell hole like this neighborhood, and I'm thinking, because of guys like you. Your craving for a little adventure, maybe even a little danger, after being cosseted in your stupid, safe towns."

"I'm not like that," he said quietly, arms once again folded across his chest.

"Yeah, right. Well, let me tell you. I came from one of those towns. Except it wasn't so safe. I bet you have no idea what goes on in some of those neat little houses right down the street from yours."

"When did you leave?" He meant, how old were you?

"Two years ago. I hitched down from Bangor. Mick was the last ride to pick me up, just outside of Hampton Beach."

She stuck her chin out. "Despite what you think, he takes care of me."

"Fine. Then go. If you want, I'll walk you out to make sure the creep isn't waiting for you on the street."

She was about to refuse him, but he saw her clamp her mouth shut and nod an assent.

She moved off the bed toward the door with a seductiveness that jarred with her childlike body.

This time he asked her outright.

"How old were you when you left home?" Not, how old *are* you. Too easy for her to lie, to give the answer that glibly fell off her lips to customers and cops.

"Thirteen," she said. "But believe me, I was *way* older than that in my head."

She moved between him and the dresser, focusing her eyes on him as she let her right arm slip casually behind her back.

But Josiah was a wrestler, and like a batter who needs to keep his eye on the ball, he had trained to sense his opponent's next move. He had his hand on top of hers just as she curled her fingers around his watch. Her hand felt like the skeleton of a bird he'd once found on the beach below the house at Innisfree, stripped bare of flesh and bleached by the sun.

"Drop it."

"You're hurting me."

"You're stealing from me. Is that why the creep was beating you up?"

"If you don't have the cash to pay me for this lovely encounter, I need something else to compensate me."

"How much? And don't lie."

"Fifteen bucks."

"How much does Mick take?"

"Twelve."

"Let go of the watch and I'll give you twenty."

"I thought you didn't have any cash."

He didn't answer her, but tightened his grip on her hand.

"OK. OK. Keep your stupid watch. What was it, a present from Mommy and Daddy?"

She rubbed her hand. He could see his grip had left marks on her fragile skin.

He put the watch on his wrist and pulled out his wallet. She snatched the twenty from his hand and opened the door. In the stairwell below they could hear a commotion—men's voices, heavy footsteps mounting the stairs.

"Oh, Christ," muttered the girl as she peered over the railing. "Cops."

She turned back to the room and dragged him in.

"I need to get out. Now." She struggled with the window, her thin hands scrabbling with the lock and then heaving against the frame with her bony shoulder to lift it. As soon as it was open she clambered out onto the fire escape.

"You coming with, or hanging out to face the cops? If you're staying, shut the window."

And with that, she was gone. He watched her grip the cold metal bars as she slipped down to the street three stories below just as the police shouted, banging on the door.

"Open up! Police."

Josiah had the presence of mind to toss the bloodied towel out the window before he shut it.

The following moments were a blur of blue uniforms, the accusatory shouts of the man who had attacked the girl screaming, "That's him! Her accomplice. He was lying in wait behind the door." Then handcuffs and a push down the stairs to a waiting squad car, its garish lights competing with the neon signs of the district. They had searched the room and found neither the girl nor whatever the guy claimed she had stolen from him. His fury was notches higher than earlier in the evening when he'd had the girl cowering on the floor. He lunged at Josiah, now defenseless with his arms cuffed behind his back and unable even to block a blow. The man got in only one punch before the police intervened, but it was aimed well, and Josiah doubled over. His own rage hadn't yet focused itself in the nightmarish confusion. All he was capable of at that moment was to vomit on his attacker's polished wingtips before the police hustled him into the car. He heard someone tell the guy to come to the station to make a statement, and then the car flew off, siren bleating.

He leaned back against the gray vinyl seat and squeezed his eyes shut to keep from crying. From the moment he had opened the door to the police he hadn't uttered a word. His skin was brown, and everyone else he had encountered in this unreal night had been white—the girl, the creep with the fancy shoes, the hotel manager, the cops. He believed nothing he could say would make it better for him, and so kept his mouth shut.

At the station they gave him a receipt for his wallet, his watch, his coat and his knapsack. At least they had thrown them in the car after it was clear they contained nothing of value, nothing stolen. But they had confiscated the knife.

They undid the handcuffs when they brought him to the cell, telling him he needed to cool off for a few hours.

It was 2 am.

He tried curling up on the wooden bench, but every muscle ached and his gut was still tender where he'd been punched. Sleep did not come.

At 5 am, an officer came to the cell block and unlocked the door.

"Your accuser never showed up to make a statement. We got nothing to hold you on, but if you want some advice, stay out of the Combat Zone and get as far away from your girl as possible. She's been in here before, and someone like her . . . well, let's just say there's no help for her. She's headed for an early grave, if you ask me."

Josiah gathered up the possessions the clerk pushed across the counter to him and turned to leave the station. But then he stopped and went back to the officer who had released him. He had detected a note of kindness in him and took a chance.

"Sir, I'm trying to find my uncle, Patrick Keaney. I know he's an officer on the force. Do you know how I can find out which precinct he works in?"

The officer looked at him. "So you do have a voice. Patrick Keaney, eh? Come with me."

It took a few phone calls, but the officer put a slip of paper in his hand with the precinct address in Dorchester and directions on how to get there on the T.

Josiah wished he'd had a shower, a chance to shave and change his shirt. He'd wished a lot of things over the years—that he hadn't left Izzy at the pond, that she'd never contracted polio, that she'd walk one day without braces or crutches, that his parents had not sold Innisfree. But he was no longer the child who believed wishes might come true.

The streets of downtown Boston were not yet awake. The neon lights of the Combat Zone were now dim; a few drunks lay curled up in litter-strewn alleys. The windows of Jordan Marsh were still dark. He would not buy a blueberry muffin today.

He turned toward the Park Street station and descended the stone steps just as the gates were being rolled back and the Green Line trolleys were screeching around the corner and into the terminal. He ducked into a restroom to wash up. The man staring back at him in the mottled mirror was a stranger. The bruises he bore were hidden by his shirt. The fight had left no scratches or deeper wounds above his neck, although the knuckles of his left hand were throbbing from the blow he had landed on the guy's chin. But the combination of his shorn hair, two-day-old beard and sleepless night had left him barely recognizable as the boy who had left the island. The eyes still seethed with the anger that had driven him away, but they held something else now as witness to cruelty and loneliness and despair. The cold water he splashed on his face revived his flagging energy but did nothing to dispel the images of the night before.

He left the washroom and went to the lower level for the Red Line, clutching the scrap of paper with the precinct address. The rocking subway car lulled him to sleep, his head pressed against the window. He almost slept through the Fields Corner stop, but its lurching arrival at the station roused him enough to realize where he was and he scrambled out the doors just as they were about to close. Outside the station, he took his bearings and started walking the blocks to the precinct.

When he arrived, he took a deep breath and pushed open the door. It was still early, not yet seven, and the hall was empty except for a uniformed officer at the desk. He looked as if he'd been there all night.

Josiah stepped up to the desk.

"What's the problem?" the officer asked, his gravelly voice conveying his exasperation. Josiah guessed he was hoping to end his shift without any more problems and now one had shown up.

"No problem, sir. I'm looking for my uncle, Patrick Keaney. The sergeant at Precinct 1 told me I'd find him here."

The officer pushed his glasses up and looked at Josiah closely.

"I didn't know Pat had a nephew. What's your name, son?"

Josiah answered, but didn't add that Pat might wish to ignore he had a nephew. His confidence in the idea of seeking out his mother's brother was ebbing. For all his denial of the false hope that there was goodness and kindness in the world, he had stupidly clung to the belief that his uncle would welcome him like a prodigal son. He felt like a kid who still believed in Santa Claus and the Tooth Fairy and was about to have the truth shatter his dreams. There was a reason his mother had kept apart from her family. He was an idiot for thinking his appearance in their lives would make that reason go away.

He was about to turn and go, to tell the desk officer "never mind," but he had already picked up the phone to summon Pat Keaney.

"He'll be out in a minute," the officer said. "He's expecting you. The guys at Precinct 1 gave him a heads up."

Josiah could feel the officer's curiosity, the questions simmering just below the surface. He imagined that he looked nothing like his uncle. Everyone on the island had always commented on how much he favored his father, his Wampanoag heritage overshadowing whatever Irish blood flowed in his veins. Izzy was the one who looked more like Mae. She had Mae's thick, honey-colored hair and delicate features. Despite her thirteen-year-old awkwardness, Josiah imagined she'd one day be considered beautiful.

His discomfort under the scrutiny of the desk officer continued to build. He was sweating under his pea coat and his palms were clammy. Not good for shaking hands with the man who possibly held your future in his.

A door opened and a tall, red-haired man approached him, a look of both puzzlement and concern on his face. Instead of extending his hand to Josiah, he reached out and clasped his shoulder.

"Josiah? Is everything all right? Has something happened to Mae?"

"Uncle Patrick? Mom's fine. Can we talk somewhere?" Josiah was acutely aware of the officer behind them, soaking in the exchange like one of the Edgartown biddies who traded gossip at the market.

"Sure, sure. Have you had breakfast?"

Josiah shook his head.

"Then let's go down the street. I'm just getting off duty."

Patrick kept his arm around him as they left the building, as if Josiah might disappear as suddenly as he had dropped into his life. He seemed genuinely glad to see him. Josiah felt as if he had just emerged from a powerful wave that had carried him to shore and he was finally able to breathe.

They settled into a booth at a coffee shop and Patrick urged him to order a full breakfast.

"You look a little worse for wear. The sergeant at Precinct 1 told me what happened last night. You OK?"

Josiah was overwhelmed by his kindness. He wasn't sure what he expected—skepticism, resentment at the barriers Mae had erected between them, disapproval of the trouble he had gotten into the night before.

"If I may ask, what the hell were you doing in the Combat Zone last night? No, wait a minute. Let's start at the beginning. Did you look me up because you got arrested, or was there some other reason? I got to tell you, Josiah, I never thought I'd live to see you. After my sister Kathleen destroyed any hope of reconciliation with your mother, I didn't blame Mae for keeping her distance and especially, for keeping *you* away from the Keaneys. So why are you here? Does your mother know?"

"I don't know where to begin. And no, she doesn't know. I didn't know myself I'd come looking for you until I got to Boston. I was in Jordan Marsh and just got it into my head that I needed to know—to know the other side of me."

"How old are you now, Josiah?"

"Eighteen. Old enough." He didn't want Patrick to insist on his going back home or even contacting his parents.

"Why'd you leave home—because that's what you did, right? You're not just here for a visit."

Josiah set his mouth in a tight line. The man across from him in the booth, even though they were connected by blood, was a stranger to him. His uncle was treating him with unexpected kindness but also with an uncomfortable intimacy—as if he'd always been in his life and had a right to ask these questions. Josiah was about to tell him it was none of his business, but before he blurted out the words the waitress arrived with their platters piled with eggs and sausage and pancakes. He realized how hungry he was and how easy it was to short circuit his resentment with a meal.

"Dig in," his uncle said, picking up his fork. "We can talk after you've eaten."

The restaurant was filling up with other cops coming off duty and customers familiar enough to be welcomed by name. The bustle of the kitchen visible through an opening in the wall behind the counter, the sizzle of eggs and bacon on the griddle, even the singsong orders called out by the harried wait staff reminded him of the Boat House in high summer. If the Boat House had survived the hurricane last year, would it have been enough to save Innisfree?

The waitress stopped by to top off their coffee as his uncle wiped his mouth and leaned back against the maroon plastic seat.

"Listen, I get that I'm not your parents and you don't owe me an explanation. Even though you didn't say it out loud, you were thinking 'mind your own business' or maybe something more explicit. But you sought me out, Josiah. So what's the deal? What's going on?"

"I needed to get off the island."

"Are you in trouble with the law? Because if that's the case, I'll bring you back myself." He was Pat Keaney the cop at that moment, not his Uncle Patrick.

"No! The only thing I broke was my drum. I'm ready to be out on my own, get a job. There isn't anything for me on the island. I don't want to be a fisherman like my father."

It was the first time he had said it loud, the first time he had admitted to himself that he didn't want his father's life.

"Fair enough. I didn't want to follow in my father's footsteps either."

"What was he like, my grandfather? I have his name."

"Liam. I remember. Kathleen kept calling you that. Your grandfather was a drunk and broken man. Boston was not good for him." That appeared to be all Patrick was going to say about his father. "What about school?" He shifted the conversation back to Josiah.

"I graduated in June. I'm done."

"College? Trade school? You don't want to fish, but what do you want to do?"

Josiah shrugged. "I don't know. I figured I could get a job like I had on the island to start. I was a stock boy at the island market." As soon as he spoke, Josiah realized how lame he sounded. An after-school job for a high school kid who didn't have to pay for rent or food was hardly going to cut it in Boston.

"You left without a plan, didn't you?" Patrick shook his head slowly. "And you wound up in the Combat Zone because you don't have a place to stay."

Josiah stared at his empty plate, wiped clean of every crumb by his hunger.

"I guess you think I'm an idiot."

"No. Just young. You'll figure it out. But listen, I'm ready to hit the sack after a long night's work, and I bet you are too. Let's head home."

"Home?"

"Yeah, home. You're my flesh and blood. I'm not going to leave you fending for yourself and wind up in another fleabag hotel tonight. Come on."

Patrick paid the bill with a generous tip, Josiah noticed. Then they walked together to this uncle's car and drove home.

Home was in Jamaica Plain, a narrow street lined with triple-deckers built close together. His uncle's house was a single family set above the street, reached by a steep set of stone steps. A folded *Boston Globe* had been tossed on the porch and Patrick stooped to pick it up without opening it to scan the headlines.

Inside, the house was dark and uninhabited. No one called out to welcome his uncle home, no aroma of coffee wafted from the kitchen. A glance into the living room revealed a sparsely furnished but neat room with a brown couch, a recliner, and a TV set in the corner. Unlike Josiah's home at Cove Meadow, there were no books.

Patrick led Josiah down a corridor and opened a door to a bedroom.

"Bed's already made up. Bathroom's across the hall. I'm going to take a shower and sack out, which you're welcome to do as well. After I have some sleep we can talk again. The phone is in the front hall if you want to call your folks."

Josiah stiffened, but said nothing. He accepted that his uncle's hospitality was bound to have some strings, and communicating with his parents was more than likely at the top of the list. But Patrick hadn't demanded that he do so now and Josiah threw his knapsack on a chair by the bed, unlaced his sneakers and collapsed on the bed.

When he heard the shower stop and his uncle's footsteps retreat to his own room at the back of the house he roused himself and headed to the bathroom.

Under the hot water of the shower he scrubbed away the grime of the past two days, gingerly testing the bruises on his stomach and chest. They were now a mottled blue and purple, still tender. His grandmother would have mashed together a handful of her herbs into a paste and smeared it gently over his skin with her gnarled fingers, winding a cloth around his chest to hold the ointment in place. He would have stunk of marsh and earth for a few days. But Naomi wasn't here and he'd have to fend for himself. He checked the medicine cabinet, but aside from shaving cream, a razor, and some aspirin, he found nothing that could heal bruises or assuage the uncertainty that now left him with a pit in his stomach.

He shaved and then sought refuge once more in the bed his uncle had offered him. It was a quiet neighborhood. Despite the lack of the rhythm of the sea that had lulled him to sleep since childhood, he slept.

He woke late in the afternoon to the smell of frying onions. He pulled on his jeans and a t-shirt and found Patrick in the kitchen wielding a spatula.

"Minute steak, onions, and potatoes," he said as Josiah entered the kitchen. "You can set the table. You'll find everything you need in that cupboard."

When the meal was ready they sat together.

"Do you say grace at your house?" Patrick asked.

Josiah nodded and Patrick invited him to speak it.

"Your mom taught me that prayer," he smiled when Josiah finished.

They ate silently until Patrick pushed his chair back, stretched out his legs and folded his arms across his chest.

"Why are you here, Josiah?"

"Do you want me to leave? I don't expect you to take care of me. I'm not a kid. I didn't intend to drop into your life . . ."

"Whoa! Who said anything about leaving? You're welcome here, Josiah. I'm just trying to understand what drove you here, and why me?"

"You were the easiest to find. I knew you were a cop. I only know the names of the others—Danny and Maureen. And I remembered Maureen was a nun. I also knew the last person I should try to contact was Kathleen."

"Good decision. Do you remember anything of what happened when she tried to take you away, or were you too young?

"I was four. I remember bits and pieces. It was hot and I didn't want to wear a tie. I don't remember ever seeing Kathleen, but I do remember the fear in our house, all the adults acting like we were under siege."

"Your Aunt Kathleen's not well in her head. Even now, I don't think it would be wise for you to let her know you are in Boston."

"I don't intend to."

"Be straight with me. Your leaving the island isn't just about finding a job, making your way on your own, is it?"

Josiah was silent for a moment. Patrick so far had struck him as a man who would understand his rift with his parents. Hadn't he spoken of his own father in a way that implied he had set himself apart from his father and his past? Josiah gathered his courage and told him what had happened the night he'd left.

Patrick listened without interrupting.

Then he said, "Don't repeat your mother's past, Josiah. Her reasons for leaving were her own, but she went without a word of farewell to any of us and it broke our mother's heart. We thought she was dead, but we couldn't even mourn her."

"I don't belong on Chappy anymore. I don't know where I belong."

"I'm not telling you to go back. You have a home with me for as long as you need. But I'm going to ask one thing of you if you stay, and that is to call your folks and let them know you are safe and you are with me."

Josiah's face hardened. Maybe Patrick didn't understand as much as he'd hoped.

"Think about it. I've got to get to work. I'll be back in the morning."

He went to a drawer and pulled out a key.

"Here's a key to the house in case you want to go out. I've got tomorrow off and can show you around the neighborhood. If you want to take a look, the *Globe* has a help-wanted section. I'll also ask around on my beat if anyone's looking for help." And then he was gone.

Josiah saw the hand-lettered help-wanted sign in the window of the coffee shop when he ventured out of Patrick's house the next morning after Patrick had gone to bed.

His uncle had arrived home from his shift in a strange mix of agitation and exhaustion. He'd gone straight to his bed without breakfast and with barely a word to Josiah.

"Rough night. Need to sleep." And he had shut the door.

Josiah didn't want to hang around while Patrick unwound from whatever had occurred on his beat.

He ran his hand over the top of his head, still unused to the spiky bristles of his short hair. Another betrayal, one his father would not understand.

He left the house, closing the door quietly and hurrying down the steps to the street as if he were late, as if he had a purpose and a direction for his excursion into the neighborhood. He left his uncle's residential street and arrived on a block of small shops. To his right, a few streets down, was a trolley stop. It was rush hour and streaming around him was a steady throng of people on their way to work—nurses in white shoes and stockings; men in suits and ties, newspapers tucked under their arms; secretaries with Jackie Kennedy pillbox hats on their neatly styled hair. He even saw a nun, her rosary beads flying behind her as she led a group of small children through the gate of a playground adjacent to a brick school building with the letters "AMDG" carved in stone above the door.

"For the greater glory of God," an old woman next to him said, pointing toward the school.

Josiah looked at her in confusion. Maybe she was the neighborhood crazy, mumbling out loud to herself. She continued, directing her words to him.

"AMDG. It's the abbreviation for *Ad Majorum Dei Gloriam*. The Jesuit motto. You appeared to be staring at it and I thought you might want to be apprised of its meaning. You also appear to be new to the neighborhood. Allow me to welcome you. I'm Margaret Mary Hannon." She stuck out her hand, gnarled and knotted with thick blue veins.

"I clean for the priests at St. Thomas Aquinas, hence my knowledge of Latin. Have you had your breakfast, boy? Where did you say you were from?"

The woman spoke in an uninterruptable stream and even had he chosen to, Josiah would not have been able to answer her. When she finally stopped, he didn't know whether to make excuses that he was late and hurry off, or tell her his life story.

He settled on giving her the simplest answer to her question.

"I'm from Martha's Vineyard, ma'am."

"How'd you wind up in JP?" Josiah was just getting used to the abbreviation people used for the Jamaica Plain neighborhood. "Do you have people here?"

"I'm visiting my uncle."

"Mind you, pay attention now that you're in the city. Staring up at buildings while the world is moving at a frenetic pace around you can sometimes lead to problems. You stick out, as you did to me. If I recognized you as a stranger, I can guarantee a dozen others did as well."

Josiah suspected that he was pegged as a stranger not because of his staring at buildings but because of the color of his skin. In all the comings and goings of people on the street, he had seen only white faces.

Margaret Mary was not finished with her interrogation.

"So who's your uncle?"

Josiah hesitated. How much information did he owe this woman? How private was his Uncle Patrick and how much did he want the neighborhood to know his business? Josiah was used to the sometimes oppressive nature of island life, where the small, close-knit community on Chappy was deeply involved in one another's lives. He imagined that his absence had already been noted, dissected and judged.

He just hadn't expected his arrival in Boston to have garnered quite so much attention. He had imagined a luxurious anonymity, where he could find his way without his every move and every word observed.

"Doesn't this uncle of yours feed you? You look a little peckish to me." She pulled up a watch attached to a thin chain around her neck.

"Father Robert isn't expecting me until after he says the children's mass. That's where Sister Mary Peter was leading the little ones. May I buy you a cup of coffee and some scrambled eggs down the street at Loretta's?"

Josiah protested. "That's really not necessary, Mrs. Hannon. I've already eaten." He lied. He had waited to have breakfast with Patrick, but when his uncle had retreated in silence to bed, Josiah lost the will to cook for himself alone. But he felt awkward accepting a meal from this inquisitive woman.

"A cup of coffee then. Humor an old, curious woman. We don't get many newcomers to the neighborhood and it will raise my stature in the community when I walk into Loretta's with a handsome young man." She grinned at him, a smile that made her look both young and playful.

She took his arm and marched him down the block. Reluctantly, he fell into step beside her.

That was when he saw the help-wanted sign, and suddenly his accompanying Margaret Mary seemed like a stroke of luck. She greeted people as they entered the coffee shop and Josiah watched carefully for their reactions to both Margaret Mary and himself. He wanted to know if she was respected in the neighborhood or merely tolerated as an eccentric, talkative biddy. He wasn't sure yet himself. And he also wasn't sure what her motive was in approaching him on the street. She knew he didn't belong. Was she suspicious of his presence, worried that he was someone there only to do harm?

Margaret Mary directed him toward a booth and deposited her purse and her bulging shopping bag on the seat opposite him before sliding in herself.

"Now, what'll it be? Just coffee, or can Loretta bring you something to eat? Myself, I have a bowl of oatmeal in the morning before I leave for work. Fills me up while

I'm vacuuming and dusting at the rectory. You just visiting or planning to settle with your uncle?"

Her ability to switch from her meandering description of her own life to an inquisition about his caught Josiah off-guard.

"I don't know how long I'll stay with Uncle P..," he stopped himself before spilling Pat's name, but Margaret Mary caught the slip and pounced.

"P, eh? What is that short for? Pablo? Pedro?"

Josiah realized she thought he was Portuguese. It was a reasonable assumption since she knew he was from the islands. He wondered whether it would be better for him to let her continue thinking that, or if he should just admit defeat and tell her who he was. He figured she'd find out eventually with her dogged inquisitiveness, especially if he stayed. He threw up his hands.

"I give up. You win. My uncle is Pat Keaney. I've come to Boston to find work."

"Officer Keaney? Well, what do you know! Who knew he had a nephew? I thought one sister was a nun and the other one, well, no one knows a damn thing about her except that she's rich. So whose son are you? The brother in the army?"

Josiah was reeling from how much Margaret Mary knew already about the Keaneys. But she didn't know about his mother, and he preferred to keep it that way.

He was about to mumble something, anything, to get off the subject of his origins, when Loretta arrived with her order pad.

"Mrs. Hannon, what can I get you? Your usual coffee and Danish? And what about your young man?"

Margaret Mary beamed with ownership of Josiah.

"My young man is protesting that he's already had breakfast, but I do know one thing he'd like." She looked across the table, defying Josiah to contradict her. "He'd like a job," she announced with authority.

Loretta glanced between the two of them.

"Is that true?"

Josiah nodded and then found his voice.

"Yes, miss. I worked in my mother's café on Martha's Vineyard ever since I was old enough to handle a knife." He looked around the shop. "It was a little bigger than this place and I did everything over the years—waited and bussed tables, washed dishes, caught and cleaned fish and clams and swept up at the end of the day. My mom did the baking, though."

Margaret Mary sat back with an expression of gleeful satisfaction on her face.

Loretta put her hand on her hip and appraised him.

"I suppose you have some references, beyond your sponsor here."

"He's Pat Keaney's nephew, Loretta, for God's sake! You think he'd put his hand in the till with a cop for an uncle?"

Josiah winced.

"I'm interested in knowing whether he can do the job, Mrs. Hannon. I don't care if he's an altar boy; I just need somebody who can keep up the pace. Ever since Janine left for college I've had my hands full and I've been run ragged. So," she turned to Josiah. "How about I give you a two-week trial while you get me somebody I can call who can vouch for your experience? When can you start?"

"I can start right now. I'll need to let my uncle know later today where I am, but just point me where you want me."

Josiah stood and put out his hand. "Thank you."

Loretta stuck her order pad in her apron pocket and shook his hand.

Margaret Mary pointed to her cheek.

"Right here," she smiled. "I get a kiss for setting you on your path to success."

Loretta quickly led him behind the counter, introduced him to Sal at the grill and then thrust an order pad and pencil in his hand.

"I'll give you a tour after the breakfast crowd thins. Sal can tell you the lunch specials then. We close at four, with everything wiped down, the floor mopped and tables prepped for the next day. We open at six. Any questions?"

Josiah shook his head.

"How about 'what are you going to pay me?'" Loretta smiled.

Josiah reddened and rolled his eyes at his own naiveté. He felt like a kid instead of the independent man he imagined himself to be. The whole experience—Margaret Mary accosting him on the street, her persistent questioning, even her role in announcing his need for a job—left him embarrassed. He was grateful, no question. But he now felt burdened. What more would Margaret Mary expect of him besides a kiss on the cheek?

He watched her gather up her things and button her coat after she finished her Danish and coffee. She waved to him as she left.

Loretta came up to him when the door closed behind Margaret Mary.

"Don't worry. She's one of the good guys in the neighborhood. She's helped both of us. Now get over to table five with the coffee carafe and refill their cups. The guy in the gray suit is on the City Council. We don't want him unhappy."

The day moved in a steady, familiar rhythm. He got a feel for how Sal liked to get the grill orders. He learned where the storeroom was in the basement. He mopped up a careless spill quickly with an apology to the customer and an extra cinnamon donut. He refilled all the salt and pepper shakers, the sugar canisters, and the plastic squeeze bottles of ketchup and mustard. He carted the trash to the alley.

"You did well," Loretta told him at the end of the day. "See you tomorrow, quarter to six."

He climbed the hill to Patrick's house, tired but buzzed. In his pocket he felt the satisfying weight of the coins left as tips for him. He smiled as he turned the key in the door.

Pat was up, dressed in a t-shirt and jeans, his feet bare and his hair still wet from the shower.

"Where the hell have you been?"

Josiah recoiled from the assault of Pat's words. His excitement at not only finding the job but earning Loretta's approval at the end of the day vanished in the silence following his uncle's harshly phrased question.

Josiah realized that Pat might have been worried about him, especially given his arrest. And he had meant to let him know where he was, but somehow the demands of the day had swallowed up his good intentions. He knew he should apologize. It was what they would have expected him to do at home. But he wasn't home. And Pat wasn't his father. Even his father wouldn't have spoken to him like that.

Instead, Josiah dug the coins out of his pocket and dumped them on the hall table.

"I was out looking for work. And I found it. Here are my tips. If it's not enough for the night I spent here, I'll drop off more tomorrow."

He turned and went to his room and started to pack up his knapsack. How could a day that had started out so weirdly with Margaret Mary and built to such a deeply rewarding sense of accomplishment at Loretta's blow up so quickly? He was both angry and shattered.

What was it about his mother's family that made them want to possess him, take over his life? He should never have sought out Pat. He was thrusting stuff into the bag with such vehemence that he wasn't at first aware of Pat standing in the doorway. It was only after he turned, swinging the pack over his shoulder, that he saw him, his arms braced against the door frame and his face conveying the same kind of turmoil Josiah was experiencing.

"Shit, Josiah. I was worried when I woke up and saw that you hadn't been here all day. I know you're not the little boy Kathleen wanted so desperately, but I also don't know who you are now or what you need. You're my sister's kid and you've got a home here if you want it. But we need some ground rules. I had visions of you winding up in another cell tonight. Whatever life was like on your island, that's not what it is here. But I think you know that."

Josiah put a brake on his anger and his desire to get out of the house. He didn't want to spend another night in jail or in the Combat Zone either.

"What kind of rules?"

"Let me know where you are when you go out. Keep the place clean. No girls overnight or alone here with you in the house when I'm not around. Help out with the grocery bill. Call your mother once a week. Fair enough?"

Josiah had started to protest about the girls rule, but decided to keep his mouth shut. He had no girls to bring home, so why piss off Patrick now. He'd negotiate that one when he had a reason.

He nodded his head. "Fair enough."

"Congratulations on the job. Where'd you find work?"

"Loretta's, the coffee shop down the block from St. Thomas Aquinas."

"You sound like you're getting to know the neighborhood. Good, good. Are you hungry? I'm off tonight. How about we celebrate. My treat. What do you like to eat?"

They went downtown to Durgin Park, feasted on thick slabs of roast beef and baked potatoes mounded with butter and sour cream, and climbed to the house with full bellies and a bit more knowledge of one another.

Josiah got up the next morning at five, made a pot of coffee he left for Pat with a note scribbled on a scrap of paper.

"Gone to work. Back around 4 o'clock."

He got home later than he expected and discovered that Pat had already left for work. Josiah made himself some supper, cleaned up the kitchen, and then roamed restlessly through the house. On the wall in the hall was a cluster of old photographs. A bride and groom, a group of children—two boys and three girls who must have been his mother and her siblings. Mae looked about ten years old in the photo, her hair in braids with big bows. She had her arm around an older girl, who Josiah realized must be Kathleen. All the children were grinning except for her. He was struck by the affection he saw in his mother's pose, how close she stood to Kathleen, leaning into her. She must have loved Kathleen deeply, making Kathleen's later betrayal so much more painful. The last photo was of a cottage that Josiah recognized. It was the

Keaney's former home on Chappy. His mother had taken him there once, an abandoned ramshackle place falling down in the midst of a weed-filled yard. But in the photo it was trim and welcoming, with window boxes full of flowers and surrounded by a well-tended garden. Over the door, Josiah recognized with a jolt of memory a carved wooden sign that he knew all too well. It read "Innisfree."

He reached out with his fingers and traced the letters. Then he turned down the hall and picked up the phone.

When Mae answered, he spoke.

Chapter 11

"Love is the crooked thing"
Mae

Tobias was right. Josiah did call. But not until they had all—Mae, Tobias and Izzy—spent two long days of anxiety and questioning. Each of them faced the loss in some ways alone.

The storm had not abated but also had not yet been designated a hurricane, and Izzy reluctantly arrived at the breakfast table the morning after Josiah had left with the puffy, blurred look that often followed a long night spent reading or, more recently, writing.

"What time did you go to bed, Izzy? You look like you didn't sleep much."

"I dunno. I guess around 1:00." She grabbed the orange juice and poured herself a glass.

"I suppose they haven't canceled school."

"No, the storm's still quite far off shore."

"Who's driving me to the ferry, Dad or Jo?"

Mae and Tobias exchanged looks and in unspoken agreement decided they would wait to tell Izzy that Josiah was gone. Mae was glad she had put away the shattered drum.

"I can run you all the way to school. I've got some errands to do in town. Finish your breakfast."

Tobias got up from the table with his plate, still filled with half-eaten eggs and a cold slice of toast without even a bite taken out of it. He left it on the counter and grabbed his Mackinaw.

"I'll be out packing up the truck."

Mae stared at the door after he left.

"What's up with him?" Izzy asked, her Cheerios-filled spoon halfway to her mouth.

Mae shrugged.

"We're all a little tired from the wind. Do you have any forms I need to sign?" Mae busied herself with clearing off the table, scraped the remnants of Tobias' breakfast into the garbage and emptied the coffee grounds from the percolator into a compost bucket next to the sink. She filled the wash basin with hot water and dishwashing soap, placed the dirty breakfast dishes beneath the expanding suds to soak, swiped a sponge along the spattered surface of the stove. She was aware that she was performing these myriad housekeeping tasks at an unrelenting pace, as if to stop would allow the fissure in their lives caused by Josiah's departure to widen, and her pain would spill out. For Izzy's sake, she told herself, I will not speak of Josiah until I absolutely must. Let her have one more day of our old life. One more day when the filaments that hold us together are still intact.

She didn't want to rush Izzy. She couldn't say "Hurry up and finish or you'll be late for school," because Izzy still had plenty of time. But she wanted Izzy out of the house before she realized that Josiah was no longer in it. Finally, after tipping up the cereal bowl to drink the last of the milk, Izzy pushed back from the table and grabbed the crutches propped behind her.

"I left my homework on my desk. Got to grab it. Tell Dad I'll be right out."

Mae watched her daughter's stiff gait as she traversed the hallway, holding her breath that she wouldn't poke her head into Josiah's room. But Izzy was either too focused on retrieving her homework or still too drowsy to bother her brother and ignored the closed door behind which no one slept.

When the truck at last had left Cove Meadow and Mae could put aside her worries for Izzy for a time, her own fears surfaced. She wanted desperately to do something, if not to bring her son back, then at least to reassure herself that he was safe. Where would he go? He had a few friends on the Cape. Her fingers flipped through her address book and saw the name of Tobias' cousin Sadie in Mashpee. Was she frantic enough to call Sadie? They had never reached an understanding after Sadie had been so rigidly opposed to Tobias marrying Mae. But they had at least been civil to one another at tribal functions, and Josiah knew her. Would he have turned to her last night when he landed in Woods Hole? And if he had, would Sadie have taken him in? Mae had mixed feeling about such a scenario. She wanted Josiah to be safe, not sleeping rough in some damp field in the middle of a storm. But if given the opportunity, would Sadie turn Josiah even further away from Mae than he already was? Would she feed his anger and alienation along with his empty belly?

Mae caught herself. For twenty years she had ignored Sadie's disapproval and antagonism toward her. Why allow her now to disrupt her thoughts. Besides, she was only speculating on the path Josiah might have taken. It was pointless to add to her already overwrought anxiety. Let it go, Mae, she reminded herself.

She needed to calm her brain with her hands, and pulled her pastry board from the cupboard along with flour and butter and shortening, and threw her energy into baking a pie.

While the dough rested she fought the wind outside and liberated a pumpkin from the tangle of vines in the garden.

She was peeling and dicing it, setting aside the seeds to roast, when Tobias returned from Edgartown. She could see through the kitchen window that he had brought Naomi with him.

The wind accompanied them into the house. Mae wiped her hands on her apron and reached out to embrace her mother-in-law.

"Mama! I hope you plan to spend the night with us. The weather looks like it's getting worse."

Naomi unwound the densely knit scarf she had wrapped around her head and neck.

"Power's out at my place. Tobias tells me you lost it last night but have it back this morning. I could use a hot cup of anything, right now."

"I've got some soup—lentils and ham. Will that do?"

Naomi got settled at the kitchen table and withdrew a paring knife from the drawer.

"I'll help with the pumpkin while you heat up the soup. There are some late greens from my garden in my bag. Did you bring it in, Tobias?"

Tobias was laden not only with his mother's bag but also the accumulated results of his errands—nails and tarpaper to repair a small leak in the porch roof; bags of ice; kerosene for the generator; milk and bread that Mae had asked for.

"Coast Guard has revised the storm warning. They've raised it to a Category 1 hurricane. Probably will hit sometime tomorrow. I ran into Dan Bergen at the hardware store. He crewed on the boat last night. Said he saw Jo and that he told him he was spending the night with a friend in Falmouth."

Mae tried to be grateful that Josiah hadn't taken the Sunfish and *sailed* off the island. At least Dan confirmed he was on the mainland. But as far as she knew, none of his friends lived in Falmouth.

Naomi kept her eyes on the pumpkin but interjected her own thoughts on Josiah's departure.

"I didn't recognize it at the time, but our boy has been pulling away all summer. He came to see me on Sunday, which he rarely does anymore. He wandered around, following me while I weeded, hauling away a bin full of dead flowers and vines, and hardly speaking a word— which is not unusual these days. It seemed he just wanted to be with me. I guess it was his form of leave-taking. They all need to do it, one way or another. Tobias did it by marrying Hannah, a wild and rebellious girl herself. I'm ashamed to say we were more unhappy she was a *white*, wild girl than if she had been Wampanoag, and Tobias was very aware of that. He may have stayed physically close to home, but when he took Hannah as his wife he took leave of us. It pained me to see my son suffer so for his decision, but the only person who could set him to rights was himself."

"I want to understand Josiah, Mama. I *should* understand him, given that I left my family as well when I was around his age. But I still ache for him. I want him to be safe."

Naomi put down the knife and stilled Mae's agitation with the touch of her hand.

"Of course you do. And if he'd said goodbye would he have been any safer? You're hurting, Mae, as we mothers do when our babies no longer need us. Do you remember how it felt when Josiah no longer wanted to nurse?"

"Oh, Mama. I remember it vividly. He turned his head away from my breast one night. I cried."

"If we are doing our mothering well, there will be many nights when our children turn their heads away from us and out to the world. He's a good boy, Mae. Almost a man. Safe may not be the best thing to wish for him. Safe can shackle him, make him afraid. Give him time. Trust him."

The next day, Mae stood at the window facing the bay as the rain pelted the island, obscuring the familiar landmarks of her world. The house at Cove Meadow was wrapped in fog, invisible to the outside world.

When she had first returned to Chappy twenty years before, Mae had treasured the invisibility and isolation that life at Innisfree had offered her. She had wanted nothing more than to be alone on the moors and meadows, her life in rhythm with the tides and the wind and the sun. When Tobias had entered that world, she had pushed him away, unwilling to open up the old wounds that were her only experience of men. When she finally let him in, their shared love of the land had been the bridge over which they walked toward one another— like a sandbar at low tide. Not always visible, but revealing itself when one needs a pathway.

It had broken her heart to sell Innisfree.

Every ripple of the wind that caused the marsh grass to bend in a dance; every moonrise over East Beach that cast a silver cloak over the cedar grove; every deep-hued sunset, its bold swaths of vermillion and goldenrod and orchid splashed against the canvas of the sky, was precious to her. Innisfree had been her refuge and her salvation. It was only her love for her family—for Tobias and Josiah and Izzy—that surpassed her love for Innisfree. Sacrificing Innisfree had been bearable only because of what it now represented for Izzy's future.

Mae knew it was a risk. The doctors had told them repeatedly there was no cure for polio. But a new surgery developed in Boston—so close!—could mean the difference for Izzy between a life confined and a life of freedom. That Josiah had not understood both Mae's desperation and her sense of loss was crushing to her. But perhaps Naomi was right. In her instinct to keep her children safe, she was denying them the opportunity to understand what it meant to let go—of a crutch, of a symbol—and grow.

The phone rang.

"Mom, it's me, Josiah."

She held back the rebuke that was an echo of her own mother—the refrain of "how could you do this to me?" She was trying to understand that Josiah's leaving was not about her, but about him. She also stopped herself from uttering the litany of worry that had taken up residence in her brain. Instead, she let him lead the conversation. It was enough that he had made the call. Now she knew he was alive, she could breathe and, as Naomi had urged her, trust him.

"I'm in Boston. I've found a job."

"You're amazing! Fast work! What kind of job?"

Silence on the other end of the line. She waited, holding back again. Had that really been such an intrusive question?

"It's a coffee shop."

She recalled the conversation she had had with him the previous year when he wanted to find another job and not work at the Boat House. He had presented it as an opportunity for him to contribute financially to the family.

"You are contributing with your time and talent in the kitchen. If you go elsewhere, I'd have to hire someone to replace you."

In the end, they had compromised. He worked at the café in July and August, but when school started in September and the Boat House was only open on weekends, he'd applied for the job at the market in Edgartown. She realized it was the beginning of his pulling away. She had mixed feelings now hearing where he was working. A part of her smiled. He hadn't moved so far away from the life he'd known on Chappy if he'd sought work at a restaurant. He couldn't have hated the Boat House too much. And he must have learned a few things over the years if he'd been hired so quickly.

But she kept all that to herself. Don't mess up, she told herself. Keep him on the phone, but don't pry, don't gush, don't worry.

"So, have you also found a place to live?"

The silence this time was longer, as if he were weighing how much to tell her. How bad could it be? As long as he wasn't sleeping under a bridge.

"I'm staying with Uncle Patrick."

Now it was her turn to be silent. Of all the answers she had anticipated, this was not one of them. She truly did not know how to respond. But she felt both a deep sense of hurt and a chilling fear. Had he turned to her family out of need or defiance? She couldn't imagine that Josiah had gone to Patrick deliberately to hurt her. That's not who she knew him to be. But now she doubted that she knew her son at all.

She wanted to know how he had found Patrick, whether he had seen Kathleen, how Patrick had reacted. Most of all she wanted to know why. Why would he seek out the Keaneys when Mae had spent his whole life protecting him from the threat Kathleen posed to their happiness?

But she didn't ask any of those questions. She kept her voice neutral, swallowed the pain and responded with a simple "OK."

"Say hi to Izzy for me. Tell her I miss her."

"I will. Do you need anything?"

"No. I'm fine. Uncle Patrick's place has everything. Look, I gotta go. Just wanted you to know I'm OK."

"Take care, Josiah. I'm glad you called."

The click on the other end of the line severed the tenuous connection to her son. Trembling, she hung up the receiver. Were all those years she had kept Josiah close for naught? In his already angry state, would his newly found connection with the Keaneys now drive him further away from her and Chappy?

All the old alarms were clanging in her head. She tried to remind herself that Josiah was no longer a four-year-old in danger of being snatched from his mother's arms. But he was still her child, still vulnerable, no matter how old or strong he was. Her descent into the maelstrom of anguish that her relationship with her family represented for her was almost complete. The memories that had been hovering in dark corners, banished there by her will to create her life anew, now were stirring, awakened by Josiah's inexplicable decision.

Mae felt suddenly claustrophobic in the house, and despite the pelting rain and the wind churning the usually placid bay, she grabbed her slicker, pulled on her rubber boots and strode out into the weather. She needed to walk off what she acknowledged was her own anger. Josiah had delivered a second blow to her today. His leaving had been bad enough. But to compound it by seeking out her family had completely blindsided her.

She left Cove Meadow, finding even the grassy expanse of the property too confining, and pushed on down the road toward the Dike Bridge and the beach. The hard-packed dirt road to the bridge was muddy and riddled with deep puddles. The rain stung her cheeks and found its way down her neck despite her tightly drawn hood. It was quite far to the beach but she forged on at a furious pace, her energy fueled by the demons released by her fears.

By the time she reached the water's edge she was soaked and chilled, but oblivious to her discomfort. She opened her mouth and howled, her voice joining the chorus of the wind and rain and pounding surf. When her voice was spent, she turned back toward home.

The house was blessedly quiet when she got back. Tobias was in the barn tinkering, unable to be out fishing. Izzy, school finally called off because of the hurricane, was behind closed doors typing away in her room. They had told her about Josiah when she got home from school the first day. She had not taken it well.

"I knew it."

"Knew that he was going to leave?" Tobias asked her.

"Not when, exactly. Just that he was unhappy enough to do something stupid like this. I hate this. Everything is changing. If it weren't for these, none of this would be happening to us." And she pushed her crutches away, letting them clatter to the floor. "If I were normal, Jo wouldn't have left."

Mae wanted to pick up the crutches but held back. If that was how Izzy needed to let out her emotions, let her be. She had wanted to throw something herself. But she didn't want Izzy to carry the burden of Josiah's departure as her responsibility.

"You had nothing to do with Jo's leaving, Izzy. That was his decision alone."

"You keep telling me that. But if I didn't have polio, we'd still have Innisfree. And if we still had Innisfree, Jo would still be here."

"There are many reasons why we let go of Innisfree, all of which we've thoroughly dissected. We are not defined by Innisfree anymore than you are defined by polio. And Innisfree isn't the only reason Jo left."

"Did he tell you why?" She searched both Mae's and Tobias' faces for an answer, expectant, hopeful. As if knowing why would somehow quell her loneliness and loss.

"No, Hummingbird. We're just piecing together our understanding. He's trying to figure out his life and doing that here was holding him back. Sometimes leaving home and everything familiar is the only way to discover what you truly want." Tobias answered her, underscoring his gentle explanation by using their term of endearment for her. Mae, her own emotions still raw, found it hard to find the words to comfort Izzy.

That had been two days ago. Izzy had spent most of that time in her room, composing on the typewriter. The hurricane and their forced confinement weren't helping any of them to adjust to the emptiness. Mae had to catch herself the night before from setting a place for Jo at the supper table.

It was therefore something of a relief for Mae to enter the house and find everyone occupied elsewhere. Mae hung up the slicker, turned her boots upside down to drain, then stripped off her soaked clothing on the back porch and gathered the sodden mass in her arms to deposit by the washing machine. She toweled off in the bathroom and climbed into a dry pair of slacks and a sweater before building up the fire in the woodstove. The power had gone out again and she knew she'd be cooking dinner over the fire later. She felt ready for a nap, drained both by Josiah's announcement and her own frantic excursion to the beach. It occurred to her, now that she was safely back, how insane it had been of her to venture out in the middle of a hurricane. She gave herself permission to curl up on the sofa wrapped in one of Naomi's afghans and promptly fell asleep.

Tobias found her there and sat next to her, the warmth and weight of his body a comforting familiarity. She stretched and reached out for him.

"What time is it?" The house was dark around her. It could have been midnight. She had no idea how long she had slept.

"Around five. The barometric pressure seems to have put all my women to sleep."

"I couldn't keep my eyes open. Has the fire gone out?"

"Almost. I put some logs on and got it going again."

"I'll start dinner." She swung her legs to the floor and started to get up, but he put out his hand.

"Don't rush off. Sit with me a moment. I was watching you sleep. There was just enough light from the stove once the wood caught."

He stroked the side of her face. "You looked at peace for the first time since Jo left."

"Did I? Just before I fell asleep I didn't feel at peace. I'd been down to the beach, screaming at the sea. Jo called."

His hand stilled.

"What did he say?"

"He's in Boston. Found a job. Found my brother Patrick. That's where he's staying. Those four sentences. That's all he offered. No apology. No grasp of the turmoil his disappearance caused, except to tell Izzy hi and he misses her."

"At least we know he's OK. But that's not why you went down to the beach." He was holding her hand now, running his thumb over her palm. It soothed her, as his touch always did. His scarred, weathered fingers had enfolded her, wiped her tears, held her hair back when she vomited, carried her when she'd had no strength, cradled their children, built the walls that sheltered and protected them. She pulled his hand to her mouth and kissed those fingers.

"No. I'm grateful that he's safe. That he called. But I am torn apart that he chose my family as his refuge."

"He's not a four-year-old who can be enticed with a set of trains from a fancy toy store."

"I'm actually astounded that Patrick took him in."

"Why wouldn't he? I think Patrick—and Danny and Maureen as well—understood what a danger Kathleen was to Jo. I don't think any of them would blame you for keeping him away from Boston. But given the opportunity, why wouldn't they want to know him? There aren't any other kids, right? Are you afraid that you'll lose him even more profoundly than the loss we feel now with him gone from the house?"

"How is it you know me so well? Am I so transparent? Yes, I'm afraid that the path he's on, propelled by the anger he's feeling toward us, will drive him even further away. I don't share your generous view of my siblings. I think they've never understood nor forgiven me for leaving. And now our son has left us, repeating the sins of his mother. They probably see it as divine retribution."

"Mae, the reason they don't understand is because you never told them."

"I don't think I can ever tell them."

"You told me. And I'm still here."

"Somehow, I don't believe it's the same." But she smiled, kissed him on the lips and got up to make supper.

By the next morning the hurricane had subsided, with only remnants of its trailing edge dousing the already soaked land with intermittent showers. The damage at Cove Meadow was slight, a few shingles torn from the roof, a shutter hanging on only one hinge. Tobias was up on a ladder making repairs when the phone rang.

Mae heard Lydia Hammond's voice on the other end of the line. "Mae, it's Lydia. I'm calling to see how you folks weathered the hurricane."

Mae heard the unspoken question: how had Innisfree held up? Lydia's concern for them was genuine but her worries for Innisfree were palpable. The property had only been transferred a few weeks before. It was the Hammond's land now. But Lydia needed Mae's eyes, Mae's intimate knowledge of every tree and blade of grass, every roof and shingle, to reassure her that she had not wasted her dreams on a folly that could be hurled onto the sand in a single wild night.

"I haven't been out to Innisfree yet, Lydia. We're still cleaning up here. Do you plan to come up to see for yourself? We'll try to take a run out later today, latest tomorrow. It's still raining here and the seas are still restless. Don't worry. I'll call you."

She hung up the phone.

She didn't think she could bear going out there, and she wasn't sure Tobias was ready either. Once they had decided to sell, it was too painful. Jo was right to have called Innisfree sacred land. It wasn't a Wampanoag burial ground, but Mae had buried her past there, had emerged from the forest fire that nearly destroyed the Boat House tempered by the flames to a new strength, had fallen in love with Tobias on its moors and conceived their children under its canopy of stars. She had signed away a piece of herself, her history, when she signed over the deed to Lydia.

She'd find someone else to go check on the land.

The hurricane had delayed the mail boat, so when the letter from Boston Children's Hospital arrived, it was buried in a thick pile bound with rubber bands. Tobias was out at sea for the first time since the storm and Izzy was back at school. Naomi was still with them, and it was increasingly clear to Mae and Tobias that she ought to stay, at least through the winter. Although her mind was still sharp, Naomi's limbs were stiff with arthritis and her once energetic pace had slowed. They hadn't broached the idea with her yet. Power was still out on Naomi's side of Chappy, so she had accepted that she couldn't go back to her own place yet. But the time for the conversation was coming. She was sitting at the kitchen table shelling peas as Mae sorted through the accumulated mail.

"Oh!" Mae exclaimed when the hospital's envelope fell out of the pile. She slit it open immediately and scanned the letter.

"What's got you so intent?" Naomi asked.

"It's from the orthopedic surgeon in Boston. He thinks Izzy may be a candidate for the leg surgery Lydia told me about. They've set up an appointment for her."

"How soon?"

"Next week."

"Does Izzy know about this possibility?"

"I didn't want to raise her hopes if he wasn't going to consider her. It's still not clear he'll do the surgery until she has some tests."

"Seems to me this appointment in Boston might be an opportunity for more than Izzy."

"You mean to see Jo? I'm not sure he'd see it as an opportunity."

"It's worth asking, don't you think?"

"Yes, Mama. It's worth asking."

That night Mae called Patrick. She had to call information first to get the number. After the custody hearing, she had put away in a trunk all the paperwork that accumulated and had never gone back to it. The names and addresses of her siblings were in those papers, but the thought of sifting through the layers of official documents had the potential for pulling her back to a time when everything was under threat—her custody of her son, the survival of the Boat House, her own life. She could not afford to be reminded of her fragility—not when she was facing another round of crises. So she had called information instead for the number of the Patrick Keaney in Jamaica Plain.

The phone rang seven times and she was about to hang up when a man's voice answered.

"Patrick? It's Mae."

"So Josiah called you."

"Yes, he did. I thought you might have had something to do with that."

"Yeah, I told him if he wanted to stay, he had to pick up the phone and let you know where he was."

"Thank you. For that, but also for taking him in. It's a lot to ask."

"He's my blood, Mae. And, so far, he's been a good kid. I don't know what was going on between you when he left home. He's not exactly a Chatty Cathy. But he isn't any trouble. He already got a job."

"I know. He told me. I thought he hated the restaurant business, but I guess it's all he knows. Is he there now? I'm coming into Boston with his sister for a medical appointment and I thought we might find a time to get together."

"He has a sister?"

"Didn't he tell you? She was born after . . ."

"After Kathleen's debacle. Which is why we didn't know about her. What's her name?"

"Isabella. We call her Izzy. Is he there?"

"He's out. Working late. The coffee shop isn't open in the evenings, but Loretta was getting a new refrigerator and Josiah was staying to help."

"I see."

"I'll tell him you called."

"Thanks . . . Patrick, do you think he'll see us?"

"Honestly, I don't know. Probably not. But I'd like to see you."

His offer stunned Mae. She didn't know how to react, wasn't anticipating the olive branch he seemed to be extending.

"That would be very nice."

"When will you be in the city? Where's the appointment?"

They arranged to meet in the Children's Hospital cafeteria. Patrick would try to encourage Josiah to come.

Then they hung up. Whatever more they had to say to one another, they'd do it in person.

Chapter 12

"Dance upon the level shore"
Mae

The following week, Mae and Izzy left the island on an early boat and took the bus to Boston. They hadn't been to Children's since the previous spring—nearly six months. Izzy's face was tight with worry as she stared out the window. They had missed the morning rush hour but traffic on the Expressway was still sluggish because of construction.

"Are you hungry? I packed some snacks." Mae gestured to her capacious purse.

Izzy shook her head. "My stomach is queasy."

"Nervous?"

"Not really. Just not looking forward to being poked and prodded and asked the same questions as last time, only to have them stand around in their white coats and tell us there is nothing they can do. When can we stop doing this? I'm a cripple. I will always be a cripple. You give up what you love, Jo runs away, our family falls apart. All because of my stupid legs."

This bitterness and hopelessness was something new in Izzy. She'd always been a gentle, perceptive spirit and a willing participant in her treatment, even when she was in pain.

"Has something happened at school?"

Izzy mumbled something into the window.

"Did you say 'dance'?" Mae asked gently.

Izzy nodded. "A harvest dance at the community center, with a rock-n-roll band from Hyannis. Everyone is talking about it. But as soon as I come over, they all stop. It's like Mrs. Hamilton told them not to hurt my feelings by talking about it, because I wasn't going to be able to participate. They pity me. I hate it."

Although she hadn't been able to run or jump rope or ride a bike as a child, Mae and Tobias had encouraged Izzy throughout her childhood to do as much as possible. She had learned to sail, attuned to the wind and the currents and positively joyful as she skimmed over the water in ways her legs could not take her over land. And she had always had friends to play board games and do puzzles, even put on backyard plays. Izzy had done most of the writing and costume making and had been at the center of the action, even if she wasn't swashbuckling across the stage. But ten-year-old girls were a lot more adventurous than thirteen-year-olds. There was a lot less room for outliers at thirteen. If you didn't fit in, weren't like the others, Mae understood it was pretty miserable.

Mae wanted to put her arms around Izzy, but she knew what Izzy wanted was a boy to put his arms around her at the dance. Instead, she echoed Izzy's frustration.

"I hate it, too." She didn't offer Izzy platitudes like "Maybe this time the doctors at Children's will have a miracle up their white sleeves." She didn't advise her to ignore the pity of the other girls. She didn't promise her that when she got older, none of this would matter. Izzy didn't want to hear those things any more than Mae wanted to say them.

Mae was confronting the realization that Izzy was a teenager, filled with all the angst and unsettling doubts that accompanied adolescence, but compounded by the very real presence of the effects of her polio. She had fought over the years not to have Izzy defined by her paralyzed leg. Polio was something she had, not who she was. But now, to Izzy, polio *was* defining her.

Mae felt helpless, a state she seemed to find herself in more and more these days as a mother. A miracle, she told herself. That's what we need today at Children's.

They took a cab when they got to Boston. Longwood Avenue, where the hospital was, was complicated to get to from the bus station. Mae didn't want Izzy to be exhausted from navigating the subways and trolleys of the MTA. The tests would be exhausting enough.

When they arrived, Mae braced herself for the assault of images and odors that greeted her every time she entered a hospital. Because of Izzy, she had learned to endure the onslaught of emotion, but it never abated, never slipped in her awareness. Children's was especially challenging because the children whom it served were so seriously ill. By the time your kid got to Children's, you'd run out of options.

On their way to orthopedics they passed waiting rooms of pale children tethered to IVs, their heads snugly wrapped in hand-crocheted caps whose bright colors exaggerated the pallor of the faces under them. The corridors were silent except for the hum of wheelchairs or the muffled click of rubber-tipped crutches. No exuberant chatter or unruly running. Occasionally they would pass parents whose faces revealed the diagnosis just delivered, the weight of the knowledge expressed in eyes wild with rage or sucked dry of tears. Mae knew it was the face she had worn six years before when the word polio had been uttered with such precision and finality.

Izzy was breathing and walking now, albeit with crutches and a brace on her left leg; no wheelchair bound her within its metal and rubber-padded arms. And yet, Mae knew, for all her relief that Izzy had survived, she would always carry the grief and guilt and desperate quest for answers to why this had happened to her daughter as if she had just been told the diagnosis.

As always, she and Izzy spent a lot of time waiting, punctuated by brief intervals of X-rays and questions and connections to machines taking measurements. The early hours of the afternoon trudged by, unmarked by changes in the light because they were encased in windowless rooms. Like the children's caps, the walls were brightly hued, but a meager substitute for yellow sunlight and blue sky.

By three o'clock, the list of appointments was only three-quarters complete and Mae was scheduled to meet Patrick, and maybe Jo, for coffee in ten minutes. She'd have to slip down to find them, and hope they'd come back up with her. She hadn't told Izzy, afraid that Jo might not show and crush her already trampled spirit. Izzy was engrossed in a book, *Wuthering Heights*, her armor on this battlefield.

"Honey, I'm going to the coffee shop in the lobby. Do you want anything? Hot chocolate?"

"I'm OK. Actually, no, I'm not OK. But what I want you can't bring back from the coffee shop. How much longer do you think this is going to take?"

"I'll see what I can learn. I'll be back in fifteen. Love you."

"Love you back." She returned to her book and Mae moved swiftly down the corridor to the elevator, tempering her hopes.

The lobby was crowded and Mae scanned the space for a blue uniform and red hair. She hadn't seen Patrick since he was a boy and didn't know any other way to identify him. There was no sign of Jo. Then she heard her name being called.

A tall man in uniform approached her, his face a faint echo of the ten-year-old boy she had left behind, but there was no doubt that he was Liam Keaney's son. She quickly glanced behind him, but he was alone.

She moved toward him, propelled by a longing she did not know she harbored. For the seconds it took her to reach him, she did not question whether he would forgive her. She only wanted to close the years between them. When they were face-to-face she wavered, remembering his reserve on the phone. But he had been the one to propose this meeting. He was the one who had called Jo "his blood."

She lifted her hand to his cheek and called him the name that had been his when she left.

"Patsy."

With her other hand she wiped the tears that had sprung from her eyes.

"It's been a long time since anyone has called me that. It's been a long time since I waited to hear *you* call me."

She understood he wasn't going to make this easy for her. "Thank you for coming. Thank you for everything.

How much time do you have? Things are running late. I've left Izzy upstairs waiting for her next appointment and I need to get back. Can you come up with me?"

"I don't go on duty until five o'clock. I've got some time."

They walked to the elevators, Patrick taking in the swirling dramas of families surrounding them.

"A lot of sick kids here. How is your daughter? Josiah told me she's got polio."

"After this battery of tests we'll know more. There is no cure. But there's a surgery that might help reduce her limp, give her more mobility. Do you have children?"

He shook his head. "Never married. Took care of Ma after Da died. With Mo in the convent, Danny in the service and Kathleen unwilling to come down out of her palace on Beacon Hill, there was only me."

He hadn't said, "And with you abandoning us," but she heard it nevertheless. She had known this was coming when she agreed to see him. But she didn't know how far he'd go in laying at her feet the blame and responsibility for all that had gone wrong in the Keaney family. She'd certainly laid it on herself.

They reached the orthopedic floor and Mae led him to Izzy. She was still buried in her book, twisting a strand of her hair and oblivious to everything else around her.

"Honey, I'm back. I want to introduce you to someone. This is my brother Patrick Keaney. Pat, this is my daughter, Izzy. Jo is staying with Uncle Pat."

Izzy lifted her head from the book and took a minute to refocus. She looked from Mae to Patrick, trying to make sense of this new fragment of information, a puzzle piece in both her brother's and her mother's life. She remembered her manners and put out her hand.

"Hello. I didn't know Mom had a brother."

Patrick raised his eyebrows toward Mae. "Actually, she has two. And two sisters. Perhaps now that Josiah has found us, you can get to know all of us."

Mae felt like an idiot for not preparing Izzy. Instead she had persisted in hiding her family. She knew she'd face a barrage of questions from Izzy on the ride home. But the damage was done.

At that moment the nurse called Izzy.

"One more X-ray, Izzy. Mrs. Monroe, you can wait here. We should be done in about 15 minutes."

Izzy slipped her wrists into her crutches and followed the nurse. Whatever questions she had would have to wait.

Mae watched Izzy until she was gone and then turned to Patrick.

"We can talk out in the hall."

"I'm sorry about Izzy. She reminds me a lot of you. Not just her looks, although the resemblance is powerful. It's that directness you always had. I remember you saying what you thought, without flowering it up. Without compromise."

"Was that a good thing or a bad thing?"

"I always admired you. Looked up to my big sister. And then you left."

"I'm sorry, Pat. I felt I had no choice. Believe me, if I had stayed it would have been much worse."

"For you or for us?"

"It's not an excuse, but I was young and I was scared. I made a huge mistake and I ran."

"But why did you never come back?"

"After what Kathleen tried to do, I felt the only way to protect Josiah was to stay away. After Izzy was born, I had even more reasons to keep Kathleen at bay. And then, when Izzy got polio, our whole world fell apart. I had no energy to try to repair the rift between us."

"I understand about Kathleen. We've all suffered from her behavior. But if you had turned to us, we could have helped to protect Josiah. We're not the enemy, Mae."

"I know that now, Patsy. Especially now that you *are* protecting him. I don't know how to thank you."

"You could start by explaining why you left."

Mae knew she was vulnerable, standing in this empty corridor, surrounded by dying children who confronted her not only with her daughter's fragility, but her own. And she knew that she could not give Patrick what he was asking for at that moment.

"I can't today. Not here, and not now with this decision about Izzy's future about to be handed down by some almighty surgeon. Give me time and probably a stiff glass of whisky. When we've got hours to rewind the years. Just not today."

"I guess that's all I'm going to get. At least it's not shutting the door completely. I've waited all these years. I can wait a little more."

"Thanks. Give my love to Jo. Not ready to come, not even for his sister?"

"Not yet. The chip on his shoulder hasn't gotten any lighter. A lot like his mother." But he smiled when he said it. "I got to get to work. Let me know what happens with Izzy. If we can do anything, we're here. We need to start being a family again."

"Thanks, Patsy. I promise. I will."

She thought he would just turn and go. But instead, he bent and kissed her on the cheek.

"Take care of yourself and Izzy. I'll take care of Josiah."

Mae had a few minutes to recover—from the unexpected kiss, from the anticipated litany of Keaney grievances, from the unforeseen opening of her heart when she saw her brother cross the lobby floor. Jo's decision to find Patrick, whether it was deliberate or spontaneous, had set in motion an enormous sea change in their lives. Mae's especially. It was entirely unclear to her where the disruption would lead.

By the time Izzy returned Mae had blotted her tears and calmed her agitation. They had one final appointment—the meeting with the surgeon. Mae encircled Izzy's tense shoulders as they walked down the corridor.

"What do you think he'll say?" Izzy asked, relaxing only slightly under her mother's touch.

"I have no idea. Let's try not to go in there with fixed ideas, or feeling like he's about to pass judgment."

"But isn't that what he's doing? Judging whether I'm a 'candidate.' I feel like I'm applying to get into Harvard. Actually, it's more like walking down the runway in a bathing suit in the Miss America pageant."

Mae squeezed her shoulder and laughed. "That's a perfect description. Maybe he's waiting for you with a tiara and a bouquet of roses."

For a change from the earlier part of the day, they didn't have to wait, but were ushered immediately into the surgeon's office. There were no roses, but he had a smile on his face as he stood next to the light box displaying the shadowy images of Izzy's legs.

By the time they left the hospital, they had a date for the surgery less than two weeks away, a mountain of documents to sign and a level of excitement that wiped away the fatigue and discontent that had pummeled them all day.

The first hour on the bus ride to Woods Hole Izzy was full of energy, a transformation from the irritable, skeptical teenager who had endured the exhausting medical marathon of the day. Mae shared her excitement with relief, and did not want to temper it with cautions about setting her expectations too high. She had time enough before the operation to bring Izzy down to earth. Let her savor this gift of hope.

Mae's relief extended to Izzy's preoccupation with her own news. She had no room right then to question Mae about the instant set of aunts and uncles Patrick had revealed. They celebrated with Cokes and deli sandwiches picked up on the way to the bus station. Izzy fell asleep against Mae's shoulder and stayed asleep all the way to the ferry.

It was after ten when they finally arrived at Cove Meadow. Mel Brown had kept the Chappy ferry at Edgartown waiting for them. Tobias' truck was silhouetted against the harbor lights as the boat churned through the channel and deposited them at the Chappy ramp. On the way to Cove Meadow, their headlights cast the only illumination on the darkened, empty road.

Izzy, revived by the nap on the bus, had her second wind and regaled Tobias with the events of the day as the truck carried them home. Mae waited for Izzy to announce the meeting with Patrick, but apparently the appearance of her uncle got swallowed up by the momentous news of the surgery. Mae was grateful. It was too late and she was too tired to have to answer whatever questions Izzy was sure to have.

But after Izzy had retreated to bed, Tobias pulled Mae to his side in bed.

"How did the meeting with Patrick go? I assume Jo didn't show or Izzy would have been as bursting with that as she was about the surgery."

"You're right. According to Pat, Jo's not ready to loosen the albatross he's determined to lug around. But Pat was . . . well, let's say willing to open up channels of communication for Jo's sake, but not about to let me forget that I caused a lot of pain to my family."

"It was brave of you to face him. Don't let him beat you up. He's not ten years old anymore."

"Thanks. I told him it wasn't the right time or place to talk about it, especially not with Izzy's future weighing so heavily on me. I promised I'd talk to him about it someday, just not today. He seemed to accept that."

"Even if *he* doesn't forgive you, forgive yourself. You taught me that, a long time ago."

She kissed him. "As long as I have you, I can do anything," she whispered. And then fell asleep.

Izzy's excitement spilled over into the next morning as she told Naomi, who reacted with all the joy and exuberance a grandmother can express to a grandchild who has good news to share.

"God bless you, child! You and I will dance around the room when you get back."

Mae bit her tongue. She wasn't ready to be the realist quite yet. Walk without a limp and perhaps only a cane, yes, that was the expected outcome. But dance?

The reprieve from questions about her family lasted until Izzy returned from school later in the day.

She dumped her books on the kitchen table and grabbed an apple from the bowl. Mae was glad to see that her euphoria hadn't yet subsided.

"How come you've never mentioned Uncle Patrick and your other brother and sisters?"

145

Mae turned around and leaned against the kitchen counter. She'd had some time to think about her answer, had even rehearsed with Tobias in the morning. She had decided to be honest, without opening the Pandora's Box of Ned Bradley.

"I left my family when I was nineteen. Ran away, because I had made a mistake that I thought they wouldn't forgive."

Izzy stopped chomping on the apple and listened intently. She seemed about to interrupt and then stopped, waiting for more.

"I was frightened, and I thought it would hurt my family, especially my mother, if they knew."

Izzy then spoke. "What did you do that was so terrible?"

"I got pregnant, Izzy. By a boy who didn't care about me or my baby. In the eyes of my church and my family, I had committed a terrible sin. I knew about a home in Connecticut run by nuns that would take me in, and I went there to have my baby and give it up for adoption."

Izzy's mind was faster than Mae's story.

"Does that mean Jo and I have a sister or brother, in addition to aunts and uncles? Wasn't it awful to give up your baby? Elise Waterman's sister has a baby and isn't married, but she got to keep her baby."

"It would have been truly awful, but what happened was worse. My baby died."

"Oh, Mom." Izzy moved from the table, holding onto the edge instead of using her crutches and reached out to hug Mae. Mae wrapped her arms around the daughter who lived, now grieving for the daughter who had not.

"What was her name?"

"Catriona. It was my mother's name."

"How could your family not take you back?

"I didn't ask them to. I left the home and went even farther away. I was so unhappy and so lost, that I couldn't go home. I was wrong not to try, but I didn't understand that then. And the longer I stayed away, the harder it was to return and ask their forgiveness.

"So why now?"

"There's more. When Jo was four and I was very sick, my older sister Kathleen found out that I had come back to Chappy. She wasn't well mentally and tried to take Jo away from us. We were able to prevent her, but after that I was afraid she'd still try, even after the court told her she couldn't. To protect Jo, and then you when you were born, I cut off any more contact with her and the others. I didn't trust them."

"But you said Jo was staying with your brother. I don't understand. Do you trust them now?"

"I don't know, Hummingbird. Patrick and I are feeling our way here. I'm trying and he's trying. He's looking out for Jo, which is a good thing, and Jo is certainly no longer a little boy. I don't know how it's going to turn out."

"Why did you change your mind?"

"For Jo's sake. If I had had someone to turn to, an aunt or uncle, when I got into trouble, it might have saved everyone a lot of pain."

"I wish Jo had found someone closer to home to go to when he left. I miss him."

"I miss him too, Izzy. But I also understand what he's going through. I just don't want him to follow the path I took and wind up a stranger. Now, how about helping me with supper. Granny is still napping and I could use somebody handy with a chopping knife."

That night, enfolded in Tobias' arms, Mae recounted the conversation with Izzy.

"You did well, Mae. You answered her honestly without leaving a lot of blood on the floor."

"I just wish one thing about our talk."

"What's that?"

"I wish I could have told Jo."

"You'll have that chance. You will."

Chapter 13

"A prayer for my daughter"
Mae

The day of Izzy's operation arrived quickly. The smile on her face as she was wheeled toward the operating room filled Mae with a hope that she had not experienced in years. She knew it was still early, that it would be months before they would know if Izzy could give up her braces and crutches and walk unassisted. They stood in the corner of her hospital room, both necessary and despised, a silent reminder rather than the click and drag that had accompanied Izzy for nearly six years. Keeping her upright but weighing her down. Mae wanted Izzy to soar, to fly free of metal and twisted limbs. *Let this work*, she begged silently as she paced the halls outside the surgery waiting room, too agitated to sit and read one of the tattered magazines stacked on a table. Tobias had gone to the coffee shop to find them some breakfast.

They had been at the hospital since six in the morning and had been awake for hours before that. They had come to Boston the night before and stayed at a Howard Johnson's. Tobias hadn't pushed her to let Pat know. She was sure Pat would have offered them his place to stay, and that would have forced a scene with Jo. No, the last thing any of them needed, especially Izzy, was to intrude on Jo's space before any of them was ready. One thing at a time. One child's needs at a time.

She promised herself she'd let Pat know once Izzy was out of the operating room. If Jo wanted to see his sister, it would be up to him.

Tobias returned with a cardboard tray piled with coffee and Danish. The caffeine and sugar recharged her but did nothing to soothe her anxious pacing.

"The number of times you cover this hallway is not going to speed up Izzy's surgery." He gently guided her to a quiet corner in the waiting room and held her hand.

"No 'what ifs' this morning," he said. "We went through them all with the surgeon; we made sure Izzy understood there were no guarantees. We made the right decision, and we will live with it." He squeezed her hand, passing his strength and his confidence to her through the gesture.

She squeezed back and nodded.

The surgeon arrived hours later, more than they had anticipated, but the expression on his face spoke to them before he uttered a word.

"It went extremely well. Her youth, the flexibility in her tendons, even her attitude going into the surgery contributed to the outcome. She's an extraordinary girl. The nurse will bring you to her when she wakes up. The hardest part of her recovery will be the patience she'll need to heal, but she should be walking without braces or a limp within two months. Just in time for Christmas."

After he was gone, Mae leaned against Tobias, the tension in her body shedding itself like sheets of rain sliding off the picture window during a wind-driven Nor'easter.

Tobias returned to Chappy that night. Naomi's brother was staying with her at Cove Meadow, but both he and Tobias needed to get back out to the fishing grounds while the weather still held. Mae remained in Boston with Izzy, arriving at the hospital after breakfast and staying until after supper. She had sat these vigils many times over the years, but never with such optimism. She knew the post-operative discomfort Izzy was experiencing was temporary; that at the end of her recuperation, when the frame encasing her leg was removed, Izzy would be a different girl. It sustained them both.

On the evening before Izzy was to be released, Mae left the hospital early to pack so that she'd be ready first thing in the morning to bring Izzy home. An ambulance would take her all the way to Cove Meadow. Before she left Izzy, Mae gathered up the cards and stuffed animals her classmates and island friends had sent to cheer her up.

When she arrived at Izzy's room to help her dress the next morning she saw another stuffed animal perched on the bedside table.

"How did I miss that one yesterday? It's certainly colorful enough!" It was a multicolored hummingbird, brilliantly iridescent from the tip of its indigo beak to its violet wings and orange tail.

"That's because it wasn't here when you left." Izzy picked it up. "Jo brought it."

Mae saw the look of hesitation in Izzy's eyes, as if she thought Mae would be angry that Jo had come to see her. Mae reassured her immediately.

"Oh, Izzy, that's wonderful! Seeing him must have been very special."

Izzy let out the breath she was holding. "I'm sorry he waited until you were gone. I know you miss him, too."

"I do. But it makes me happy that you are still so important to him. He's a good brother."

Mae turned away to open Izzy's suitcase but also to hide her tears. She could bear Jo's departure for herself, but Izzy's loneliness for her brother was breaking her heart. When she was about to burst out of her chrysalis, when he could be a witness to her transformation, his absence had been another virus, robbing Izzy.

Thank God he had come. She wondered if he had been watching in the lobby, waiting for her to leave last night so that he could come up and be with Izzy alone. Whether he had or not, purposefully avoiding her or simply arriving serendipitously to find his sister alone, all Mae wanted was that he continue to seek her out.

It would be a challenge once Izzy was home. But he could write or call, couldn't he? *Please*, she thought, *hold your sister in your heart. Don't do what I did.*

When they reached Oak Bluffs, Izzy asked the ambulance driver if he could turn on the lights and siren just for a few minutes on Beach Road. To Mae's surprise, he agreed. It pulled her back to the afternoon they had arrived at the dock from Innisfree, Izzy collapsed and feverish in her arms and then lifted to the waiting ambulance. Izzy understood that this time, she was riding in triumph. Mae hugged her and shared the laughter that bubbled out of her.

Chapter 14

"Someone called me by my name"
Josiah

Over the fall, the days settled into a predictable pattern, Josiah often leaving the house before Pat arrived home from his shift. As the days grew shorter he walked to Loretta's in the dark, leaves skittering across his path or a cold drizzle finishing the task of waking him. After two weeks and a phone call from Betty as a reference, Loretta gave him a key and he was often the one to open the kitchen door on the alley and haul in the bread, egg, and milk deliveries deposited there during the early hours. As he had at home, he started the coffee, handed a mug to Sal when he arrived and then switched on the lights, lifted the shades and unlocked the front door.

The earliest customers were guys coming off their shift at the Holtzer-Cabot plant, school crossing guards about to take their posts and weary nurses and orderlies heading home from the VA hospital. They were the ones Josiah felt most at home with. They had no need of smiles or banter, just a hot meal and a hot cup, served with the least amount of fuss. It never bothered him that they were the least likely to leave a generous tip. They were also the least likely to make note of his brown skin or try to figure out where he came from. It was enough that he brought them their sunny side eggs and bacon, remembering who liked ketchup and who always asked for a French roll slathered with sticky icing.

They were gone by 7 a.m., followed by the commuters wolfing down their donuts as they checked their watches and kept a close eye on the tracks across the street, ready to grab their briefcases and their *Boston Globes* as they threw down the cash for their sugar-coated breakfasts. By 9 a.m. the café was a haven for the lonely widowers in the neighborhood who no longer had someone to cook them breakfast. They were the most suspicious of Josiah, the ones most likely to ask Loretta pointedly about when Janine, the former waitress and Loretta's daughter, would return. They also weren't easy to please or placate if Sal had left the eggs on the griddle a little too long or if the shop ran out of jelly donuts. Josiah saw no reward in attempting to cajole or engage them in the kind of breezy joking Loretta was so adept at. If they saw him as sullen when, in his opinion, he was simply taking their orders and delivering their food with a minimum of conversation, so be it.

Early on, Loretta had taken him aside.

"If you're in the front of the house, you don't have to like everybody who comes through the door, but you also don't have to let them *know* you don't like them. Loosen up. If somebody comes in with a Red Sox cap on and his *Globe* is open to the sports page, ask him how he thinks the Sox will do in the playoffs."

He knew the business and he knew she was right. But that didn't overcome his reluctance to be a master of small talk. It was only when Margaret Mary popped in for a cup of coffee on Wednesday mornings that his face brightened and he said more than "What can I get you this morning?"

"How's life, Josiah? Is Loretta treating you well?"

He assured her that life was fine; Loretta was a good boss—demanding but fair; Sal was giving him a shot at the griddle when he took a smoke break out back. It was partially the truth. He felt as if his life was on hold. He was doing essentially what he'd done all his life—"helping out" in someone else's restaurant. First his mother's, now Loretta's. It wasn't where he had imagined himself when he left Chappy. He had expected the city to be freeing. An adventure. But he felt as confined in this pocket of Jamaica Plain as he had at Cove Meadow. Sometimes on Sundays he went to Jamaica Pond and ran on the path around the water, the Boston skyline just visible over the treetops. He didn't know what he wanted. But he knew it wasn't spending the rest of his life in a place like Loretta's. He appreciated the work. He was even good at most of what a busy neighborhood place like Loretta's needed, except for the small talk. He knew he had his mother to thank for that. But his mother's dreams were not his—especially since she had given up the land, the one thing that could have held him, rooted him, on Chappy.

He moved through his days like a canoe through the still waters of Poucha Pond. Occasionally a swell might disturb his rhythm—like a brisk wind stirring the reeds along the shore. Someone new might come in, not fitting into any of the categories of Loretta's regulars, and he would try to place them in the urban landscape that was beginning to be familiar to him. But for the most part, he was bored.

And then Pat announced that it was time to start planning the Keaney Thanksgiving dinner. He rushed to assure Josiah that only Danny and Maureen were coming, not Kathleen and Ned. As far as Josiah knew, Pat had not breathed a word to Kathleen about his arrival in Boston or his presence at Pat's.

"Danny has a week's leave. He arrives by train on Wednesday night. On Thursday we'll pick up Maureen at the convent for the day. Have you ever cooked a turkey?"

Josiah didn't know if Pat would understand that Thanksgiving was a day of mourning for the Wampanoag, not a time to celebrate. But he let it go. He was curious about Danny and Maureen, and willing to help cook a meal for them.

His Uncle Danny filled up the house when he arrived, taller than Pat and lean where Pat had begun to soften from too many hours in a squad car. But it wasn't just his physical presence. He carried himself with an authority and power that Josiah remembered his father once had. Danny was the younger brother, "the smart one," Pat had called him. An officer in the Special Forces, the son who had made their mother proud, with a medal Jack Kennedy himself had pinned to his lapel.

Josiah was awed from the moment Danny walked through the door. Josiah gave up his room and moved to the couch in the living room. The first night he sat with his uncles at the kitchen table over pizza and beer, sensing the change that had rippled through the house. He was aware of Danny's curiosity about him, the appraisal that had begun as soon as Josiah had put out his hand to greet him.

Danny had taken it firmly, his blue-gray eyes focused intently on Josiah's brown ones. Josiah had returned the glance without looking away, without acknowledging that yes, this was his first test. Then Danny had broken into a broad grin and thrown his free arm around Josiah, pulling him close.

"Come here, Jo. We're not going to be strangers anymore."

No one had called him Jo since he had left the island, not even Patrick. To have Danny use his shortened name from the start gave Josiah a sense of kinship he hadn't known he missed.

"Pat wrote me about your arrival on our doorstep. Not exactly Moses in a basket, but we're happy to finally welcome you to the family. How's your Mom?"

Josiah answered as well as he could. The weekly phone calls home had been strained. Often his father had been out to sea fishing and Mae's pain at Josiah's departure hovered over the calls, effectively silencing any excitement he might have shared with her for fear of causing her more anguish. Even Izzy, at first, had been reluctant to say more than a few words. She had made it clear to him she felt he had abandoned her, and in her piercingly clear way, had said to him, "I know you left because of me, Jo. If I hadn't gotten sick, if they hadn't needed the money from the land for me, everything would still be the same. We'd still be a family."

He had denied that she was the cause for his leaving. But if he were honest with himself, he had to acknowledge that Izzy was indeed at the heart of his decision. Just not in the way she believed.

He felt profoundly responsible for Izzy's polio. Despite all the assurances from his parents, he had not been able to forgive himself for leaving her at the tidal pool that hot day in July six years before. The image of her in the isolation ward was etched in his memory as if acid had carved it. Every clank of her braces, every scrape of her dragged foot, every tap of her crutches had been a drumbeat in his head.

She needed the undivided attention of their parents. She didn't need his guilt and shame as yet more obstacles in her already hampered life.

So, no, he didn't have a lot to tell his uncle about Mae. He also wasn't convinced that Danny was deeply interested in Mae's welfare. Like Pat, he had probably not thought about his sister much when so much time, so much emptiness had intervened. It wasn't until Josiah had shown up that the tangled emotions had begun to emerge for all of them.

Now they sat together at the kitchen table, the remnants of a pepperoni pizza congealing in its oil-stained box and empty beer bottles cluttering the space between them. Pat got up to pull three more bottles out of the refrigerator. Ever the cop, Pat had never allowed Josiah to drink before, but Danny had prevailed upon him to open a beer for Josiah from the case he had presented as his offering for the Thanksgiving feast.

"Come on, Pat. It's not like the kid is going to go for a joy ride afterward. If we were in New York, he'd be legal. Besides, he's probably had his share of alcoholic beverages growing up on the island. Remember what our summers were like on the Cape when we were his age?"

Danny's mention of the Cape was a revelation that startled Josiah. How close they had been physically to Mae, and yet, the waters separating the Vineyard from the mainland might as well have been the Atlantic Ocean.

"So, Jo, why now? Why us?"

Josiah wasn't prepared for the abrupt redirection of the conversation. Up till that moment, he'd been lulled by the beer and the banter between the two brothers, each one trying to outdo the other with cop vs. soldier stories. It struck him how unlike his father they were. How unlike him.

He took a swallow of the beer.

"Why now? Because it was time. I'd finished school and I didn't want to fish. Not much else to do on the island."

"No thoughts about going to college?" Danny repeated the question Pat had asked him when he first arrived.

It was an odd question, Josiah thought, coming from guys who hadn't gone to college themselves. He wasn't about to tell them that, even if he had wanted to go to college, there'd been no money for it. He was certainly smart enough, but it was Izzy who was going to need an education. The polio had affected her legs, not her brain. If she was going to have any kind of life, it would be as an intellectual. But Josiah didn't mention Izzy to his uncles.

"Not for me. I wanted to get out into the world, start making a living."

"Pat tells me you're working at Loretta's. Is that the kind of living you intend?"

Josiah wasn't sure where Danny was going with his questions. Was he baiting him, or had he truly figured out in the short time he'd been here that Josiah was restless, anxious to move beyond the familiar but stifling world of a neighborhood café?

"Loretta's is a stop along the way. I wanted to be able to pay my share. I didn't look up Pat for a handout."

"Ah, now we get to the second half of my questions. Why *did* you come looking for the Keaneys? Hadn't your mother warned you against us?"

"Only against Kathleen." Josiah wasn't going to get pushed into Danny's game, whatever it was.

"Give the kid a break, Danny. Who else was he going to turn to, just starting out?"

"So we're not all monsters, populating your nightmares as a kid?"

"No, sir." He didn't add that he'd hardly been aware of the Keaneys as a child, so thoroughly had his mother obliterated her family from life at Innisfree.

He decided to answer Danny truthfully.

"I was curious." He shrugged. "I'm half Keaney. I wanted to know who you were, so I could understand better who I was."

"Fair enough," Danny answered.

Pat started clearing off the debris on the table.

"We can sit here all night delving into family history, or we can get this place into shape before Mo arrives and gives it her Sister Mary Holier-Than-Thou critical eye, accusing us of living like slobs. And if we don't get started with some of the food prep, we won't be eating until midnight tomorrow. So how about it, Loretta's jack-of-all-trades. Can you chop some onions and celery for the stuffing? And Mr. Green Beret, do you think you can handle setting the table?"

Josiah didn't believe for a minute that Pat was concerned about his sister's opinion of the state of cleanliness of the house or the need for getting started prepping the meal. He was convinced Pat didn't want to talk about the past. But he didn't protest, and got up to dig around the fridge for the vegetables.

Danny seemed to share his perception, and when Pat had left the kitchen to take out the garbage, he turned to Josiah.

"When Dudley Do-Right isn't around, I can fill you in on some of the family secrets he seems to want to stay buried. Maybe it's a family trait, secret keeping."

"Why is it you're willing to break the silence?"

"Maybe because I'm the only one who got out, got away from Boston. You might want to think about that. Getting off the island may not be enough."

With that, Danny went to the cupboard in the dining room and rummaged in the bottom drawer until he found a lace tablecloth. He shook it out and spread it over the dining room table with a gesture Josiah had often seen his mother make.

Danny looked up at him.

"Your great-grandmother tatted that tablecloth. On Sunday afternoons my mother spread it on our table at North Neck. Do you know the cottage?"

Josiah nodded. Mae had taken him there once. The place was falling down, overgrown with weeds and faded by the maritime weather to a color not far from the vegetation that surrounded it. If you weren't looking for the cottage, it could disappear into the landscape, a forgotten place that reflected the disappearance of the Keaneys from Chappy.

"Do you remember it?" He asked his uncle.

"Snatches of memory. We had a piano in the parlor and Kathleen played. I was maybe four or five years old. Not old enough to hold onto anything more than fragments. But I remember being happy there."

"That's what my mom said. That she had been happy there."

Pat had returned to the kitchen. Danny and Josiah turned back to their assignments.

The next morning, Jo rode with Danny to the convent while Patrick put the turkey in the oven. Danny was wearing his dress uniform.

"It impresses the nuns and makes it easier for Mo to escape for a few hours. Pat wears his uniform when he goes to see her, too. How much more respectable can we be—a cop, an army officer and a nun? Not bad for an immigrant caretaker and housekeeper who found themselves descending into hell when they left Chappy and came to Boston."

Danny spoke not with pride, but with bitterness.

"Does Maureen need to escape often? I can't imagine living the life of a nun."

"Your mother couldn't either. That was why we thought she left. To answer your question about Mo, I think she appreciates her outings with the family, but each time I see her—which isn't often—she seems more comfortable in her habit. I don't suppose you went to Catholic school."

Josiah shook his head. "There isn't one on the island."

"Were you raised Catholic? Or some Indian religion?"

Josiah stiffened at Danny's dismissive tone.

"We went to church. The Wampanoag have been Christian for centuries. Our church is the oldest Indian church in the country." Josiah surprised himself at his vehemence. Sometimes white people were so ignorant. He felt a surging need to defend his heritage, despite his alienation from it. He held back, however, from describing the deeper spirituality that informed the religion that had surrounded him growing up. It was none of Danny's business, and Josiah doubted he'd understand it.

They arrived at the convent, a crenelated Victorian brick building attached to a more modern school and adjacent to an imposing church. Danny parked in the empty lot between the convent and the church and they approached the door.

They didn't have to wait long for their knock to be answered by an ageless nun whose face brightened at the sight of Danny.

"Captain Keaney! Welcome home. Sister Immaculata told us at dinner last night that you were on leave. And who is this young man?" She turned to Josiah, curious but not disapproving.

"This is our nephew, Josiah Monroe, recently arrived in Boston."

"I had no idea there was another generation. Sister hadn't mentioned Josiah."

Josiah could sense that the nun had more questions, but she kept them to herself. No doubt she'd be reporting to the other nuns about his existence and wonder out loud why Maureen had kept quiet about him.

She left them in the vestibule while she swept down a hallway to announce their arrival to Maureen. Josiah looked at their surroundings. Dark wood paneling on the walls, maroon carpeting on the floors, a wooden crucifix on the wall above a narrow table that held a red votive candle. A thin slant of light illuminated the hall from the stained glass panels that lined each side of the front door. Everything about the space, despite the flickering candle and the window light, was dim, as if it were twilight instead of late morning. Not only the light but the sound was muted. They didn't hear any footsteps approaching and weren't aware of Maureen until she appeared in the archway.

"Mother Mary Bernadette reported that we have a new member of the family. She implied I was keeping secrets from the sisterhood."

Maureen reached out her hands with a smile on her face. "You must be Josiah. Pat told me you've come to us."

She held both his hands and studied his face. He didn't know if she would find the glimmer of Keaney he thought she was seeking. He had never seen it. Everyone in the tribe, on the island, had always said he was his father's son.

"Welcome, Josiah." She squeezed his hands and turned to Danny, throwing her arms around him.

"You do know how to charm an old nun with that uniform. Let me look at you." She pulled away, appraising her brother. "You'll do," she smiled.

"Let's get going before Pat overcooks the turkey or half the convent wants to come with us." She pulled both of them out the door and toward the parking lot, her veil lifting in the wind.

Josiah hadn't known what to expect from Maureen, but he was definitely surprised by her exuberance and directness. She didn't strike him as someone who tolerated dishonesty—either to others or to oneself.

On the ride to Pat's she sat in the front seat next to Danny but turned her body so she could face Josiah in the back, peppering both of them with a barrage of questions. What daring missions was Danny engaged in these days, what did he think of Kennedy's handling of the Bay of Pigs, did he think we were going to get involved in the crisis between North and South Vietnam, had he read Tom Dooley's book as she had recommended? When she had exhausted her interrogation of Danny she focused her brightness on Josiah, flooding him with her interest and curiosity. Unlike her brothers, she hadn't started with questions about Mae. She asked instead about him.

"Pat hasn't told me much, other than that you showed up one morning at the precinct a little worse for wear. Tell me about yourself. What do you like to do for fun? What do you read? Are you working? Where? Do you like it? Is that what you want to do, run a restaurant? No? Then what?"

She was relentless. Josiah wondered if she had to keep a vow of silence in the convent and therefore had all these words pent up inside waiting for the release of being beyond the convent walls.

He caught Danny's eye in the rear-view mirror, an expression of mirth on his face as he listened to Maureen bombard Josiah and Josiah attempt to sputter his way through the thicket of questions.

Finally, Danny interrupted Maureen.

"Give it a rest, Mo. He looks like a deer in the headlights. You've got all day to conduct your inquisition. Besides, we're here, and I can see Pat at the window. He's probably been pacing the floor waiting for us, having timed the meal to the minute."

As they got out of the car and Maureen raced up the steps, Danny threw his arm around Josiah.

"I probably should have warned you that Mo has a motor mouth. She started talking before any of us and hasn't shut up since."

It was Josiah's first holiday meal away from home. He had expected it to be different—two bachelor uncles and a nun at the table instead of the constancy of familiar faces who had populated Monroe holidays since his childhood—Mae and Tobias, Izzy, his grandmother Naomi and her brother, his great-uncle George; Betty; and the occasional guests for whom there was always room. But Josiah was surprised by the unexpected similarities, especially in the food. It had not occurred to him that Mae had learned to cook from her mother, but he came to understand that day that his grandmother Keaney had been a silent presence at Innisfree his whole life. The stuffing for the turkey, the scalloped potatoes, the lima beans, even the apple pie that he had associated so keenly with his mother, were all on the table in Jamaica Plain. If he closed his eyes, he could taste Innisfree.

Maureen had curbed her inquisitiveness during the meal, when most of the conversation had been good-natured banter among the three siblings, with Josiah mostly observing and listening. But as the meal wound to a close, the tone shifted as the light-hearted ribbing turned toward Kathleen.

It was Maureen who broached the topic.

"I'm the one behind the wall, so I have to ask—have either of you heard from Kathleen?"

Josiah had wondered if her absence from this family celebration had been because of him. But Maureen's question and Patrick's visible discomfort led him to believe that it had nothing to do with him.

"Anything I know is what I read in the *Globe*. They were at the Inauguration in January. One of the guys at the precinct moonlights as a security guard on Beacon Hill and told me he saw Secret Service outside her house a couple of months ago. For whatever reason, Ned appears to be pretty tight with Jack Kennedy. During the campaign last year Kathleen couldn't stop talking about how much the Kennedy people were depending on Ned."

Danny directed his question to Pat. "Has she found out yet that Jo is in Boston?"

Maureen chimed in. "That's the $64,000 question, isn't it? Although I suppose Jack Kennedy is a good substitute as an obsession. Maybe it will keep her occupied long enough for Jo to sort out what he wants to do with his life before Kathleen comes swooping in."

Her next words were for Josiah.

"I know you're no longer a vulnerable child. But Kathleen will try to seduce you with something more than a steady stream of toys from F.A.O Schwarz."

"You knew about the gifts?" Josiah looked from one to the other.

"Kathleen couldn't keep what she called her 'generosity' to herself. This time the gifts will be more dangerous, because she can offer you something you may want desperately."

"And in exchange, she'll demand more and more of you. And when you can't give any more, she'll turn on you."

"That's why we've been asking you, Jo. What do you want to do with your life?"

Josiah shook his head.

"I wish I knew. But are you all telling me that whatever it is, I shouldn't be doing it here in Boston?"

It was Danny who answered.

"There are entanglements here, Jo, probably more than you left behind on Chappy. My advice to you is to let go of both the Keaneys and the Monroes and find Josiah where no one else is going to define you—not your parents, not us, and certainly not Kathleen."

Later that evening, it was time for Pat to bring Maureen back to the convent.

As she was leaving she took Josiah's face in her hands and looked at him as she had in the morning. This time she found what she was looking for.

"You are your own man, Josiah Liam. And I will keep you in my prayers."

Danny and Josiah remained behind to finish cleaning up the kitchen. Josiah took the opportunity to ask his uncle the question that had been simmering in his head since Danny's arrival the day before.

"What if I told you I was thinking of enlisting?"

Danny stopped scrubbing the roasting pan and faced Josiah.

"I would say to you it damn well better be the army."

1961
Cove Meadow
Chappaquiddick Island

Chapter 15

"All disheveled wandering stars"
Josiah

When Jo wrote to Izzy at the end of November that he was enlisting, she had called him at Patrick's.

"You can't leave without saying goodbye, and there's no way I'm getting off the island with this metal frame holding my leg together. So you have to come, even if it's just for a few hours."

He had said yes. Cautiously, reluctantly, but out of love for his sister. He steeled himself for the meeting with his parents, anticipating their disapproval of his decision to enter the military. He remembered it hadn't been Tobias' choice during World War II not to serve; the army had declared him unfit because of his damaged hand. Jo had assumed Tobias' opinion of soldiers stemmed from his rejection by the army. Jo realized he was erecting another barrier between himself and his parents with his decision. He knew Mae supported

Tobias in distancing himself from any contact with the military. He couldn't imagine her doing otherwise. He also knew that as a mother, her fears for his safety would be magnified. No, his visit home to say goodbye to Izzy was not going to be easy or comfortable for anyone. But he went.

Patrick drove him to Woods Hole. Jo wondered if he was doing so to make sure he got on the ferry. He hadn't been sure himself that he'd make it all the way. Too many places to step off the path, wander in another direction that did not lead to home.

That's what enlisting was. Another direction. A different definition of home.

He bought his ticket—round-trip—and climbed the metal ramp to the waiting steamship. It was both familiar and strange. Gulls circled overhead, well-conditioned to associate the giant boat with an opportunity to snag an errant French fry or crust of pizza, although the pickings were meager in December, when few people braved the outer decks. Jo pulled up the collar of his pea coat and slapped on a watch cap. He wanted to ride in the open air despite the biting wind and low clouds scuttling across the horizon, likely ready to dump some icy rain on the Sound.

The horn sent out its clarion warning and the big ship rumbled to life. Jo watched the scattered buildings on the shore recede and then turned his attention to the east and the open water. He breathed in these moments of peace, between the life he'd chosen on the mainland and the life he was coming to bid farewell on the island. Both shores held tensions for him, not just Chappy. As supportive as the Keaneys had been, Patrick especially, his relationship with his mother's siblings was fraught with their own pain and anger toward his mother. Although they understood why she had kept Jo away, none of them could fathom why she had chosen to abandon them in the first place, least of all Jo. There were secrets buried in her decision— there had to be. He understood on a visceral level that something had driven her away, just as he had felt compelled to leave home that night at the Burial Ground. But the last thing he wanted to feel was sympathy for his mother. The last thing he wanted to admit was that he was anything like her. He hated it when Patrick made pointed comments about his resemblance to his mother. No, he had not felt any more at home in Boston than he had in the last year on Chappy. He was still an outsider, a stranger in their midst.

But he didn't expect a warm welcome at Cove Meadow, either, nor did he feel any sense of longing to see Chappy again. He was going back for Izzy and Izzy alone. He'd accepted that he'd have to see his parents. He expected that they'd challenge him about the decision to enlist. For Izzy's sake, he'd endure their inquisition. It was only for a few hours, and then he'd be gone again.

The Oak Bluffs harbor shimmered in the winter sun as the ferry slowed and eased into its berth. From his vantage point on the deck, Jo could see the line of cars and trucks waiting for passengers to disembark. He wished Izzy could have greeted him at the boat. They could have walked over to Circuit Avenue for some fudge and hot chocolate, said their farewells, and he'd be on a ferry to the mainland in a few hours. But it would be weeks before her doctor removed the contraption that kept her leg immobile while it healed.

He took a deep breath and left the boat.

Tobias was standing at the end of the pier, apart from the bustle of reuniting families and tourists arriving for the Edgartown Christmas tree lighting and its attendant hoopla. Jo couldn't read the expression on his father's face, but that was nothing new. Whatever he was thinking, Tobias had it well-guarded.

"Welcome back, Jo."

Jo refrained from pointing out that he wasn't "back" in any sense of the word. "Back" implied a return to the past, to the way things had been. He wasn't sure exactly what lay ahead for him in the army, but he knew he was never going "back."

"How's Izzy?"

"Improving every day. This visit of yours is lifting her out of a slump. It hasn't been easy for her."

Jo wasn't sure if his father was referring to Izzy's recovery from the surgery or her sense of loss since Jo had left. She'd made it excruciatingly clear to him she was feeling abandoned. He wished that leaving her behind hadn't been a part of the equation and it continued to gnaw at him. That was certainly why he'd agreed to come today. To explain. To talk through the tangle of loneliness and alienation and loss that had led him to leave the Burial Ground and board the ferry. He hoped she, at least, would understand. But she was still just a kid, with her own burdens of isolation and not fitting in.

"Let's go home. I know you don't plan to stay the night, and Izzy, Mom, and Granny want as much time as possible with you. So do I."

The ride to Cove Meadow was spent in silence. Jo stared out the window at the winter landscape along Beach Road. Sengekontacket Pond was already frozen. The reeds and cattails along its shore were bent and tattered, coated with a layer of sleet that had started soon after the ferry had docked. Everything was dun-colored. The water of Cow Bay churned and surged, throwing gray waves along the state beach. Jo shivered and Tobias flicked the dial of the heater up a notch.

As they approached the house, Jo could see the windows lit with a warm glow and smoke puffing out of the chimney. He tamped down an unexpected tug of homesickness and climbed out of the pickup.

Naomi was waiting at the door and he bent to kiss his grandmother and inhale her familiar lavender and chamomile smell. Mae stood back, her face still, and her hands at her side.

He approached his mother and kissed her cheek, but did not embrace her. She lifted her hand and stroked the side of his face.

"Thank you for coming, Jo. It means a lot to Izzy . . . and to us."

"Where is she?"

Mae led him to the living room, where a hospital bed had replaced the couch. Izzy was propped up and clearly impatient.

"Get over here, as you can see I can't come to you!" She patted the side of the bed.

He sat and leaned over to hug her, hard.

"Jo-Jo! You came. I was really scared that you'd ditch the trip at the last minute."

"I thought about it, but I realized not only would you never speak to me again, you'd probably induce Granny to put a curse on me if I didn't come."

"Granny wouldn't do it for me. I was preparing to call down a plague of some kind myself. But here you are!"

He was aware that his parents and grandmother, instead of hovering over his reunion with Izzy, had retreated to other parts of the house. He and Izzy were left alone for almost an hour, and after they had exhausted the teasing, got honest with one another.

"I hate that you are going into the army. Boston was far enough. Where are they sending you?"

"After basic training, I'm going to Texas. I've been accepted into the medic program and that's where they train."

"Then what?"

"Don't know. I could be assigned anywhere. But it will be almost a year before I finish my training. I wish I could be here when you get this contraption off."

"So do I. I'm getting nervous. Walking on my own. I keep having nightmares about falling with nothing to grab onto."

"Hey! It's going to be fine. Not only fine. It's going to be amazing."

"I hope so. After so many years of wishing for a miracle, it feels eerie that I might actually get one."

Naomi poked her head into the living room.

"Is anybody hungry?"

Instead of sitting around the dining room table, which Izzie obviously couldn't do, they ate seated in a circle around her bed. The meal was a venison roast and Jo felt a twinge of longing. He'd missed the hunting season, the only time since he'd been ten, when Tobias had first taken him. He shook off the regret. He couldn't afford to be pulled into memories, not when he was leaving for basic training in a few days.

To his surprise, his parents refrained from challenging him about his enlisting. They also were silent on his angry departure in September. No accusations of ingratitude or selfishness were thrown at him or even implied. It was a startling contrast to his last night at home, and he finally understood that everyone was trying very hard to make this visit a peaceful one. He realized with relief that there'd be no confrontation today; he also acknowledged

176

that nothing was resolved between him and his parents. He honestly didn't know if that meant the issues had simply been postponed or if they'd never reach an understanding. It was an uneasy peace. But it was enough.

He left after dinner, stuffed with his mother's abundant cooking. Her silent offering. He was able to thank her with a hug, and he saw the tears in her eyes as he embraced her. Izzy clung to him tightly, whispering in his ear. "Be safe. Come back to us."

1962
Cove Meadow and Innisfree
Chappaquiddick Island

Chapter 16

"These are the clouds"
Mae

Ever since she strode across the meadow and into their lives seven years before, Lydia Hammond had been both a force and an enigma. Mae acknowledged that Lydia had saved them twice. First in 1955 when she had diagnosed Izzy's polio and again in the summer of 1961, when she had bought Innisfree.

For all Lydia's confidence—as a mother, as a nurse, even as an athlete who waterskied with abandon—Mae recognized in her a loneliness their quiet evenings on the porch assuaged. Lydia's husband, Lou, was a cardiologist in Philadelphia. He came up to the Vineyard for a weekend or two in the early summer and returned to spend the final week of August with his family. But the rest of the time, Lydia was alone at their cottage with the kids.

"She sure doesn't come across as needing anyone," Betty had once remarked to Mae in the early days of their friendship. "But I can appreciate her wanting to have an adult conversation now and then. Those boys are a handful."

Mae kept a bottle of gin for Lydia on the sideboard for those nights when the women could lean back into their Adirondack chairs and indulge in whatever topic was consuming them that day—concerns about the influx of new people to the island and the effect it was having; the rain that kept customers away and gave the kids cabin fever; how to encourage Lydia's middle child, a second son, to seek attention in more positive ways. They never talked about their husbands. It was territory that Mae couldn't relate to—how distant both geographically and emotionally Lydia and Lou seemed to be. She couldn't imagine being separated from Tobias for weeks at a time.

As the years went by the women supported each other through their children's adolescences, with Betty providing the wise advice of someone who had "been there, done that." They laughed through the sleeplessness and hot flashes of early menopause. They cried when hoped for improvements in Izzy's mobility failed. They cheered when any one of the kids did well.

Mae thought that selling Innisfree to Lydia would ease the pain of its loss. But she discovered in entrusting Innisfree to Lydia she also lost their friendship. At first it was a tiny tear in the fabric of their connection, a shift in the balance. It was Mae who started to pull back as a way to protect herself. The morning of the closing, she had sailed the Sunfish over to Innisfree to do a final walk-through of the property, ostensibly to check that everything was in order. But in reality, it was to say farewell. She beached the shallow boat and climbed out onto the flat, letting her feet sink into the wet mud of low tide. She made a slow circuit around the perimeter of the beach, brushing her fingers along the reeds and cattails, moving inland to the meadow and the woods, passing the roofless Boat House and ending up at the house.

Her breath caught as she saw what she had left behind and climbed the porch steps to reach for it—the wooden nameplate of Innisfree, carved by her father and carried by Mae from her childhood cottage on North Neck to its place of honor above the door to the house. She pulled off the sign, its weathered surface a testament to the decades it had marked a Keaney home. She cradled it in her arms as she leaned her forehead against the glass of the door.

Then she turned and descended to the boat, not looking back.

Through the fall and winter that marked Jo's angry departure and Izzy's life-changing surgery, Mae did not once look across the bay.

When the summer of 1962 arrived and word rumbled through Edgartown that the Boat House was going to be torn down, Mae stayed away. When Lydia called to invite her and Tobias for dinner, Mae stayed away.

Betty had left for Key West, the New England winters finally defeating her. Izzy had a new-found independence and was pulling away from her mother as any fourteen-year-old would. Without her closest friend and no longer bound by the needs of her daughter or the demands of running the café, it would have been natural for Mae to renew her friendship with Lydia.

But she could not.

She could not bear to see Lydia as mistress of Innisfree. She had heard that the Hammonds were keeping the name and she was torn in her reaction. A piece of her screamed that the name Innisfree was hers, that she had not sold its deep significance along with the land. But another voice whispered that she had called the land Innisfree and it would always carry the name, keeping it alive in the memories of everyone it had touched.

She threw herself into cultivating Cove Meadow that summer, planting not only her usual vegetable garden but also a flower garden as well. She was thinning lettuce and spinach in the late June sun when she heard Tobias' truck pull up. He had been out to the Gut early in the morning to do some fly fishing. It was different from the deep-sea fishing he made his livelihood from. Casting at the Gut was his way of unwinding, of letting go the tensions and disruptions and challenges of life—leading the tribe, running his business, coping with his mother's decline, and his son's departure.

Mae knelt on her heels and watched him climb out of the truck. In their twenty years together she had never lost her delight in watching his supple, strong body. A smile edged its way across her lips as he approached her after depositing his fishing gear and a cooler on the porch. She reached out her hand he pulled her up, leaning in for a kiss.

She wrinkled her nose. "What did you do, hug the fish to bring them in? You reek more than if you'd been out all day on the water." She smiled as she teased him. She'd certainly smelled worse as the wife of a fisherman.

"Just about. But I got us a nice couple of blues for supper. I'll gut them before I head into town. Is there any coffee left?"

"I'll make a fresh pot. I could use a cup as well."

They walked to the house together and rinsed their hands at the outside faucet.

"I ran into Lydia at the Gut."

Mae stiffened.

"What was she doing there? I didn't know she fished."

"She wasn't. I think she must have seen my truck driving out there and she came to find me."

"What did she want? I've already told her we couldn't come to dinner. Was she trying to get you to convince me to change my mind?"

"No. I got the impression she's figured out you aren't ready to go back to Innisfree."

"I'm not sure I'll ever be ready."

"I know. No one is pushing you. It's hard for me, too."

"Then why did she track you down?"

"She asked if I'd be willing to do some repairs. That storm last week ripped off a section of roof shingles, and some other odd jobs."

"It's not your responsibility anymore."

"She wants to pay for the work. She wasn't asking for a favor . . . We could use the money."

Mae sighed.

"I know. I pay the bills. Without the income from the Boat House, we have to find other sources. I've been looking at jobs in Edgartown."

"Izzy still needs you and so does Naomi. Let me worry about bringing in more."

"I wish it didn't have to be at Innisfree."

"So do I. But for now, I think we have to put aside our feelings and be practical."

Chapter 17

"My wall is loosening"
Tobias

Tobias drove over to Innisfree the following evening, following the rough track that had been carved out of the narrow barrier island that ran from the Dike Bridge south to Wasque and north to the lighthouse. Only trucks with four-wheel drive and deflated tires could navigate the soft sand. At full moon high tides a good portion of the track was underwater. Lydia was waiting for him out front, which meant she'd been watching for him, just as she had the morning before when she had followed him to the Gut.

"Thanks for coming so soon. Another rain storm is supposed to be headed our way and I'd rather not be tripping over buckets arranged under the leaks."

"No problem. Did you get to Edgartown to pick up the shingles and tar paper?"

"Everything is in the shed. Do you want to see where the bare spots are?"

She led him to the northern side of the house

Tobias knew that the hurricane-ripped shell of the Boat House had been torn down, but coming around the corner and seeing an empty lot bare of even a sliver of wood shattered him. Mae was right not to come back. To have the café completely obliterated, as if it had never existed, was harder to accept than seeing it ravaged by the hurricane. That had been an act of nature. This had been a human decision.

He turned his back on the devastating reminder and focused his attention on the roof and Lydia's voice, blinking back stinging tears.

"I can probably wrap this up tonight. Do you have a ladder?"

He wanted to get to work, keep moving, anything to stave off the pain. If Lydia wanted to establish Innisfree as hers now, she couldn't have chosen a more effective action than destroying the Boat House. He pounded out his anger with every swing of his hammer, and climbed down from the roof just as the sun was setting.

"Can I offer you a drink?" Lydia stood at the kitchen door, her own gin and tonic in her hand. She seemed oblivious to the awkward reversal of their positions. She, no longer the guest; he, no longer the homeowner.

"No, thanks. Mae's waiting with dinner."

"When will you be able to come back for the pump and the steps to the beach?"

Tobias wanted to tell her he was too busy for those other jobs, that she would need to find someone else. But he smothered his pride as she handed him the cash for the work he'd done that night. *Is this what I am reduced to,* he thought. *A transaction between me and a woman we had once considered a friend; the hired help for a home that was once my own?*

He pocketed the money and told her he'd be by later in the week.

"Thanks, Tobias. You're a life saver."

As he drove away he imagined her watching from the window, behind her the empty house, her loneliness.

When he got home he put the money on the kitchen table before he washed up for supper.

"How did it go?"

He wasn't going to tell Mae about the gaping space where the Boat House had once stood or about his discomfort and sense of diminishment. The decision to sell had cost her enough—relinquishing everything she had accomplished, driving Jo away. He could not add to her burdens by revealing what it had cost him.

He shrugged. "I got the roof sealed. It shouldn't leak again. But I didn't get to the other repairs. I'll need to go back later in the week. She paid generously." He pushed the money across the table.

"I hope she doesn't view us as charity cases."

"I don't know what she thinks, except that she seems lonely."

"That's nothing new. It always surprised me, her need to be surrounded by other people, hanging out with us at the end of the day. She seems so self-confident, so clear about who she is and what she wants. And yet there's a need to share her life that never quite gets fulfilled for her."

"Well, she definitely wants things fixed."

Two days later Tobias steeled himself for his return to Innisfree. The work itself, while it wasn't the same as fixing up his own home, wasn't challenging. But Lydia's watchfulness was unsettling. She seemed on the verge of asking for something, but then held back. From what he knew of her over the years, he thought she had been more forthright and direct in the past.

When he got around to fixing the pump, he realized he was going to need an extra pair of hands. He knocked on the kitchen door.

"Lydia, are any of the kids around? I could use some help."

"The boys are both working in Edgartown and won't be home till around nine. Susan is babysitting for the family that's now renting our old cottage. Is it anything I can help with?"

He showed her what he needed; it wasn't much, but it speeded up the process of dismantling the pump. Once he had it apart, she stayed, leaning against the shed while he tinkered.

"How did you learn how to do all this?" She waved her hand around to encompass the compound, the sea, the woods.

"By doing, mostly. Watching my father when I was a kid."

"There's not much my kids will learn from their father."

"They'll learn from you, then." He kept his head bent over the pump. He was no Ann Landers, dishing out advice. It was true; the Hammond kids didn't spend a lot of time with Lou. It wasn't how Tobias lived. He had loved being there for Jo and Izzy. It was what his own father had done for him.

"Mae doesn't want to come back, does she?"

This was the Lydia Tobias was more familiar with, honing in on what mattered instead of whining about her husband. Tobias looked up from the pump.

"No. She's grateful to you. We both are. But letting go of Innisfree had to be a clean break for her. Neither one of us has any regrets. Seeing Izzy walking on her own has made it worth the cost a hundred times over. But to come here would be torture for Mae, especially now with the Boat House gone." There, he'd said it.

"It was going to collapse in on itself if I hadn't pulled it down. I was afraid someone—kids—would play around in it and get hurt."

"No one's blaming you, Lydia. But it happened on your watch, even though the hurricane started it. If it hadn't been for Izzy, Mae would have rebuilt. She's done it before."

"I'm not Mae. Believe me, no one on Chappy is letting me forget that. I'll always be an outsider."

"You know, there was a time when Mae was the outsider, when the community, especially the women, ostracized her. She built Innisfree without their help and certainly without their approval."

"Those are very big shoes to fill."

"No one expects you to, least of all Mae. Look, Innisfree is yours now. Make it your own. I think all we ask is that you love and respect it. We were its stewards, not its possessors. If anything, I think the land possessed us."

"Will you help me?"

"You mean with repairs? When I have the time, if you can't get anyone else. But I need to let go, too."

"I don't mean with repairs. I mean understanding how to love it."

"Lydia, I can't teach you that. You've spent how many summers at Poge? If you didn't love it already, why did you continue to return? If you weren't already spellbound by its beauty and tranquility, why take on a responsibility like Innisfree? You already know how to love it. You don't need me."

"I need something. I can't believe I'm admitting that, especially to you. I've always been the strong one, who had it all figured out. The one who could identify what everyone else needed and make it happen. But the ground is shifting under my feet. My kids barely need me; Lou is both emotionally and geographically on another planet, not understanding the balm Cape Poge is and why I stay; and the one friend I had on Chappy can't bear to see me because all I do is remind her of what she's lost. I thought Innisfree would be my salvation and all it has done is alienate everyone from me."

Tobias had never seen Lydia cry—had actually never imagined that she was a woman who would allow herself to cry, especially in front of others.

His irritation with her and his discomfort at the change in the dynamic between them when she took over Innisfree began to slip away as he listened to her bare her soul. He might have dismissed her words as fueled by gin, but as far as he could tell she hadn't been drinking. Something about her honesty touched him.

Without thinking, he reached for her and took her in his arms.

It was at that moment that Izzy looked up at her former home with longing as she drifted past on her way back from a sunset sail.

Chapter 18

"Here we will moor our lonely ship"
Izzy

All of Edgartown had been buzzing about the final destruction of the Boat House and she had been driven by a morbid curiosity to see for herself. What she had overheard in town had been mixed. To some people, pulling down the half-destroyed building had been an inevitable necessity, the removal of something that was both dangerous and an eyesore. But to most people, the disappearance of the Boat House signaled the end of an era, the wiping away of the last vestige of a simpler time. To Izzy, the Boat House was her childhood and her mother's legacy. The story of its transformation from a decrepit fishing camp to a thriving restaurant was the story of Mae's survival and resilience.

Izzy knew something had changed in her mother when she gave up the Boat House, a change that made Izzy's gut hurt. Despite all the reassurances from her parents, Izzy felt herself at the molten core of the catastrophic changes swirling around her family. She had set out in the Sunfish that afternoon with the specific purpose of bearing witness to the Boat House's demolition. She wanted to see for herself that it was truly gone. One of the boys she knew had been out to the Gut to fish and had told her he had looked across the bay to where the Boat House had stood.

"It's as if it was never there."

Izzy wasn't convinced. Sure, from across the water it might look like that. But if she sailed close to shore, where the dock had once stood, wouldn't there still be some fragment of its once solid and comforting presence?

She reached Innisfree and stared at the former landing. The water lapped at the embankment that was eroding with every severe storm. Above the bank was only air. It looked as if everything had been carted away—the splintered wood of the frame, the dark brown linoleum on the floor that had always accumulated half the sand from the beach by the end of the day, the weathered shutters that had flown off during Hurricane Donna and been scattered across the meadow. It was truly, totally all gone.

Something welled up inside Izzy. She had expected to feel sad. She'd come alone, rather than with Susan Hammond, even though they sailed together all the time ever since Tobias had taught them how to handle the Sunfish when they were ten. She thought she'd cry when she saw the empty lot and she didn't want Susan to know how upset she was.

But instead of crying, she was angry. Instead of a torrent of tears, she unleashed a scream, a howl, as if she was calling down a curse. If she had had something in the boat to hurl at the mocking emptiness, she would have.

She startled a flock of cormorants wading at the water's edge. They flew up in a raucous black cloud, echoing her hoarse condemnation of everything that had brought her to this moment of loss. When the birds were a distant speck in the sky and she had exhausted her curses, she tightened the sail and steered with the tiller in the direction of Cove Meadow.

As she rounded the slight bump in the coast where Betty's cottage stood, she couldn't help herself and cast a longing gaze at their old house, the windows of its familiar western façade reflecting the lowering sun. But then another image seared itself into her brain. It took a few seconds to register. She was already distraught from the sight of the now barren plot of land that was once the Boat House.

What she saw was an image that she didn't want to believe, an image that hurt more than the emptiness of the vacant lot. Her father holding Mrs. Hammond in his arms the way he held her mother. And Mrs. Hammond— her mother's friend, Susan's mother—wrapping herself tightly around him, burying her face in his chest.

Izzy could not see their faces. Mrs. Hammond's blond hair spilled over her father's arm, catching the sunlight, and her father was bent over her as if he was whispering something to her. He stroked her hair. They did not see Izzy.

This time Izzy did cry. She swung the tiller violently and pointed the boat in the direction of the Gut rather than Cove Meadow. She couldn't go home at that moment and face her mother. Her tears splashed down her cheeks and sobs rose gulping from a deep and painful place in her chest. As if losing Jo and Innisfree were not enough, she was now going to lose her father.

She sailed on, navigating the narrow, shallow waters of the Gut without a destination except for the compulsion to get as far away from Innisfree and Cove Meadow as possible. She hated her father at that moment and she was afraid for her mother and what her father's betrayal would do to her.

In the midst of all the uncertainties in Izzy's life, her parents' love for one another had been an unwavering anchor that she had clung to; a brilliant star in the night sky that had been a reassuring constant. How could it now be a sham? She searched her memory for signs she might have missed, for a loving gesture that wasn't offered or harsh, impatient words expressed and not repented. But she couldn't find any. Tobias must have carefully hidden his betrayal by pretending to still care for Mae. If the loss of Innisfree hadn't done so, this was going to kill her mother's spirit. One more blow to their fragile family that could be laid squarely at Izzy's feet. Feet that now could walk on their own—but at such a huge cost. She wished she had died that day on the beach when the polio had attacked her.

The wind had picked up as it often did near sunset and Izzy was flying northward, leaving Chappy and Edgartown behind her. She didn't care where the boat was taking her as long as it was away. She paid no attention to the deepening hues in the sky or the chill that was settling on her bare arms and legs. She had been reveling in her first summer without her braces. Mae had taken her to Filene's when school let out and let her pick out brand new shorts and matching tops. She had felt like a normal teenager.

She hardly felt normal now.

Chapter 19

"While day its burden on to evening bore"
Tobias

He held Lydia while she cried into his chest. Her vulnerability struck an unexpected chord in him and turned around his reluctance to engage with her. But at the same time, it set off warning bells that forced him to step outside himself and ask what the hell was going on. Lydia's body was wracked with sobs that gradually subsided, but instead of pulling back, she relaxed against him, a giving way physically that was as surprising to him as her letting go emotionally. For a woman who had always held herself aloof, the self-contained WASP, her transformation was startling. He could not deny that a part of him responded to her need, the way he had tried to save his first wife, Hannah. But Lydia was not his wife. If anyone should be rescuing her it should be Lydia herself. Not him and not even her husband, Lou. He had learned that much in his painful loss of Hannah and in his marriage to Mae. Mae. She had struggled already to accept his taking on the repairs for Lydia. The last thing she—and he—needed right now was an emotional entanglement between him and Lydia.

"I'm sorry, Lydia," he whispered. He meant, *I'm sorry for your loneliness. I'm sorry I can't be the one to fill the emptiness in your life. I'm sorry that by selling Innisfree to you we have severed our friendship.*

And then he stepped away. The space between them grew cold as the evening air blew in from the water. Neither one of them noticed the green and white sail riding the wind away from the shore and toward the Gut.

The pump still lay in pieces on the wooden table.

"I'll pack this up and rebuild it at our place."

He didn't want to spend another minute there, didn't want to risk that the resolve that had made him let go of Lydia might weaken. The crossing over into intimacy and revelation, even when it is unwanted, is too fraught, too powerful.

He did not look at Lydia's face as he gathered up the pump parts into a box. He was afraid of what he would see there—the raw need or the humiliation of rejection.

She did not stay, perhaps recognizing what could so clearly be read on a face that was no longer a mask of detachment. He heard her go inside, her footsteps retreating through the house to her bedroom.

He carried the box and his tools to his truck on the other side of the shed and climbed into the cab. He had his key in the ignition when he heard her call his name.

He pressed his head against the steering wheel. *I should just turn the key and go, pretend I don't hear her.* But he didn't.

She came around to the driver's side. Her face was blotchy in the way fair skin reacts to sun or stress. Her hair had slipped out of its ponytail when he had stroked it and she hadn't yet pulled it back. The wind was lifting it in a halo around her head.

"I can send Rich to pick up the pump when you're done. No need to come back."

She extended her hand through the open window and put an envelope on the dashboard.

"I think that will cover everything."

Her voice was barely above a whisper and he could hear the quaver as she struggled to regain what she had lost in those moments on the other side of the shed. He gripped the steering wheel to keep his hands from grabbing hers. He nodded, and started the engine.

She stepped away from the truck and he pulled away. In his rear-view mirror he saw her standing in the deepening twilight, watching.

By the time he reached Cove Meadow it was dark. The house, although lit, was unusually quiet. No music coming from Izzy's room, no TV on in the living room where Naomi normally spent her evening hours crocheting and watching Gunsmoke. He found Mae in the kitchen on the phone, her back to him.

"No? You haven't seen her at all today? Thanks, I appreciate it." She hung up and crossed off a number on a list next to the phone. She was about to dial another number when he came up behind her and hugged her.

She stiffened instead of softening as she always did.

"Why are you so late? I called Lydia but there was no answer. I've been trying to reach you for the last hour. I've been frantic."

"What's wrong? Is it my mother?"

"Mama is fine, although as worried as I am. It's Izzy."

"What's happened?

"She took the Sunfish out around four and isn't back. You didn't see her on the bay did you, when you were out at Innisfree?"

"Is that where she said she was going?"

Had he been so focused on Lydia that he hadn't seen Izzy's boat? Is it possible that Izzy saw them?

"She didn't say, although I suspect that was her intention. She knew Lydia had demolished the Boat House last week. It's been the only topic of conversation around Chappy, although everyone gets suspiciously silent if I happen upon a discussion. I'm afraid she went over to see for herself and got upset."

"And now she could be anywhere, in the dark and with no running lights."

"Do you think she'd be foolish enough to leave the bay and head out into the shipping channel?"

"God, I hope not. You were on the phone when I came in . . ."

"I've been calling around to her friends, hoping she'd stopped at one of their houses, but so far no one has seen her."

"I'll head out and patrol the bay. If I don't see her, I'll move out into the channel."

"It's going to take more than you to find her. Naomi wants me to call George and get some help from the tribe."

"Do that. I'll get started and I'll keep the radio on. You stay close to the phone in case she calls or someone finds her."

"I'm afraid, Tobias. All these years I kept her safe, but I knew how hard it was for her to be held back because of her legs. I thought, she's waited so long to be independent. Let her go this summer. As difficult as it was for me, I thought it was the right thing to do, to give her some freedom. Now, it's a terrible thing to say, but if she were still in her braces, she'd never have been out in that boat alone."

Tobias pulled Mae toward him. "Don't beat yourself up. You were right to loosen the ties, Mae. She's a good sailor. She won't do anything stupid. She probably tied up over at the ferry landing, ran into friends and is hanging out in the parking lot eating ice cream, oblivious to her parents' worry."

He wanted badly to believe what he was telling Mae. But gnawing at him was his memory of those minutes with Lydia in his embrace and how they might have appeared to Izzy watching in confusion and then disgust. He prayed that his fears were unfounded, but every moment that Izzy stayed away reinforced for him that he had failed both his daughter and his wife. He knew he had to heal this breach of trust. Not only by finding Izzy, but by being honest with Mae. But right now there wasn't time. They had to get Izzy back first.

Tobias left, unsure of whether Mae would forgive him, especially if Izzy came to harm. He could not blame her, since he hadn't forgiven himself. He raced to the dock, fired up the engine on his fishing boat and turned the spotlight on the water. Somewhere in the darkness his daughter was floundering in pain.

He made the circuit of Poge Bay with no result while the radio crackled with intermittent messages from Mae. At least three other boats were now trolling Chappy waters searching for Izzy. He convinced himself that she had left the bay and was more than likely on open water. If she were distraught, he expected that she would have let the prevailing wind carry her, rather than tacking against it. That meant she was headed north. His hope was that she would have tired enough by the time she reached Oak Bluffs to pull in there rather than keep going into the open water of Nantucket Sound and the ferry channel.

He relayed his suspicion to Mae to ask her to convey it to the other boats. God willing, one of them would spot her distinctive green and white sail. He prayed that it would be him.

He patrolled slowly close to shore, training his spotlight along the beach, but saw nothing but a group of teenagers around a bonfire. There was no sign of Izzy's boat and he moved on. He passed a few boats heading into Edgartown Harbor, mostly off-islanders with large yachts arriving for the Fourth of July events. The radio continued to sputter with sporadic updates from Mae, each time her voice more anxious, her messages shorter. It was after nine when the lights of Oak Bluffs illuminated the skyline and reflected off the water. Tobias hoped his hunch was correct, that Izzy would have made for the shore here. He scanned the town beach running south of the ferry pier. He saw a white overturned hull in the sand that could be the Sunfish and steered toward it. It was high tide, deep enough for him to move in fairly close before he had to drop anchor. He was going to have to leave the boat, however, to really see if the hull was Izzy's. He slipped over the side and waded in. It was only late June and the water hadn't warmed up yet, which his legs registered with discomfort. He shook off his realization that he must be getting old if a little cold water could bother him. He was more concerned about what effect the water might have had on Izzy, out for hours after the warming sun had set.

He strode up the damp sand to the hull. Lying next to it, neatly rolled and tied, was a green and white sail bound to the mast and boom. Just as he had taught her.

Everything was there except Izzy. He raised his flashlight and ran it along the sea wall, but no one was anywhere on the beach, so he trudged up to the street and walked toward the pier. Izzy knew there was a phone booth there, and the police station was across the street. Both opportunities for her to call home. For him, as well, if he didn't see her along the way. He'd let Mae know the boat had been beached and she could call off the water search.

As he approached the steamship office he caught his breath. Someone was sitting on one of the benches outside, a slight girl with her bare arms wrapped around her knees, her legs pulled up onto the seat. It was Izzy. He began running toward her.

"Izzy! Izzy!"

She looked up.

"Go away! I've already called Mom. She's coming in the truck to get me. I don't want to talk to you."

He didn't have to ask if she'd seen him with Lydia. It was written all over her face, in the way she shrank from him when he approached her. Both his children broadcast their emotions without filters. When they were happy, their ebullience had been infectious, filling their lives with laughter. But when they were angry, great storm clouds spread over the Monroe household, with flashes of lightning and rumbles of thunder that disrupted everyone's equilibrium. This was one of those times.

He knew now was not the time to offer explanations or apologies. She'd been known to shut her eyes and hold her hands over her ears when she didn't want to be told something. He had no doubt if he tried to talk to her now she'd do the equivalent, probably get up and walk away. Instead, he sat at the other end of the bench, as far as he could get from her. He slipped off his windbreaker and held it out to her. He could see she was wet and shivering.

"Don't want it. I'm fine," she insisted.

He didn't push, just left it on the bench between them.

"You can go back to Innisfree for all I care."

"I'm not going back to Innisfree—not tonight and not again. I'm going to wait here with you until Mom comes and then we'll load up your boat in the truck. I left my boat at the beach near yours. I'll meet you at home."

"Suit yourself. I don't care what you do."

They sat silently for about ten minutes. At this hour Mae would have to wait for the ferry to get across the harbor at Edgartown. Izzy continued to shiver and he let her, despite how hard it was for him not to wrap her in his jacket and then pull her close for warmth. That was what he did; hold people in his embrace—for comfort, for strength, for love.

Eventually, Izzy slid her hand along the bench and dragged the jacket toward her. She wrapped it around herself like a blanket. He knew she was going to be stiff with pain when she stood—if she could stand. After hours in the boat in the cramped position required by the shallow well of the Sunfish, and then who knew how long she'd been sitting, damp and chilled on the bench, he wasn't at all sure her legs would function. He doubted she realized how much she had compromised herself. He prepared himself to catch her, carry her, even if she didn't want him to.

Tobias saw the lights of the truck before Izzy did, since she was trying so hard not to look at him and had kept her eyes away from Beach Road. Mae pulled up next to the bench and rushed to Izzy's side. Tobias stood ready to catch Izzy. Mae looked at him, but did not speak—it was a look at once relieved but also questioning. Tobias could not tell if Izzy, in her call home, had told Mae what had driven her on this wild ride. But now was not the moment to ask.

Mae hugged Izzy.

"Let's get you in the truck."

As Tobias had suspected, Izzy was barely able to stand, let alone walk. As her legs buckled under her he scooped her up. She stiffened in resistance, but was too exhausted to put up much of a fight. He carried her to the truck and gently settled her in the cab.

"The Sunfish is on the beach. If you drive down the ramp I can hoist it in the back of the truck."

"How long do you think it will take? I should get her home and into a warm bath as soon as possible."

"Why don't I tow it then? I can run a line through the bow handle and stow the mast and sail on my deck. Get her home. It'll be a couple of hours before I'm back."

Mae nodded. Her focus was entirely on Izzy. Whatever she knew or thought about his role in Izzy's reckless escapade she was holding within her.

He closed the door after Mae climbed into the truck. He leaned in through the open window to kiss her. She turned her head so that the kiss landed, unreturned, on her cheek. Then she pulled out, made a U-turn and sped off in the direction of Edgartown.

He made the lonely trek back to Izzy's boat. She had kept his jacket. He spent the next hour loading and tying off the various elements, wading in water up to his waist to make sure everything was secure.

By the time he docked at Cove Meadow, it was nearly midnight. The house was dark; not even the porch light left on for him.

In the living room he found a stack of sheets on the couch and it was pretty clear they weren't there because Mae had been interrupted folding laundry. They were meant for him.

He peeled off his damp clothes in the bathroom and only then caught on his shirt the scent that he remembered wafting in the air when he had bent to comfort Lydia.

Shit, he thought, as he ducked under the hot shower, its searing temperature dispelling the chills and aches of this long night, but not the sense of foreboding that he had betrayed the two women he loved the most.

He tossed most of the night on the couch, not because his back ached but because his heart did.

He rose before Mae and Izzy, folded up the sheets and stowed them in the laundry room. He was torn about leaving the house to check on the Sunfish, which he had left lashed to his own boat, too tired the night before to deal with it. A part of him was more than happy to escape the heavy mood in the house, put off what he knew was the inevitable confrontation. But another part was anxious to get everything out in the open, as painful as he knew it would be for all of them.

He decided to stay and make breakfast for everyone. It occurred to him that he felt outnumbered, a stranger in his own family. The intensity of the past year had put an unfathomable strain on them—losing the Boat House to Hurricane Donna; making the decision to relinquish Innisfree for the sake of Izzy's future; Jo's angry departure and his decision to enter the army; Izzy's operation and rehabilitation. The cumulative effect of all these assaults on their happiness had been to fray the cords between him and Mae. He saw that now. Not as an excuse for his vulnerability in the face of Lydia's need for him, but in his understanding of how fragile they all were right now. Mae had borne the brunt of the losses and he had not been there for her as much as he could have and should have been. No wonder she had turned away from his kiss, turned him out of their bed. It wasn't just about one misstep with Lydia, but about his emotional detachment when Mae needed him most. He had felt on the periphery this year, especially as Mae had thrown herself so completely into securing Izzy's surgery. What an idiot he'd been not to see it.

He began pulling eggs and bacon and flour and blueberries out onto the counter. If nothing else, he could start making them the blueberry pancakes that were the Monroe signature breakfast. If he was lucky, the aromas would wend their way to them and pull them out of bed and into the conversation they all needed to have, especially him.

It was Mae who emerged first, still in her bathrobe, the strain of the evening before evident on her face. It also looked as if she hadn't slept much either.

She poured herself a cup of coffee.

"We should talk before Izzy wakes up."

"I wanted to tell you last night, but the importance of finding Izzy outweighed everything else."

"It would have been better for me to hear it first from you. I was blindsided. All I have is Izzy's version. An adolescent who has adored her father as a hero suddenly sees him doing something that so repels her it wipes out everything she has ever believed about him. Did you know that she had seen you?"

"I didn't know at the time, but I suspected that she might have when you told me she'd been out to Poge. All I could think about last night was finding her. I thought, once she's safe, we can unravel what happened."

"So what exactly did happen?" Mae was still standing, arms folded across her chest.

"Lydia broke down. All that pent-up loneliness and hurt that you are avoiding her came spilling out. She was so unlike the Lydia I thought I knew. I felt . . . I guess what I felt was compassion for her and some foolish idea that I could rescue her."

"What did you do?" Mae's voice was cautious, tentative, fearful.

"I took her in my arms and let her cry it out on my shoulder."

"That's why your shirt smelled like her Jean Naté."

"Her what?"

"Jean Naté. It's the fragrance she wears."

"So you suspected something last night, and then Izzy confirmed it by describing what she saw—her father embracing another woman. God, Mae, I'm sorry."

Every muscle in his body, every yearning in his soul wanted to reach across the gulf between them. But he knew if he took one step toward her, she'd see it merely as his reflexive solution to anyone in distress. Give them a hug, make it all better, even when he couldn't. So he remained apart, waiting.

"What happened after that?"

Did she really think it had gone beyond the embrace? He was shaken by her suspicion, and angry. Had he ever given her a reason to think he'd betray her?

"Nothing."

He searched her face, looking for a spark of recognition, an acceptance that he was telling the truth. But all he saw was doubt and hurt.

"Why did you stop?"

"Because I came to my senses. I realized that comforting her as I had was too open for misinterpretation . . ."

"By Izzy or me?"

"No, by Lydia. I pulled away as soon as I felt things shift."

"From comfort to something else . . ."

"Yes. Mae, I'm sorry. It was a stupid, unthinking action. Please forgive me."

"I do forgive you. But I need some time to sort through this. I'm not surprised—not by you, but by Lydia. I knew something was going on with her and I suspected that her following you out to the Gut that morning had more to do with her emotional needs than a leaky roof she could have gotten Mel Jeffers to fix. She wanted you, plain and simple. I think that's why I was so reluctant to have you take on those repairs. I didn't know if you were simply oblivious to why she had turned to you or if, at some level, you were drawn to her. Look, I know I've been so focused on my own pain this year and on Izzy's health, that I've pushed you away. I was scared that I had pushed you too far. When Izzy told me what she had seen, it just confirmed my worst fears. Not only had I lost Innisfree and Jo, but I'd lost you too."

"Oh my God, Mae! You haven't lost me. I've been tortured since finding Izzy that I'd lost you."

She opened her arms and he stepped into her embrace.

"How do we make this right with Izzy?"

"She may not understand at first. Life is still very black and white to her. You've toppled from the pedestal, and it may take some time to climb back up. Take it from the mother of a teenage girl, it ain't easy."

They were still in each other's arms when Izzy came into the kitchen. They didn't step away from each other when they realized she was there, but instead faced her together. Her ever-expressive face floundered between disbelief and relief. She seemed torn between railing against her father—"How could you do it?"—and her mother—"How could you forgive him?" And yet, simmering under her fury it was apparent to Mae and Tobias that she wanted everything to be all right.

Mae reached out her hand.

"It's OK, Izzy. Dad has told me what happened. I both understand why he was holding Mrs. Hammond and I forgive him. Sometimes we make judgments about what we see before we have all the facts."

"I'm sorry that my comforting Mrs. Hammond upset you so much, Izzy. I can understand that what you saw disturbed you. Will you forgive me?"

"Only if Mom has. It's Mom you hurt, not me."

"But I think I did hurt you, Izzy, by making you doubt my love for Mom and our family."

"Izzy, I *have* forgiven Dad. That's between him and me. You need to hear Dad out and look in your own heart." Mae's tone was gentle as she spoke to her daughter.

"Izzy, Mrs. Hammond was crying and upset. Maybe she shouldn't have shared her troubles with me, but I was there and she did. I held her while she cried. That's what you saw."

"But . . . but you whispered in her ear, the way you do with Mom."

"I was telling her goodbye, Izzy."

"Goodbye for then, or goodbye for good?"

"I won't be going out to Innisfree to help her anymore. I think that's best for all of us."

"OK." It was said grudgingly, a tentative assertion that seemed to be saying, "I'll wait and see." But Tobias accepted that was all he could expect right now.

"How about some blueberry pancakes?"

"You made them?"

"Is that so hard to believe? Sometimes we can try to do new things, especially for one another."

She slumped into her chair. "I guess I'll try to eat them, then."

It was a small concession, but he welcomed it.

He and Mae put off for another time a discussion with Izzy about her recklessness in taking the Sunfish beyond the bay alone after dark.

Chapter 20

"A grey gull lost its fear and flew"
Izzy

The summer eased into fall with no more crises. Izzy called it boring, especially after her parents laid down a rule about where and when she could sail. Tobias stayed away from Innisfree and Lydia and found extra work at a boatyard in Vineyard Haven. Mae and Naomi tilled and harvested and put up the bounty from the garden. About once a month Izzy got a letter from Jo, training for the Special Forces in Texas, and she read parts of it out loud to her parents and grandmother at the dinner table. But not all. Some of his words were just for her. Words of encouragement, words of sympathy, words of humor that staved off her loneliness and frustration and hunger for a life that extended beyond the boundaries of Chappy.

Gaining the use of her legs had unleashed in Izzy a longing to experience what she had only been able to read about before her surgery. She had been an early reader and then a voracious one, spurred by the stillness of her limbs to exercise her brain. She had skipped sixth grade, excelled in junior high and then flown through her freshman year of high school, acing all her exams even though she had spent three months recuperating from her surgery.

With the opening of school just weeks away, a letter arrived from the principal of the high school to her parents. She assumed it was the usual blather about rules and dress codes and vacation schedules, and tossed it on the table with everything else she had pulled from the mailbox at the end of their lane. But it wasn't. At dinner, her mother brought up the contents of the letter.

"The administration wants to move you up again, have you skip sophomore year and go directly into the junior class. It would mean taking a couple of courses next summer to make sure you cover the state history and math requirements. You'd be out of sync with your friends, but it will probably be more stimulating for you academically. If I recall, you chafe sometimes when the class is moving too slowly for you, especially when, as you put it 'I read that book when I was ten.' What do you think?"

Izzy seized on the idea of moving up. It meant she'd graduate in two years. She could barely contain her excitement.

"Of course, I'll do it!"

She wrote to Jo that night.

Chapter 21

"Together in that hour of gentleness"
Mae

In December Izzy had her annual follow-up exam at Children's Hospital and she and Mae made their usual pilgrimage to Boston.

The tests took longer than they expected and, as a consequence, the orthopedic team wanted to keep Izzy overnight. Izzy groaned. "Really! How much more do they need to know. I can walk. Maybe I won't ever climb Kilimanjaro or run the Boston Marathon—although, I guess because I'm a woman, even if I *could* run, I wouldn't be *allowed* to run. But jeez, Mom. What a waste of time."

"I hear you. But the great Oz has spoken. We both are going to have to deal with it. Here are the menu choices for dinner. The nurse said we need to fill out the card now if you're going to eat tonight. Then I have to find myself a hotel room. The snow is getting heavier, which means we might not have been able to get back to the island tonight anyway. Look at it this way. You're snug and warm and not stuck in a freezing bus on the Expressway. I'll see you in the morning."

She gave her a hug. "I love you."

"Love you back. I'll just sit here and read *War and Peace*. I'll probably be able to finish it by the time they let me out of here."

Mae gathered up her coat and purse and went to the phone booth in the lobby. She saw the coffee shop was still open and slipped in to grab a cup of coffee and sandwich to go. She didn't think she'd have another opportunity to find some place to eat, especially with the snow.

As she was standing in line waiting for her food she heard her name being called. Mae Keaney, not Mae Monroe. It took her a moment to grasp that the voice was seeking her, and another moment to recognize the voice. She turned and saw a nun crossing the café toward her.

"Maureen?"

Despite the wimple and veil, the long black habit and sensible oxfords, Mae saw the face of her baby sister—a light dusting of freckles, gray-blue eyes and a generous mouth set in a wide smile.

Maureen held out her hands to Mae and clasped them. Mae saw the gold band on her left ring finger in the shape of a delicate cross. A bride of Christ.

In all the years she and Izzy had been coming to Boston, she had never encountered Maureen. She admitted to herself that she also hadn't deliberately sought her out after connecting with Pat the year before. Although she and Pat had continued to take their tentative steps toward reconciliation, Mae had been reluctant to meet with Maureen. Her perception of the judgmental nature of nuns had been shaped so harshly by her experience with Catriona's birth and death, and she feared that Maureen, of all her siblings, would not find room in her heart to forgive her.

But now, she had no choice but to speak to her sister. "What brings you to Children's?"

"One of the children in our school has just been diagnosed with juvenile diabetes and I've been visiting him and his mother. They're frightened and overwhelmed. But I'm sure you know . . . Is everything OK with Izzy?"

It seemed odd to Mae that Maureen was familiar with Izzy's situation, when the two sisters had not seen each other in decades. But then she realized that Maureen must be in close touch with Patrick. And with a sharp pang, Mae grasped that she might even have spent time with Jo. Of course she knew about Mae's family.

"Everything's fine. Izzy's here for her annual follow up and they're unexpectedly keeping her overnight. I'm just on my way to find a hotel."

"Stay with me."

"What? In the convent?"

"We have a guest suite, and I know it's available tonight. It's miserable out and the convent isn't far. I've got our station wagon and can take you right now. Please come."

The thought of finding a room at a price she could afford on a night when hundreds of people stranded by the snow were trying to do the same was enough to outweigh any reservations she had about accepting Maureen's invitation—although she knew she was saying yes to more than a bed for the night. She was agreeing to let another one of her siblings into her life.

She followed Maureen to the hospital parking lot and helped her scrape off the accumulated snow on the wagon. By the time they were on their way their cheeks were red and their hats were dripping with melted snow.

The convent was exactly as Mae imagined it—brick Victorian, heavy drapes, dark wood paneling, images of the Virgin Mary and the Sacred Heart on the walls. When they arrived, Mae was surprised to hear the nun who greeted them address Maureen as "Reverend Mother."

"Reverend Mother? My little sister is Reverend Mother?"

Maureen lowered her eyes. "I got elected in September. It's taking everyone a bit of getting used to, including me. I'm shaking things up, which in the Catholic Church isn't always welcome. But Pope John XXIII is giving me some help." She smiled, a glimmer of the mischievous little girl Mae remembered.

Maureen got Mae settled in the guest quarters, which included a sitting room along with a bedroom and bath.

"Thank you, Mo. This is beyond luxurious."

"I'm thrilled to be able to offer it to you, and for the opportunity to have time with you. I know you've had your reasons to stay away, but I want to get to know you. I've missed my big sister. I've got to hustle to the chapel. You're welcome to join us for prayer, but it's not a requirement of being a guest. But even if you don't pray with us, please eat with us. I'll come get you when it's time for dinner. A hot meal will be so much better than a plastic-wrapped sandwich from the hospital coffee shop."

Mae stayed away from the chapel, but Maureen was right, the prospect of a hot meal had a strong appeal. The convent was larger than Mae realized—nearly twenty-five nuns—all of whom were curious about Reverend Mother's unexpected guest.

"Do they know I'm your sister?" She didn't want to put Mo in an awkward position.

"Oh, yes. And the older nuns will try to pump you for your life history, but save that for me." She answered with a twinkle and led her into the dining room.

Mae escaped from the inquisition relatively unscathed, mainly by asking more questions of the nuns than they did of her. After dinner she retreated to her rooms, with a promise from Maureen that she would stop by later.

Around nine, a knock on the door indicated that she was keeping her promise. When Mae opened the door, she found Mo, her arms laden with a flannel nightgown, a pair of wool socks and a bottle of whisky.

"I thought of all the things that could warm you on a snowy December night and I scrounged around till I found them."

Mae laughed. "You're not exactly the kind of nun I've ever encountered. But you are definitely a Keaney!" She took the bottle first.

"Will you have a drink with me?"

"Oh, I am definitely a Keaney in that regard. Danny gave me that bottle."

She opened a cabinet and retrieved two glasses and poured for both of them.

"To sisterhood." She raised her glass to Mae and Mae reciprocated with a clink of her own glass.

Then Maureen got down on her knees by the fireplace. Mae thought she was about to pray, but instead Maureen expertly built a fire and had it spreading its heat within a few minutes.

"I have something else for you," she said, and dug out of her voluminous pocket a stack of letters—the pale blue, tissue-thin airmail kind. She handed them to Mae. It took Mae a moment to register the return address. They were all from Jo to Maureen.

"I thought you would want to read them."

"Thank you." Mae put the letters aside. She didn't want to read them in front of Maureen. Maureen must have known that Jo had cut off contact with Mae and Tobias. Was this a gesture of compassion, to share the letters with her, or a demonstration that Maureen was closer to Jo than his own mother?

Despite Maureen's hospitality and generosity, Mae felt uneasy. Maureen wanted something Mae was unsure she was able to give.

Maureen sipped her drink and studied Mae.

"I've often dreamed of this moment, especially when I was a little girl . . . that my sister would come home and we would be a family again."

"Please don't start the litany of how my leaving destroyed the family. Kathleen began on that note fifteen years ago and then proceeded to try to destroy *me*."

"Mae, I'm not blaming you for what happened to us. There are so many reasons—the forced move to Boston, Da's drinking, Ma's depression, Kathleen's instability. I was just musing on my dreams as a little girl, and how one of those dreams was fulfilled today when I saw you at the hospital. To have you here now with me is a blessing. You know, when we thought we were on the brink of war in October, with those Russian missiles in Cuba and the world holding its breath, we were praying around the clock in the convent. I was in the chapel at three o'clock in the morning with only the lights from votive candles and God's presence in the silence all around me. I prayed for the world, but I also prayed for us, for our fragmented family. I was filled with such a longing for us to come together, to make amends. Jo's arrival on Patrick's doorstep has brought us closer to that possibility. He's a wonderful young man, but I'm sure you know that."

"I do know that. And in losing him last year, I am so aware of the heartbreak I must have left in my wake when I disappeared. Please believe me that I didn't leave in anger. I didn't leave to hurt anyone. If anything, I left to save you all from hurt—especially Ma."

"Is there any reason now holding you back from telling me why? Ma and Da are both gone. You can't cause them pain."

Mae studied the amber liquid in her glass, its fragrance an evocative memory. Whisky was indelibly linked to her first night with Tobias so many years ago, begun on the stone porch at sunset, turning the pages of the *Collected Works* of William Butler Yeats.

She might have labeled that a simpler time, but she knew that it had not been, any more or less than other moments in her life. She had described Izzy this past summer as seeing the world in black or white, defined in absolutes. Perhaps when it came to her family, Mae was doing the same, believing that no one among the Keaneys could understand or forgive her.

"There is still the possibility that someone will be hurt by my secrets. But I'm willing to share them with you, if you can help me find a way back—at least with Patrick and Danny. Maybe even with Jo. He must trust you, to have written so many letters to you."

"Oh, Mae, please don't think I have usurped you! I am only a stand-in until he figures out who he is and where he fits in the Monroe-Keaney constellation. I will be honored to have you tell me your story. And I will hold it in my heart as we figure out together who needs to know what."

"You have to understand how difficult this is. Tobias and Izzy are the only ones who know."

Maureen grasped her hand. "And how blessed you are to have them to love and protect you. I hope I can do the same."

Mae began.

"I don't know if you ever knew that I had encountered Ned Bradley about a year after we moved to Boston. The presence of a childhood friend, who cherished the memories of Chappy as I did, was a balm in the drudgery and ugliness of our tenement life. But I knew Da hated the Bradleys and blamed them for our changed circumstances. So I kept my friendship with Ned hidden. My first secret."

Maureen nodded. Her gaze was focused intently on Mae, listening without interruption.

"Eventually our friendship started to change—a kiss, a caress, desire overcoming childish games. I became Ned's lover one Saturday afternoon when his parents were away and we were alone in the house on Beacon Hill. I was stunned by the opulence. I thought they had lost everything in the crash, but that was obviously a lie. They had closed The Knolls and banished Da and Ma, but they still had most of everything else."

If Maureen was shocked, by either Mae's admission of her sexual relationship with Ned or the duplicity and callousness of the Bradleys, she managed to contain it. Mae observed her sister keenly, ready to shut down her story immediately if she detected any signs of judgment or accusation that she was a sinner. Maureen was unlike the nuns who had sheltered and then condemned Mae when she had sought refuge with them. Mae suspected that Maureen's acceptance of her was not only because she was Maureen's sister. Mae imagined that Maureen would listen so unconditionally to anyone who had sought her help. She took a deep breath and continued.

"I convinced myself that I was in love with Ned. How could I think otherwise? I was sleeping with him, defying every precept of chastity and purity we had learned not only in our catechism but also at Ma's knee. His love was the only beacon in my bleak life.

"And then I found myself pregnant."

"Oh, Mae! It's all becoming clear to me." Maureen reached across and squeezed her hand. Then she poured them each another shot.

"I told Ned. Despite the shame, a part of me was excited. A child. A product of our love. It never occurred to me that Ned would be angry. He accused me of deliberately getting pregnant to trap him. Told me I should have been smarter, known how to prevent a baby from happening like the girls in his set. Frankly, I didn't know there were ways either to get pregnant intentionally or avert a pregnancy. I knew we had been taking risks, but I was more concerned about getting caught than getting pregnant."

"What did Ned do?"

Mae took a moment to tamp down the pain that, even now, thirty years later, rose up in the memory of that ugly, devastating conversation.

"He told me to 'get rid of it' and flung a hundred dollars in my lap. 'There are ways,' he said, and even got me the name and address of someone in New Haven who would give me an abortion.

"I went home that night shattered. I had begun the day believing Ned would take me in his arms and ask me to marry him. I was petrified, but I couldn't talk to anyone—certainly not Ma. I thought it would kill her to find out I was pregnant, and I thought Da would kill Ned.

I couldn't even talk to Kathleen, who was so perfect and good. A saint."

Maureen winced. "We all thought she was."

"I spent a week in escalating panic, going through the motions of getting up every morning to go to work, coming home in the evenings to help Ma with supper and housework and you kids, all the time trying to find a way to save both the family's honor and my baby's life. Then I remembered that a sister of one of the girls at the bakery had gone away to have a baby. No one was supposed to know, of course, but word had gotten around, and the place where she had gone in Connecticut had been passed from ear to ear and then put away for safekeeping. I had written it down and put it in my missal. I had the hundred dollars still from Ned. I thought it would be enough to get me to Connecticut, have my baby and figure out the next step in my life.

"I planned everything carefully and carried a few things I'd need for the trip to work each day and stored them in my locker. On the day I left, I bought a valise in the luggage department, packed everything up and walked to the bus station. I was four months' pregnant.

"I didn't know the home was run by nuns until I got there, and I also didn't know I wouldn't be able to keep my baby but would have to give it up for adoption. I was so naïve, such an innocent despite my sexual history. I thought I could somehow raise and support a child on my own, at the age of nineteen. I almost left when they put the papers in front of me to sign. I got up from the table and picked up my valise when the sister in charge described in excruciating detail the meager circumstances and disgrace of life as an unmarried mother. She went on to accuse me of selfishness for wanting to keep my baby when a good, Catholic family could provide everything—

stability, education, respectability—for the child. She left out one thing. I asked her 'What about love?' and she told me if I truly loved my baby I would give it up. At that moment the baby kicked inside me for the first time, a flutter pushing off against the inside of my belly. It suddenly made her real, and an overwhelming sense of responsibility descended on me. I knew I had no way to keep her safe. So I signed the papers."

"Oh, Mae, you mean you have a daughter somewhere in the world? Do you have any idea where she might be?"

Mae held up her hand and shook her head.

"No, Maureen, I don't." Just as Izzy had, Maureen had rushed ahead to the assumption that there might be a happy ending to this story. Mae had to stop her before her imagination had invented the scenario of a touching reunion between mother and child.

"Catriona was stillborn."

"I am so sorry! You named her after Ma."

"It was the only way I could think of to have Ma close when I so desperately needed her. The nuns, well, they saw Catriona's death as God's punishment for my wickedness. I have never understood why those women felt called to care for mothers and their babies. They did all they could to berate us that we were not fit to mother our children because they had been conceived in sin."

"I know women like that in the sisterhood. Sadly, too many of them, bitter because they feel trapped in a life they did not choose or did not fully understand."

"May I ask why you are not bitter? Kathleen led me to believe you were forced into the convent in place of me."

"It sounds like Kathleen was doing her best to lay a very heavy guilt trip on you. The answer is complicated. Yes, I knew it was important for Ma to have a daughter enter the convent. More than important, actually. It was critical to her. As we all knew, when she didn't become a nun herself she made a vow that one of her daughters would. But I never felt forced or resentful. My experience with nuns was very different from yours. One nun in particular, my teacher in sixth grade, was a role model for me. To be honest, I know part of my motivation to become a nun had nothing to do with Ma's expectations or Mother Mary Campion's encouragement to be open to the 'calling.' I became a nun to escape the squalor and misery of life in the Keaney household."

She stopped, as if to digest what she had just revealed.

"I've never admitted that to anyone before, not even to myself. A surprising statement for the leader of the community, don't you think? But somehow, I felt you would understand."

"I do, Mo, I do. But what about now? Is your life still defined as 'not Keaney' or has it changed?"

"Oh, Mae! My life is so much more than I ever imagined. The order sent me to college, encouraged me to grow intellectually as well as spiritually. I've found both peace and power I don't think I'd have been able to wield in a world where women are defined by what their husband does. For all her money and social status, Kathleen does not have the authority and the capacity to effect change as I do. I am not just inured to my life as a nun. I have embraced it and rejoice in it."

"That requires another drink!" Mae poured this time and raised her glass to her sister.

"To peace and power! Who knew?"

"I suppose all of us were looking for a way out— Danny by becoming not just a soldier but a member of an elite team; Pat defying Da's view of the police as a tool of oppression; you building a life for yourself with your café on the Vineyard; Kathleen taking refuge in marriage to a rich scumbag."

Mae nearly choked on her drink.

"Did Reverend Mother just call her sister's husband a scumbag?"

"I did. And from what you told me tonight about his response to the news he had fathered your child, the opinion I've had of him since he began courting Kathleen has simply been confirmed."

"When exactly did he begin seeing Kathleen?" Mae had her suspicions.

"It was before you left. I remember that he came to pick her up in the evenings only after Da left to go to the bar. But I don't recall you being home those nights."

"I worked till six on Thursday nights at the bakery and then did office cleaning until eight."

"So Ned was dating both of you. Do you think he was sleeping with Kathleen as well?"

"Who knows? It would have killed me then to know what he was doing behind my back, but now, well, everything I saw in his behavior during the custody hearing disgusted me. I am frankly stunned that he and Kathleen are still married."

"Part of the peace I've achieved in the convent has been my relief that I'm not married. I knew only two marriages—Da and Ma, and Kathleen and Ned. Both were disastrous, especially for the women. Kathleen is a harpy, although a sick one, but I'm sure her marriage to Ned has only exacerbated her illness. The convent has protected me from her destructiveness, but I berate myself for not doing more for her than praying. I have felt recently, especially since Jo's arrival in our lives, that perhaps this is the time for reconciliation. I think she's very isolated. Ned is part of Jack Kennedy's entourage, as far as I can tell from the newspapers, and Kathleen seems to have been left behind in her empty mansion."

"I don't think you need to feel any guilt about leaving Kathleen to her own twisted view of what the world owes her. Just as I did what I knew I had to do to protect Jo from Kathleen, you did was necessary to protect yourself. Look at who you've become and what you've accomplished! Do you honestly think you would be who you are today if Kathleen had been a part of it?"

"I hear what you are saying. But deep in my heart, perhaps in my hopes, I feel that we are finally at a moment when we can heal as a family. Look at the two of us! Who could have imagined even a year ago we would be having this conversation?"

"For us, and Danny and Patrick, yes, I think we can come together without flinging a lot of blame, especially at me. Patrick, especially, in welcoming Jo last year; and you tonight, so willing to listen without judgment. But I cannot imagine Kathleen being anything except a source of pain for me. I have my own family to heal, Mo. A son thousands of miles away, who more than likely will be sent to the other side of the world; a daughter just emerging from years of crippling pain; a husband who has borne the weight of our disintegration. I don't have the energy for Kathleen and I won't be sucked back into her vortex. Keep up your prayers—for all of us—but don't reopen wounds we all seem to have worked very hard to heal."

"I understand. The time isn't right for you. Maybe it will never be, as far as Kathleen is concerned. But I'm grateful I have you back in my life. Thank you for trusting me. I'm sure you want to get some sleep, and I'm going to have a full plate tomorrow dealing with the snow. I'll say goodnight."

Maureen got up and threw her arms around Mae. "Goodnight, sis. Welcome back."

1963
Dak To
South Vietnam

Chapter 22

"And the cries of unknown perishing armies
beat about my ears"
Josiah

The copter descended quickly, its rotors pushing the
grit of the landing zone into dun-colored plumes that
shot out from under the metal bird like the splash of a
surfacing whale off the cliffs at Gay Head. But he was a
long way from Aquinnah.

The orders had said Dak To, a remote outpost on the
Cambodia-Laos borders. He had been in country only a
week, listening to the unfamiliar cadences of the
Vietnamese language, the raucous advice of the soldiers in
the Saigon barracks and bars, the tumult of motor bikes
and ancient buses in the congested streets. But as soon as
the pilot killed the engine, Josiah was struck by the silence
of Dak To. He adjusted his pack, slapped on his baseball
cap and leaped from the copter onto a barren scrap of
sand.

No one was there to meet him.

Around the perimeter of the landing zone he saw clusters of flimsy wooden structures and some scattered tents. Beyond them, a flat, open scrub land and then the mountains, thick with vegetation and, more than likely, Viet Cong.

"The landing zone is the most vulnerable," one of the old timers had told him the night before. "No cover and the noise of the copter announces your arrival long before you're on the ground. Get out of the open as soon as you land."

Josiah swept his eyes over the encampment, searching for the symbol that marked where he belonged. He found it quickly, the peeling red paint barely visible above a screen door. A red cross. The medic cabin.

He set off across the field as the copter roared to life again, once again spewing the choking dust into obscuring clouds. When he emerged at the edge of the field, he saw a face at the window of the cabin. A woman's face.

Nothing in his training had prepared Josiah for his arrival. Not his nine months of field medicine instruction, not his month of jump school. Not even his Special Ops training. But the isolation of Dak To and the disturbing sense that he was being watched, set off alarms in his brain.

His CAR-15 was slung over his shoulder, but his .45 pistol was within easy reach. He moved along the outer walls of the buildings leading to the medic cabin. A dog barked in the distance. Insects whined in the low brush stretching across the plain to the mountains. He wondered if the camp had been abandoned. But he could see clusters of equipment under camouflage netting and, as he got closer to the clinic, he could hear the lilt of women's voices. He hadn't been mistaken when he had seen a woman at the window.

A screen door slammed and Josiah flinched, flattening himself against the building. He watched a soldier leave the clinic, half-raising his slinged arm in a gesture of farewell to someone inside.

"I'll be back, Liz, for some more of your TLC."

Josiah relaxed. Another human being. Two, if he counted Liz. He hadn't expected there to be nurses at such a remote camp.

He left the shelter of the neighboring building and strode more purposefully to the field hospital. The chatter he had heard increased as he approached, then stopped abruptly when he pulled the screen door open and stepped inside.

His eyes adjusted to the dim interior; his nose detected the familiar odors of a military clinic: the sharp, sweet tang of alcohol; the slightly bitter scent of industrial disinfectant; the metallic trace of blood; the yeasty simmer of infection. Overlaying all the odors was the unexpected note of lilies. The nurse, Liz, was wearing perfume. The scent wafted toward him before she did. Then he heard her voice, saw her face.

"You the new medic?" She smiled, her English tinged with an unfamiliar accent, one he hadn't heard in Saigon. He realized she must be Montagnard. One of the tasks the unit here was charged with was recruiting native troops, the mountain people.

"I am Nguyet, but the guys here call me Liz, Liz Taylor. They can't say my name easily." She turned and waved at three other Montagnard women hanging back in the shadows. "And this is Kim Novak, Betty Grable and Olive Oyl. We've been waiting for you. The last medic, he left two weeks ago with a bullet in his spine. There's work to do..." she gestured to the folding chairs lined up against the wall, filled with men—both GIs and Montagnard. "They need shots, wounds cleaned, stitches. You ready?"

"I need to report to the commander first. Where can I find him?"

"He's out on patrol. Be back before dark. We work now, you report later."

Josiah understood with clarity that Liz Taylor was a force to be reckoned with. He slipped off his pack, stowed it and his rifle in a corner, rolled up his sleeves, and plunged in.

By dusk he had treated about twenty soldiers. As soon as word got around that the new medic had arrived, the camp that Josiah had thought abandoned was swarming with guys seeking help for what ailed them.

He bent to his tasks, ignoring the muttered comments coming from voices waiting their turn.

"Christ, another kid. We should get a pool going to see how long this one lasts."

"If he's got an attitude problem like the last one, I'll be the first to ante up."

Josiah was tying off the last stitch in a jagged arm wound caused by barbed wire when he heard a commotion at the front of the clinic and the scrape of boots on the plywood floor as soldiers pushed back their seats and stood at attention. Josiah didn't stand until he'd finished the stitch and snipped the silk.

The commander took in the scene with a sweeping glance—pails filled with bloody swabs, empty vials of antibiotics and vaccines, and a waiting line still six deep.

He approached Josiah, the dust and grime of patrol still clinging to him along with faint traces of a fired weapon. Josiah saluted, the needle and trailing thread still in his hand.

"I heard you'd arrived, Specialist Monroe. I see you've wasted no time in making yourself useful, and I'm not going to hold up the line now. Come see me when you're finished here."

"Yes, sir."

The commander strode out of the clinic and the room settled again to a low buzz. The next guy in line needed a tetanus shot and rolled up his sleeve.

"He's a decent commander. He gets that those of us in Special Forces are renegades. He's not going to cite you for a sloppy uniform. Just don't do anything sloppy in the field."

It was full dark when Josiah finally closed his suture kit and the last soldier had grunted his thanks. From Josiah's perspective it had been a good day, despite the unveiled skepticism of the men in the unit. He'd felt confident that he'd handled everything that confronted him. He was glad he hadn't landed in the middle of a firefight. None of the wounds he'd sewn up today had been caused by the enemy; no one had been bleeding out; no one was going to lose a limb or a section of his gut. It surprised him, even though he was grateful for the relatively easy start, that a part of him itched to be put to the test under fire. In training he'd scored at the top of his class in every challenge. Technically, he knew his stuff. But he knew he wouldn't be considered a good medic—wouldn't consider himself one—until he saved lives in the midst of battle.

He left the clinic and made his way to the commander's headquarters, where he could see a dim light burning behind the drawn blinds. He was waiting for Josiah.

He knocked on the door. Like the clinic, the structure was flimsy, patched with odd pieces of wood or metal and surrounded by four-foot high walls of sandbags. Any paint had long since blistered and peeled. Josiah suspected that in the rainy season most of the buildings scattered around the camp would be leaking and the dusty roads would be mired in mud.

He pushed open the door when his knock was answered. Inside an anteroom at a battered metal desk sat a corporal. "Commander Jackson's waiting for you. Go on in."

"Sir." Josiah saluted as he entered the commander's office. He'd learned well. Not only field medicine skills had been drilled into him in the year since he had enlisted. He was a soldier, and it had been a surprise to him that the persona as well as the uniform had fit him so well. His parents, both rebels in their own time, would not have recognized him nor understood him.

"At ease, Specialist. Welcome to Dak To. We weren't expecting you so soon. But as you could tell by the number of men at the clinic today, we need you. A unit like ours, as remote as we are and with the kind of exploratory patrols we engage in, we can't be without a medic for long."

The commander had Josiah's file in front of him on the desk.

"I'll be blunt with you, Monroe. Our last medic was a first-timer like you; maybe not as skilled with a needle and thread as I saw you handling those sutures today, but a good medic. But he went out of here on a stretcher and I'll tell you why. He thought he knew it all, resented being given advice and was slow to follow orders. He was a smart-ass and now he's a smart-ass who's paralyzed from the waist down. Being a good medic is not the equivalent of being a good soldier. I need you to be a soldier first. Understood?"

"Yes, sir."

"Good. Be ready at 04:30 tomorrow. We're heading out again for a few days. You've patched up enough guys here for the time being. Make sure you've got enough gear in your combat medic bag to get us through the next week. Now go get some grub and some sleep. Anybody showed you where the mess and your quarters are?"

"No, sir. I've been at the clinic since I arrived."

The commander called out to the corporal.

"Hank!"

"Sir?"

"Point Specialist Monroe in the direction of food and a bed. Then get Colonel Meeks on the phone."

"Yes, sir."

The corporal was a few years older than Josiah and not much of a talker. He hadn't been one of the men Josiah had treated earlier in the day. He followed the commander's orders to the letter. With his hand, he pointed to his right.

"Mess is the next building. Your bunk is the one left by your predecessor, in the cabin behind the clinic."

Josiah hefted his gear one more time that day and found the mess with his nose. He'd eaten only a chocolate bar since arriving, too focused to stop for sustenance. But now, adrenaline draining from his system, he acknowledged his hunger.

There were still guys in the mess, playing cards with mugs of coffee at their sides. Josiah filled his plate with some mystery meat in a brown sauce and slipped onto a bench at an empty table. The card players didn't even look up. Josiah dug a well-thumbed paperback out of his pack and read, ignoring the others as firmly as they were ignoring him.

When he left, he heard the laughter and the same disparaging comments that had greeted him earlier in the clinic. He was too tired to care.

The cabin behind the clinic held four beds, but no one was there when he entered. He made up the one bare bunk, found the latrine and then crashed.

"Welcome to Dak To," he murmured as sleep overtook him.

It was dark and cold when he woke up to his alarm. From the other beds came a mixture of groans and curses.

"Shut that fucking thing off," someone shouted.

Josiah slammed his fist on the clock and pulled himself up and out of bed. He had been too tired the night before to supply his medic bag and scrambled to dress and make his way to the clinic for whatever the patrol might need. He went through a mental checklist as he grabbed bandages, syringes, bags of IV solution, and suture thread. Using the keys the corporal had issued him the night before he unlocked the med cabinet, scanned its contents and pulled what he thought he might need. But with no experience of what they might be facing in the field, he tried not to panic, tried to remember the basics from training. He made a mental note that when he got back from patrol he'd put in a requisition for the drugs he expected to find in the cabinet but weren't there. He wondered whether the specialist before him had really been a "good medic" as the commander had described him. Whatever he had been, however, didn't matter. Placing the blame on him for a nearly empty med closet wasn't going to help Josiah out in the field. He locked the cabinet, grabbed his gear and found the small group gathering by the commander's quarters.

It was still dark and Josiah could just make out the faces of the six soldiers. Two were Montagnards, four Americans, all in the same tiger stripe camouflage fatigues that he'd been sent to a tailor in Saigon to procure for himself. "You don't want to stick out in the jungle, boy. Forget about what they issued you in Texas and get yourself to Mr. Diem before you head north," the Special Forces commanding officer had ordered him. The unorthodox uniform was only the first sign that things were going to be different. No one in the patrol this morning wore a helmet or a flak jacket but instead all had on floppy bush hats. They were gathered on the ground sorting out their packs and weapons and ammo. Josiah felt for his pistol and his knife. He knew guns. He knew how they fit his hand, how to make his rifle an extension of his arm and his eye. He had hunted with Tobias from the time he was seven and had earned high grades on the firing range during training. He hadn't chosen to be a medic because he was a bad shot or afraid to fight. He had asked for a medic assignment because his uncle had told him it was the best way for an inexperienced soldier to get into Special Forces. Danny had been right. Here he was. About to go on his first patrol.

He told himself it didn't matter that he was on the periphery of the close-knit team crouched over their supplies and dividing up the weight of the ammo and rations and water to share the load. He knew he'd have to prove himself, not just with neat sutures. He knew his own vital signs, and he was pulsing with restlessness, hovering between excitement and terror.

"Kid, you're pacing like you got to pee. Hit the latrine before we hit the trail," the sergeant said, loud enough for them all to hear.

The darkness hid Josiah's red face.

"I'm fine, sir. Just working off some first-timer energy." Better to admit what they all already knew. The corporal had seen his file the night before and had probably filled them in. Josiah had been in the army for over a year, even if he hadn't yet seen combat. He knew no one was going to give him a break, and more than likely were going to try to break him.

He didn't blame them. Their lives depended on everyone knowing and doing their jobs and not fucking up. They couldn't afford to babysit him. He knew it. But he didn't have to like it. Just keep your cool, he reminded himself. You've learned a lot about self-control in the past year. Don't do anything stupid. It's one thing to be green. That you can't help and that you can change. But their tolerance for someone who's both green and a hothead is totally nonexistent. Keep your mouth shut and your eyes and ears open.

When the sorting and reorganizing were done, it appeared they were ready to head out. The commander showed up at that moment, apparently well-used to the team's preliminaries.

"Has everyone met Monroe?" He looked around to blank faces. "Although I expect him to treat you even if he doesn't know your names, I suggest you introduce yourselves or he might use a little more pressure when he jabs a syringe full of painkillers into you."

Names were grunted around the circle.

"Now let's make sure Monroe has nothing to do on this patrol except hand out salt tablets."

With that, they moved toward the perimeter of the camp. The sun was still below the horizon and the darkness covered their exposed journey through the brush until they reached a trail at the base of the mountains. Josiah had oriented himself the day before to know they were heading northwest, toward the border. Toward Laos.

They climbed for hours through the thick vegetation covering the mountain, the guys up ahead hacking through the brush with their Ka-Bar knives. They met no one and nothing except the insects and the heat. Josiah found himself observing the others with a medic's eye. When they stopped this evening he expected to be dealing with nothing more than sunburn, blisters, and bug bites. One of the things of use he'd found in the medicine cabinet had been calamine lotion. He was concentrating on the terrain, steep and rock-strewn, pulling himself back to the present whenever he found his mind wandering in the excruciating boredom of the trek. It was easy to get lost here, he realized. Not just physically in the dense and tangled underbrush, but mentally in the equally tangled nest of his own thoughts.

War had barely been a whisper when Josiah had enlisted, awed by his uncle's sense of purpose and direction. Enlisting had made so much more sense to him than enrolling in college and way more sense than following his father out to sea in a fishing boat. He was too young to remember World War II, although even isolated Chappy had seen its share of military operations, watching the beaches for German U-Boats. Finding himself on the other side of the world from Chappy, in the middle of a country simmering with both tropical heat and invisible Viet Cong, was not what he had anticipated when he signed up. He slapped a bug from the back of his neck, much like he had slapped himself aware that sooner or later a soldier was going to be in the line of fire. "What did you expect?" He could imagine Danny's voice when Josiah got his orders.

Despite his desire to get away from the constraints of his island home, he was distinctly uneasy when he read the word "Vietnam" on his orders. He had never been farther away from the Vineyard than Boston until he'd been sent to San Antonio to train at Fort Sam Houston. He had dealt with his disquiet by devouring everything he could find about this shrouded, unsettled land. It was why he knew this patrol he was on was heading toward Laos. The commander hadn't said where or why—yet. Josiah wondered if that was his style, keeping as much as possible close to the chest. Maybe he didn't trust the Montagnards in the unit, or it was too easy for vital information to seep out to the surrounding villages he'd seen from the air when the Huey had brought him in yesterday.

A sudden movement in the trees beyond the trail brought his reverie to an abrupt halt. The others up ahead had seen it, too, and everyone had dropped to the ground with weapons drawn. Silence. Waiting. Sweat trickled from Josiah's scalp into his eyes, but he remained still with his hands on his rifle. Then out from the overgrown vegetation, sprang not a man but a stag, leaping, its antlers ripping leaves from the overhanging trees.

"Pow," said the one who had introduced himself in the darkness as Charlie, miming the firing of his gun.

"Damn. If we'd been on our way back instead of out, we could have supplied the mess with venison for a month."

The tension eased; muscles relaxed from their straining positions holding bodies at readiness. There would have been no flight in this group, only fight. Josiah could hear the others exhale as he did. Not this time, their brains were assuring them.

Charlie was the first to stand, shifting his rifle back over his shoulder, when Josiah heard the thud of something hard hitting the ground not far from Charlie's feet. His brain registered "grenade" just before the dirt flew, spewing slivers of shrapnel and tossing Charlie into a cluster of thorned bushes. The others started to return fire that was coming from the northern side of the trail, where the stag had come from. That must have been what spooked him, thought Josiah. He slid on his belly along the southern edge, trying to get to Charlie. He was still alive; Josiah could hear him moaning. He made it to the thorn bushes as another grenade exploded, but away from them. One of their guys must have gotten it away. For a blessed moment, all was quiet. Josiah reached for Charlie and dragged him off the bush and into a slight gully. His shirt and pants were torn where the shrapnel had sliced through the cloth and into his flesh. Josiah cut off the bloody shirt with his knife, triaging the wounds. It didn't look like any shrapnel had come close to an artery, but blood was everywhere on his chest, oozing from multiple wounds. Josiah grabbed the largest, thickest compresses in his pack and held them with one hand while wrapping gauze around Charlie's chest to hold them in place. He worked methodically, focusing on one priority at a time to keep his panic at bay. The firing had begun again, but he was only vaguely aware of it as he went through his checklist. Stop the bleeding, start an IV, give him a painkiller if he needs it, sew up what wasn't going to close on its own if he had the time.

He didn't know how long it took him to stabilize Charlie, but when he did, he turned back to the rest of the unit. He counted the men on the trail, recounted when he realized he was one short. Then he saw him, the Montagnard named Bao, sprawled face down, a sticky pool of blood underneath him. Josiah crawled over to him, pulling his pack behind him. His hand was shaking as he felt Bao's sunburned neck for a pulse and found none. He eased him over on his back and saw the hole burned through his shirt above his heart and the dark, wet stain of blood obliterating the muted tiger stripes of his camouflage. Josiah smelled the urine and shit released when Bao's muscles had slackened. He knew the signs. The man was dead. And yet, he could not stop himself and began compressions, pushing with all his strength to get the heart pumping again, blowing into Bao's mouth with hopeless gasps.

It was only the hand of the commander on his that stopped him.

"He's gone, Monroe. There are others who need you."

The voice was stern, a command. But not without understanding that this was Josiah's first death.

He wiped his bloody hands on his pants and moved on to the next wounded soldier.

Josiah knew he had to focus on both the fighting going on around him and treating the men felled by the fighting. In training his instructor had stressed to them that they were no good to their units if they themselves were hit. "Be alert. Keep down. Know where the bullets are coming from, not just where they've hit."

But following that instruction in the middle of an attack was far more difficult than he had imagined. His brain kept homing in on the bleeding body in front of him, blocking out the distractions of bullets and explosions. It was how he'd always approached difficult challenges. Facing wrestling opponents in the ring in high school, he closed off the cheers and taunts of the opposing fans, kept his eyes on the wrestler in front of him, felt the solid surface of the mat under his feet, sensed the "tell" of his opponent's muscles as they pressed against his own and signaled his next move.

With great effort, he forced a small part of his brain to pay attention to the fight going on around him as bent over the third injured man. But every eruption of bullets pulled his mind away from the concentration he needed to save the life under his hands. Finally, he flattened himself as low as he could and still dress the wound, and simply shut out the battle.

Because of that, he didn't realize immediately that he was alone with the wounded and the dead. The three soldiers who hadn't been hit and the commander were gone. He scrambled over to check on Charlie and give him a few sips of water.

The bullets were no longer reaching their position, but punctuated the air further away. Charlie was alert enough to notice the change as well.

"Commander must have gone after them," he whispered.

Two explosions followed in rapid succession. Then silence.

"Where's your rifle, kid? If those explosions weren't ours, the VC will be here in no time."

Josiah scanned the blood-soaked, trampled ground and saw his gun propped next to his second pack. He crawled over to it and grabbed it.

"You know how to use that thing?"

Josiah did not answer him. He moved to a position away from Charlie and the other wounded man, whose name was lost to him somewhere in the fog of "before."

247

At the very least, he could divert fire away from the helpless men. As a medic, the Geneva Convention considered him a noncombatant. He wasn't allowed to engage in hostilities but he could carry a pistol and a rifle to protect the wounded under his care. And to answer Charlie's taunt, he *did* know how to use them.

He waited, gun propped in front of him, for a ripple in the vegetation, the snap of a twig underfoot. For what felt like an interminable amount of time, he heard and saw nothing. Were they all dead?

And then he heard the voices. American voices. Exhausted, muted, but definitely American.

Charlie heard them, too.

"How many are coming?"

Josiah counted as they came into view.

"All of them. They all made it."

With makeshift stretchers, the survivors carried the wounded and dead to a clearing about an hour beyond the ambush site and waited for the Huey they had called for to descend and carry them to safety.

The remaining soldiers walked further into the mountains before setting up camp. Even with their reduced numbers, the commander had decided to go on.

Trang, one of the other Montagnards left on the patrol, went off by himself to the perimeter. When Josiah looked, he thought he was bowed in prayer.

The next morning, he was gone.

The commander was not happy, but decided to continue the mission without searching for him. As the patrol moved on, he dropped back to speak to Josiah.

"We're heading to a key village this morning. People there we need to recruit, both as soldiers and as eyes and ears. I want you to set up a clinic while we're there. Chien will translate for you."

He moved off. That was all the background Josiah was going to get. They arrived at the village shortly after daybreak, Chien at the front of their diminished party. He spoke to a woman feeding chickens in a dusty yard next to the first hut. Her eyes flicked from Chien to the Americans, suspicious and fearful. Josiah found himself scanning his surroundings wondering if they had walked into another ambush.

The anxious chatter from the woman was echoed by the chickens scrabbling for the feed. Josiah saw Chien pointing to him and the woman nodded and came out of her yard. She took Josiah's hand and pulled him toward the center of the village.

"She wants to take you to the elder," Chien explained.

Josiah followed her, looking back to make sure Chien and the others were close behind. The elder's hut was dense with smoke and thick with the smells of fish sauce and garlic. Chien let the woman introduce them and then stepped in to offer the clinic. The old man was silent as he listened, sucking on something that he rolled over and over in his mouth. Josiah had seen some of the old Wampanoag do the same with a hazelnut, worrying it with their tongues for hours.

Chien turned to him. "He wants to know why you are brown and not pale like the others." Josiah was surprised the old man had seen only white Americans; there had been plenty of skins darker than his in Saigon. But the village was far from any major deployment of Americans.

"Tell him my people are the original people of my land, there long before the white man came."

Chien nodded, but seemed to see Josiah with new eyes. As Chien translated, Josiah realized it was the first time since leaving Chappy that he had acknowledged this part of his heritage. He had said the words with pride.

"Come," said Chien. "He's given us his sanction. We can set up under the chestnut tree in the center of the village."

For several hours, Josiah treated burns, set a broken arm and handed out Tootsie Rolls to children. The commander and the rest of the patrol had slipped out of sight. Although he knew he was helping the villagers with these simple ministrations, he was also aware this impromptu clinic was a smokescreen, a ruse to occupy the attention of the village while the commander carried out the true purpose of his mission. Whatever that was, Josiah hadn't been told. He had a part to play and he performed it.

The commander had made noises about "winning hearts and minds," and Josiah's clinic was supposed to persuade the village to support the American cause. Josiah doubted that a few bandages and chocolates were going to convert anyone—not when their houses were being burned and their children didn't have enough to eat. Josiah had seen the destruction on his way up from Saigon. Maybe *this* village hadn't burned yet, but it seemed to Josiah no matter where their loyalties lay, they were vulnerable. Trang had clearly figured that out when he had deserted during the night. Death at the hand of an enemy was encroaching upon this hidden enclave, and it wasn't clear whose guns would be firing the fatal shots.

By mid-afternoon, the line of the afflicted had dwindled and the other Americans had reappeared. It was time to move on.

Over the next three days the routine repeated itself, at villages deeper in the mountainous terrain. Josiah was sure they had crossed into Laos, although the

Montagnard dialect was the same in all the villages they visited. He had already begun to pick up words and phrases. He had a basic knowledge of French from high school and that had gotten him by in Saigon, but up in the mountains, the French occupation had not penetrated the culture as it had in the cities.

Chien was at first amused by Josiah's attempts to speak the dialect, which he tried out first on the children. Their laughter and playfulness ignored his mistakes.

"You learn fast," Chien told him as they were packing up one afternoon. "You will put me out of a job soon and I'll have to go back out on patrol." He was joking, but they both knew these clinics were a respite for both of them. In the evenings, Chien began to expand Josiah's vocabulary.

By the time they returned to Dak To, Josiah could speak rudimentary sentences to the nurses and the commander had caught on.

"Keep it up, Monroe. Anything we can do to better communicate with the native population fosters our mission. We don't need any more desertions." The commander had suspected Trang had been more than distraught over the death of his comrade. When he had assigned Chien to be Josiah's liaison in the villages he cautioned Josiah.

"Somebody alerted the Viet Cong about our presence. I don't for a minute believe they just happened to stumble upon us. It might have been Trang. But it could very well have been Chien. So keep your eye on him, especially if he engages in extended contact with any of the villagers."

Josiah had not encountered much duplicity in his life. For the most part, people on the island spoke their minds directly to you, not behind your back. But here, he felt mired in a bog of distrust and suspicion. The contradictory messages of the commander troubled him—"we're here to win hearts and minds, but don't trust any of them, especially not your fellow soldier."

He expected the return to Dak To to settle his uneasiness, as if the sandbagged buildings and continually manned watch posts could provide an end to his sense of displacement as well offer him the physical security that had been nonexistent out in the field. But physical safety was an illusion. Dak To was not an impregnable fort commanding high ground. Even Josiah, as inexperienced as he was, knew that it was vulnerable. Probably the only thing that had protected it from attack so far was that it was too small and too remote to have attracted the attention of the North Vietnamese army and the Viet Cong. But with every foray into the mountain villages to collect intelligence and recruits, Dak To became more visible, more of a target. It was only a matter of time.

One thing that did settle Josiah, as the weeks and then the months wore on, was the numbing repetition of daily life. Scorching heat blasted at them during the day, followed by temperature drops of twenty to forty degrees at night in the winter when he first arrived. Choking dust got into every crevice and filmed every surface unabated by rain, until the summer, when everything turned to mud. The monotony of waiting—for the next shipment of supplies, for the next mission from headquarters, for news of any kind—was disrupted only by dangerous assignments, great risks, the narrow precipice between survival and death.

Josiah killed for the first time two months into his deployment.

He was called to a village that had been attacked by the VC the day before. It was one where he'd held a clinic on an earlier mission. Although the villagers had fought off the assault successfully, they had sustained many injuries too severe to bring the wounded to camp. With Chien and two other soldiers, he climbed for half a day to the village, hidden under a thick canopy with no possibility for a helicopter to land. They carried everything they would need. When they arrived, Josiah led the way past charred dwellings still smoking, the air dense with the stench of burned flesh and spent ammunition. The radioed request for help had reported the wounded were in a thatched-roof long house on stilts in the middle of the village.

As they approached the house, Josiah was surprised that no children had rushed to greet them, clamoring for the chocolate they had learned he carried. But in the aftermath of an assault, perhaps their mothers were keeping them inside.

Josiah had learned in his short time in Vietnam not to enter an unknown structure without drawing his gun. The light from the door illuminated the chaos facing him, dozens of bodies sprawled across the bare wooden floor. As a medic, his first instinct was to begin triage, but another instinct kicked in, overriding his sense of responsibility to the bleeding and moaning men. It was the instinct Tobias had cultivated in him as a boy when they hunted. He dropped quietly to his knee and aimed for the glint of metal his eye had registered in a fleeting glance when he had entered the house.

He fired.

The bullet that had been meant for him went wide, lodging in the frame of the door to his left. There were no other shots, only the expletives coming out of the mouths of the soldiers behind him on the ladder. The women caring for the wounded had flattened themselves soundlessly when the firing began.

Josiah slipped along the wall to the corner where he had seen the gun. His assailant had fallen forward. When Josiah reached him, he kicked the rifle out of the way before turning over the body. Even for a Viet Cong, he was small. No uniform, just a belt of bullets draped across his chest. Bare feet.

He was just a boy.

Josiah's hand shook as he bent and closed the kid's eyes. Then he stood and demanded in Montagnard to know who was in charge. He wanted to run out of the house; he wanted to vomit. He had killed a child. But he turned his horror at his own actions into rage. Who had allowed the boy to be there with a gun? Was the plea for help with the wounded a trap? Were there more boys out there waiting to take them down?

The other soldiers were in the house by now, with guns pointed at any able-bodied person. The women were petrified; some of them were crying. Josiah swallowed the bile rising in his throat and identified one woman who seemed to have calmed down enough to speak. He approached her.

"What do you know about this?"

"They took the children to a shed at the edge of the forest. Unless we did as they said, they will kill them."

"How many?"

"Only one other."

"You're sure?"

She nodded. "All the rest, dead. These two, we thought they had fled. But they came back when we were burning our own dead. All our men are wounded. They said they wanted to kill Americans to avenge their comrades."

Josiah translated for the corporal leading the patrol.

"Can she show us where they are? Do you believe her, or is she leading us into another trap?"

The woman understood enough and flung herself at Josiah's feet.

"You can kill me if I am lying. I beg you. Save our children!"

Josiah and the corporal looked at one another over her head. Whether the children were hostages or not, the boy had probably not acted alone. They nodded and Josiah pulled the woman to her feet.

"Show us."

When they reached the shed, Josiah instructed her to tell the hostage taker that his comrade was wounded, but he had killed the American soldiers. She needed to get him out in the open, offer to take him to the wounded man.

He waited out of sight, listening to her. She was strong, a mother bear defending her cubs. Like Mae, he realized, struck by the memory of his mother in the midst of this horrific day. Would Mae understand his killing that boy? He shook the distracting question from his brain. He had to focus. Had to listen for any sign of movement, a change in the negotiation underway in the shed. He didn't want to kill another child.

He heard the murmur of voices closer to the door and the words of the woman, now distinct.

"Take me as a hostage as I lead you to your comrade. You can kill me if I am lying to you."

The same words she had begged Josiah with.

The door opened and the woman emerged first, a gun pointed at her head. Josiah realized even a sniper could not get off a shot in time to prevent the VC from killing her as well.

But he had to try.

He aimed and fired, defying the Geneva Convention. The VC assailant fell, but so did the woman. Josiah hadn't been able to stop the boy from firing his own gun.

He reached the two of them before the others. The woman was still alive, but barely. He bent over her, pressing his hand against the artery where her blood was pumping out faster than he could stop it.

She looked up at him.

"The children?"

"You saved them."

She died in his arms.

The patrol spent two days in the village treating the wounded men. Josiah went through the motions, setting limbs, stitching up jagged wounds, handing out painkillers, relying on the familiar, practiced actions to hold at bay the images that haunted him—the barefoot boy soldier, the mother bleeding out. They were not the enemies he thought he would be killing when he trained to be a soldier.

By the time they returned to base he was as adept at shutting down his own pain as he was in applying a tourniquet. He had observed how members of his unit dealt with the aftermath of combat. Some of them were constantly alert, wired, sensitive to any unexpected noise or movement, hand always hovering close to the trigger. Other guys obliterated memory in the searing fire of whisky or the haze of weed. None of those paths worked for Josiah. He had tried them all. Instead, he dug a hole in his soul, a grave, and buried it all—fear, hope, joy, despair.

He continued to do his job with precision. Wounds didn't fester; limbs were saved; airways were opened; hearts that had stopped beating were pounded back to a steady rhythm. He did it under fire and in sick call. He did it under open skies and thatched roofs.

But every life he lost diminished him and no life he saved replenished him.

By the time his tour of duty was up at the end of the year, he was a dead man.

1963
Cove Meadow
Chappaquiddick Island

Chapter 23

"Gaze no more in the bitter glass"
Mae

Mae was in the kitchen putting together a care package for Josiah when she heard the low putter of a motor boat approaching their dock. It was not the familiar rumble of Tobias' fishing rig, and was too early anyway for him to be returning home. Curious, she left the house and walked out to the edge of the yard to see who was arriving.

It was not a boat she recognized—a sleek, brand new Chris Craft Constellation that was being skillfully maneuvered alongside the landing. She walked down to see who was at the wheel—probably a lost newcomer way off course for Edgartown Harbor and the Fourth of July festival. But the hands that threw a line out to Mae belonged to no stranger.

It was Lydia.

Mae stood frozen for a moment, holding the rope in her hand.

"Will you tie up?" Lydia asked from the deck.

Mae wanted to say no, I want you to go away. But she looped the line over a piling and waited for Lydia to disembark.

Lydia gestured dismissively at the cruiser. "Lou's idea. He thinks it's a more than adequate replacement for his own presence."

Mae finally found her voice. "If you're looking for Tobias, he's not here."

"I didn't come for Tobias, Mae. I came to talk with you. Will you at least listen?"

Something in Lydia's voice pierced the wall Mae had erected the previous summer. Lydia was neither demanding nor begging, simply honest in her request to be heard. Mae nodded.

"Let's go up to the house, rather than stand here on the dock. I just made a pot of coffee."

They sat on the porch, looking out at the bay dotted with white sails and the foamy wakes of speedboats pulling water skiers.

"I'm not going to pretend this is easy. I know I stepped over a line last summer and I've spent a lot of time both regretting my actions and trying to climb out of the hole of loneliness I dug for myself. Our friendship was important to me. I know it may be impossible to recreate the bond we built summer after summer and I tore apart in a few unthinking minutes. But I'm here to ask for your forgiveness and a chance to start over."

Mae was silent for a minute, absorbing Lydia's words with care and allowing them to seep into her heart. One of the things that had hurt so much the previous summer, beyond the searing pain of her fear she had lost Tobias, was the loss of Lydia's friendship. Until their easy comradery was gone, she hadn't truly realized how much it had become a part of her experience of Innisfree. Lydia had brought energy and laughter and, as she often put it, a "no bullshit" approach to speaking her mind. Despite her original unease when she first met Lydia eight years before, Mae recognized that Lydia's differences had enriched Mae's life. She missed her.

She reached out her hand and Lydia met her halfway across the distance between them.

"I'm willing to try. Our friendship is important to me, too. So, yes, I forgive you."

Mae heard Lydia exhale in relief. "Thank you. Look, did you have any plans for the rest of the day? Let me take you out on that ridiculous boat and let's do some fishing. I heard that the blues are plentiful."

Mae laughed. This was exactly what she had missed—Lydia's spontaneity and enthusiasm for seizing the moment. They grabbed poles and nets and raced to the dock like a couple of teenagers playing hooky from school. A weight lifted from Mae's shoulders that afternoon as the two women sat on the deck of Lydia's boat, their fishing lines dangling in the water, the sun warming their faces and the cares of their complicated lives dissipating for a few blissful hours.

Chapter 24

"She carries in the candles"
Mae

Mae wandered from oven to table to back porch, her footsteps echoing the random pattern of her thoughts as the skin of the turkey deepened to a caramel hue and the butter in the sweet potato casserole bubbled up like lava. Jo hadn't been home in more than two years, when he had come for a few hours to say goodbye to Izzy before he left for Texas.

She could not stop herself from watching the driveway. Tobias and Izzy had offered to pick up Jo at the ferry, giving Mae the buffer of time and the seclusion of home rather than the bustle of the ferry pier on New Year's Eve morning for their reunion. Tobias had understood that Mae still blamed herself for Jo's departure.

"He's coming home, Mae," he had assured her the night before, recognizing the tension in her body as he had drawn her close while in bed. "He would not have agreed to come if he was still harboring the resentment and anger that drove him away."

Despite Tobias' reassurances and the gentle touch that eased the tightness in her muscles, Mae had no confidence in her son's change of heart. She ached. Not the ache that followed a long day of physical work, the kind that so often had greeted her when she locked the door of the café and headed home to the cottage. That ache had been accompanied by satisfaction. No, the ache now was amorphous, without borders, spreading pain that seeped into every corner of her consciousness like the rain that was drenching the island, sluicing through the crevasses on the gravel drive in the season's first Nor'easter.

After the initial devastating acknowledgment that Jo had left—in defiance, in repudiation of all they had tried to give him—the agony had subsided, replaced by this hollow throbbing, like a phantom limb. But Jo's letter to Izzy that he was returning safe and whole from Vietnam had reopened the wound. She was grateful, God knew, but the anticipation of a reunion with Jo had once again intensified her emotions.

The communication between Mae and Josiah during his year at war had been limited to brief notes of thanks for the packages she had sent—socks, a transistor radio, tins of home-baked cookies she hoped survived the long journey, jars of tabasco and Worcestershire sauce that he had requested to mask the flavor of army rations. He never described anything more than the weather or, once, a successful deer hunt. For all he shared, he could have been camping in the woods of Maine instead of fighting in the Vietnamese jungle.

When she heard the truck in the driveway she was reminded of the night she had waited for Jo to come home from the drum circle. The weather had been equally miserable then, nature amplifying her fears. But unless he had missed the ferry, this time Jo would be emerging from the pickup. He was coming home, she reminded herself, and that was all that mattered.

She heard the chatter of Izzy's voice trilling with one of her stories, Jo responding with a deep laugh Mae barely recognized. It was the voice of a man, not the boy who had left before Boston, before the war.

She thought she could wait, give him time to get inside, shake off the rain and the fatigue of travel. But she found herself racing out the door and into the storm, rain and tears mingling on her cheeks as she put her arms out for her son.

He saw her and dropped his duffle bag into a puddle.

"Mom," he murmured as he returned her embrace. Whatever lay ahead of them with this homecoming, in this moment he was the boy she had fought for and fought to live for.

Tobias retrieved the duffle bag and herded them inside.

The aromas of the meal simmering in the kitchen brought a smile to Jo's face.

"Let me guess—apple pie, sweet potato casserole, and turkey."

"What did you expect, rice and Spam?" Izzy punched him in the arm. "She made your favorite meal, idiot."

Jo flinched at the punch, then recovered. But his initial reaction, as if he were truly under attack, did not go unnoticed by any of them.

"Hey, I'm sorry. Just wanted to show you how well-developed my biceps got maneuvering my crutches all those years."

He rubbed his arm. "No problem. You've made your point. It's good to see you without your crutches. The last time I was here you were still immobilized by your surgery."

Izzy twirled around him like a ballerina.

"Look, no hands. I'm on my own two feet."

"Would you like to eat right away, or do you want a shower," Mae asked.

"Is that a hint that I smell like I've been traveling halfway around the world without benefit of soap and hot water?" He grinned.

"No, no," Mae assured him, although he did smell and look like he had neither slept nor changed his clothes since arriving stateside.

"It's OK, Ma. A shower actually sounds like a luxury I don't want to pass up. Do I still have a room here?"

"A room? It's a shrine, blessed weekly by my dusting and Granny's herbs." Izzy grabbed his hand and pulled him down the hall, throwing the door open. "Make yourself at home, dear brother."

Mae smiled at the teasing interplay between her children, grateful to Izzy for lightening the mood in the house. Had it been entirely up to Mae, she knew all the unspoken words, all the painful memories, would be weighing them down.

She sank into a kitchen chair as she heard Jo and Izzy continue their banter. When the pipes began to clang, signifying that Jo was in the shower, she closed her eyes for a moment. They had passed the first hurdle.

The noisy pipes woke Naomi from her nap and she tapped along the hall with her cane.

"Is our boy home?"

Mae took her hand and squeezed it.

"He is, Mama."

"Is he himself? I saw enough boys come back to the island after the last war who had lost a piece of themselves, even if they had all their limbs."

"I don't know yet. But one thing is certain. He's not a boy anymore."

"I suppose he's got a man's appetite after a couple of years of soldiers' grub. What still needs to be done that I can give you a hand with?"

"Can you watch over the gravy while I whip the cream for the pie?"

Izzy wandered into the kitchen as the two women continued their companionable chores. She twirled a strand of her hair that Mae recognized as a contemplative gesture.

"He's different," she said.

"Of course he is, child. He's been to war." Naomi chided her gently.

"But he's more different than I expected from his letters. I thought he was telling me everything."

"There are some things soldiers cannot bear to tell. Your great-uncle George fought in the Great War and to this day he will not speak of it."

"Some of the boys in my class are talking about enlisting after graduation. If I were a boy, I don't know if I would. In his letters, Jo didn't always sound convinced he was doing the right thing."

"But he was saving lives, honey. How can that not be the right thing?"

"Maybe he wished that he didn't have to save those lives in the first place."

When Jo emerged from the bathroom he was clean but not clean-shaven.

"Hey, are you growing a beard or did you lose your razor in your travels?" Izzy brushed her fingers lightly over the four days' growth.

"Beard. Now that I've been discharged, I thought I'd give it a try."

"I like it. It makes you look deep, like a philosopher or something."

"Right," he scoffed. "You've been reading too many French novels. I suppose you think I should start smoking Gauloises, too."

"M-m-m. Now that's a thought."

"Not in this house, you won't be smoking." Mae interrupted her children's conversation. Even if they were joking, she worried that they might be as susceptible as she had been to lung cancer.

"Only joking, Mom. They taste disgusting. When's dinner? I'm starving."

"Just a few more minutes. Why don't you go get Dad out of the garage?"

When the family finally sat for the meal, the table fell silent. Not just because the meal was one to savor, but because the presence of Jo in his usual chair was also something to savor. Izzy once again had a companion with whom she could exchange inside jokes. Naomi reveled in the sight of everyone together again. Tobias was relieved his son had made it home safely. Mae was simply thankful he had chosen to come at all.

After dinner was cleared and the dishes done, Tobias asked Jo to walk with him to check on his rabbit snares. It was a task they'd often done together when Jo was a boy.

Divide and conquer, Mae thought, as they pulled on boots and Mackinaws. She ached for more than Jo's presence, but knew that any attempt to get him to talk, to open up, to be their son again and not merely a visiting guest, was going to take moments like a walk in the woods with his father.

Chapter 25

"Go gather by the humming sea"
Tobias

The rain had subsided to a drizzle as Jo and Tobias ranged along the edge of the woods. Tobias studied his son as he loped ahead. His body had never been soft, but now it conveyed a tautness and an impression of coiled energy ready to spring. There was no danger in these woods; no tigers were lurking in the dense, wet greenery; no North Vietnamese soldiers were hiding in the hollows.

I can never know what he has experienced, Tobias thought. *Other fathers who went to war can understand, but that gulf will always exist between us because I did not serve. How do I reach him?*

Jo stopped and turned to Tobias.

"Did you set snares on the Porter's land? I haven't seen any yet in the places I remember, and we've reached our property line."

"This isn't the line anymore, and that land ahead isn't Porter land. It's ours. Your mom and I bought it last year. The snares are just the other side of the meadow."

Tobias did not have to tell Jo that the land beneath their feet had once been Wampanoag, just as Innisfree had.

"How's Mom's health?"

This was an unexpected direction. Had Jo seen something that Tobias had missed because he was too close?

"She hasn't mentioned anything. Why do you ask?"

"I know I haven't seen her in a couple of years, but she looks thinner, older. I don't remember her being so weary."

"We *are* older, Jo. And it hasn't been an easy time for Mom. Between Izzy's operation and Granny's decline, she's had a lot to worry about."

"Not to mention a son away at war."

"You were always on her mind. She's happy to have you back, and especially pleased you came home."

"I'm not staying."

Tobias felt the conversation advance and recede like the sea. He couldn't tell yet if the tide was coming in, bringing his son with it, or racing out away from shore.

"We hoped you might stay, but we don't expect you to. Just know that you are always welcome, anytime." He nodded toward the meadow. "The land is waiting for you."

"Don't start." Jo turned away.

They spent the rest of the walk in silence, retrieving the snared rabbits and returning to the house as the sun set.

"If you hunted in the jungle, I assume you haven't forgotten how to skin and gut game."

"Naw. I got to hone my butchering skills there. They were appreciated. There's just so much tinned meat you can eat. I can help. Just give me a knife."

Mae found them on the porch.

"Looks like rabbit stew for New Year's Day dinner."

"Make sure it's your recipe and not my Aunt Agnes' concoction," Tobias told her before turning to Jo. "Your mom's rabbit stew is what made me fall in love with her."

"Red wine, that's my secret. When you finish, Jo, can you help me in the barn with the chickens?"

She went into the kitchen.

"How did you guys get anything done without me?" He smiled at his father. The tension that he had felt earlier when they had been walking the land had lessened. He'd made it clear he wasn't staying. But the simple tasks of skinning and gutting the rabbits alongside his father triggered a lost memory to a time when he had felt connected to Tobias, and through him to the tribe. It was a fragment, nothing more. But it felt like a step toward whatever it was he was seeking, and it brought him an unexpected measure of peace.

Chapter 26

"Let us try again"
Mae

Mae handed Jo a bucket of vegetable scraps as they made their way over the muddy path to the barn. It was warm and dry inside, the only sounds the low clucking of the hens and the rustle of straw.

"Would you give them the veggies and collect the eggs while I grab a new bag of feed?" Mae handed him the pail.

When she returned, Jo was cleaning the cages unasked. Perhaps this was her moment.

"Jo, I want you to know how much it means to me—to all of us—that you have come home."

He shrugged. "I guess you know Aunt Maureen read me the riot act in her last letter. She told me it was time."

"No, I didn't know, but I suspected. She has a way of speaking the truth even when we don't want to hear it. Even if it wasn't your idea, I'm glad you listened to her."

"Are you and she friends now?"

"Let's just say we had a 'Come to Jesus' conversation over a bottle of your Uncle Danny's best whisky. She was fully into her role as Reverend Mother. But she was right to push me. So yes, we're friends."

"I thought you would like her. She's as direct as I remember you being, when I was younger."

"Am I not so direct anymore?"

"The last couple years before I left, no. You changed. I don't know, it seemed like you were giving up. I had always thought of you as a fighter. All the stories of your early days at Innisfree—building the Boat House, beating back the fire, defending Dad against the most powerful guy on the island and then enduring your cancer treatment while fighting for me against Kathleen. It was like you were another person then. I didn't—still don't—understand why you didn't fight to keep Innisfree."

Mae knew in starting the conversation she was opening herself up to fresh pain. She tried not to show Jo how deeply his words had cut. How do you explain to the child who once revered you as the heroine of their family's history that you were human, with flaws and weaknesses? How do you say, "Jo, I'm weary and tired of fighting?" She also didn't want to rehash old reasons, reasons that might seem to Jo to be either hollow excuses or confirmation that Izzy's needs overshadowed his. Instead, she was honest with him and herself.

"I guess I will have to accept that you don't understand. I don't think I can explain away the pain my decision caused you—and all of us. All I can say is that it was necessary."

"One of the hard lessons I learned in Vietnam is that doing what is necessary often goes against who I thought I was or was capable of. And even when I knew it was necessary, that no other decision would have been right, it still left me feeling angry and hollow and a stranger to myself."

"Oh, Jo, that is exactly how I feel!"

She reached out for him, catching his extraordinary moment of vulnerability while it illuminated the dim barn and their own connection. She held onto him, wishing that it could be this simple and knowing in her heart that, although he was one step closer, her son was still far from home.

She could feel the tension in his body. He had accepted her embrace, had put his arms around her in return, but the gesture was stiff and restrained. She released him, stepped back and took his face in her hands.

"We are more alike than either of us is willing to admit."

"I'm not you."

"I didn't say that. Only that I recognize pieces of myself in you—especially my young self. But you've grown beyond me. You've been to war, and I will never comprehend what that has done to you. Just remember that you are a survivor."

"I'm a survivor, Mom, but so many others were not—guys whose lives drained away under my hands, in spite of everything I'd learned and all the meds and instruments and bandages I carried. And maybe that is what none of you will ever understand. So let's not even try, OK? I'll finish cleaning up here and bring the eggs in when I'm done."

Mae left him. That he needed to be alone she *did* understand.

Chapter 27

"Now all the truth is out"
Josiah

Later that evening after turkey sandwiches and leftover pie, Izzy brought up the fireworks.

"Hey, Jo, do you want to go to the ferry dock and watch the Edgartown fireworks?"

He looked up and recognized in his sister that restless teenage desperation that, although unspoken, conveyed her real meaning: It's New Year's Eve and getting out of the house, even if it's with my brother, is better than sitting around with my parents waiting for midnight to arrive.

"Sure. Where are the keys?"

Their parents seemed more than happy to have them go off together—another step in their all-to-obvious plan to hasten his adjustment to being home. For Izzy's sake, he was humoring them. But he had no intention of prolonging his stay. He knew what could happen—the inertia that sets in on the island in winter, especially when weather isolated them, stopping the ferries from Woods Hole and knocking out power. No, thank you. He slipped behind the driver's seat of the pickup and Izzy climbed in beside him. It still left him in awe that she was walking.

"Thanks, brother dear. I appreciate your indulgence in your sister's childlike wonder at exploding chemicals."

"We both know your request had nothing to do with fireworks. You just wanted to get out of the house."

"Ah, you're on to me. But admit it, so did you."

He eased into a spot along the side of the road since the ferry parking lot was full with teenagers and also families with small kids already in their pajamas. When he and Izzy had been children they had spent New Year's Eve at Innisfree and watched the Oak Bluffs fireworks from their own dock. *Time to let go, Monroe*, he reminded himself.

Izzy was digging around under the seat and came up triumphantly with a brown bag. She pulled out a bottle of whisky.

"A little something to toast in the New Year," she grinned.

"Isabella Fiona Monroe! When did you start drinking?"

"Relax, Jo. You're not contributing to the delinquency of a minor. I'm not in the habit of doing this. In fact, I never have before. I just thought, it's a special occasion. My big brother came home alive from a war zone. I thought we could drink to that, OK?"

"As long as you promise me not to mess with this stuff after tonight."

"I promise. And I appreciate your looking out for me. I've missed that." She handed him the bottle to take the first swig.

"I've missed you, too, Bird." He couldn't remember the last time he'd called her that. Their parents had nicknamed her Hummingbird when she was a baby, but he'd found that a mouthful at the age of five and had simply called her Bird. He passed the bottle to her and watched her reaction to the volatile liquid.

"Whoa! That's not what I expected."

"Take smaller sips next time."

"I'm not sure there'll be a next time."

"Good."

She swiped at his arm. It seemed to be her main means of communicating frustration with him. But then she switched to words.

"If you missed me so much, why did you leave in the first place? Do you have any idea what it was like at home when we realized you weren't coming back? It was like all the air got sucked out of the house and we couldn't catch our breath. Mom, especially. The only thing that animated her at all was getting me the surgery, and then getting me through the surgery and rehab. She ignored everything else, including Dad. You left me with a fine mess."

"Why didn't you write me about all this crap? "

"I didn't write about it because there wasn't anything you could do from Vietnam. I figured you had enough to worry about."

"It seems like things are OK between Mom and Dad now. Or is that an act for me?"

"Have you ever known either of them to put on an act for anyone? No, all is well, as far as I can tell."

"I'm sorry, Bird."

"I survived. But I have to tell you something. I know you were unhappy they sold Innisfree. They wouldn't have had to, if it weren't for me and my stupid legs. I feel like it's all my fault that you left."

"God, Izzy, none of this is your fault! You couldn't help that you got polio and needed medical care. And it certainly isn't your fault I made the decision to leave. That was my responsibility. Nobody forced me, least of all you."

"Would you do it again?"

That stopped him. He took another drink.

"I'll tell you what I wouldn't do again. I wouldn't leave you to play at the tidal pool that day we were clamming. I'd make you come back with me instead of abandoning you. I was responsible for you and I didn't watch out for you."

Izzy looked at him with a new sense of understanding.

"You think it's your fault I got sick."

"I don't just think it. I know it."

"Jo, I probably got infected by Billy Esposito, not the tidal pool. He came down with polio before I did and died after spending a year in an iron lung. Annie Soames was diagnosed after me and is paralyzed in both legs. We were all in the second grade together. Neither of them was anywhere near the tidal pool. I thought you knew that."

"Even if you didn't get infected from the pool, I left you there and you weren't found until you were really sick. If I'd brought you up to the house, Mom could have seen it sooner. We could have gotten you to the hospital sooner."

"And so what? There is no cure, no miracle drug that, if I'd been given it an hour or two earlier, would have saved me. Forgive yourself, Jo. I do."

"You forgive me?"

"Of course. I was pissed at you for leaving us two years ago and, yeah, I blamed you for what happened afterward. But we seem to be coming through, especially now that you're home."

"You know I'm not staying, don't you?"

"No, I didn't." Izzy's voice got tight. He thought she was about to take back her forgiveness. But then he saw she was crying. All that spunk and self-confidence were dissolving in her tears.

"I can't stay, Izzy. Chappy isn't home for me anymore." He spoke gently.

"Where is home, then?"

"I don't know yet. It's not Boston, and it's not the army."

"How long will you stay?"

"I'm going to leave by the weekend."

"Where will you go? Back to Patrick's house?"

"No. Like I said, that's not home for me either. I've got a couple of contacts in Cambridge. I'll probably head there first."

"I thought you might stay for the winter. Get me through my last semester of high school. I've applied to college. You're not the only one who wants to see what life is like off-island."

"College? It's hard for me to imagine my little sister graduating from high school. See, even if I stayed, you'd be gone in less than a year. It's not like I'm disappearing again. I'll come visit. If you need me, I won't be on the other side of the world. I promise."

He hugged her.

The fireworks were beginning and he pulled her out of the cab. They climbed up into the bed of the truck and stood arm-in-arm as the colors exploded above them.

He tried not to flinch at each detonation and flash of light. He tried to ignore the trace of gunpowder that drifted toward them on the wind. Izzy seemed to sense the tension in his body and moved closer to him. It was only the familiar angularity of her body and the clean soap fragrance of her hair that grounded him, kept him in Chappy on his father's truck and not in Dak To the night the base came under attack.

"I'm here with you, Jo. I'll always be here for you."

"I know, Bird. And I'll be here for you, too."

The next morning Jo was up early and found Naomi in the kitchen.

"Happy New Year, Granny." He bent to kiss her.

"Same to you, Jo. I'm glad to have you to myself for a bit. Care to help me make some blueberry pancakes? Your mama and I froze several batches of berries this summer. Go fetch me a quart, will you?"

He retrieved the blueberries and all the other ingredients for his grandmother, who waited at the table issuing directions.

"Baking powder is in the cabinet above the breadbox and the flour is in the bin on the counter. I believe we've got some buttermilk in the back of the fridge."

"Yes, ma'am." His grandmother definitely reminded him of his sergeant. That hadn't changed. But what had changed was how frail she'd become in the two years he'd been gone. Her hands, that had gardened and crocheted and canned and doctored, were gnarled and bent. He realized that the help she had asked for was going to consist of his making the pancakes from start to finish while she supervised.

He got to work. After a few minutes he was stirring the batter and heating the griddle and she switched the direction of the conversation.

"I am the one member of this family who is not going to berate you for leaving. I have missed you as sorely as anyone, but I understand what drove you away."

"Do you? Everyone seems to believe it was Innisfree, but that was only the final straw."

"I know that, Jo. I've raised a son. You reach a point in your life as a boy about to become a man and if you have a brain and a heart, you question everything you've believed and try to understand what kind of man you want to become."

Josiah stopped stirring, surprised by Naomi's insight.

"Your parents were understandably blindsided by your decision. They had fought fiercely to keep you and then raised you to honor both your heritages. They thought they had done their best for you."

"I know that, Granny. But the older I got, the harder it was for me to feel I belonged in either culture."

"I know a young man who wrestled with his identity when he was your age. You might want to talk with him."

"Who's that?"

"Your father, Jo. It was not an easy time for him; he struggled to find himself."

"Granny, I appreciate the suggestion, but Dad cannot possibly understand. It's a different world. I'm a different man."

Naomi said no more, only shook her head and studied her grandson with sad eyes.

Neither one of them saw Tobias quietly slip out of the house. A few minutes later, they heard the repetitive thwack of an ax hitting wood. They did not hear the sobs.

1964
Western Massachusetts

Chapter 28

"Once more the storm is howling"
Josiah

The VW van that had picked him up at the Concord rotary stopped at the intersection of Routes 2 and 112 outside of Shelburne Falls, the cryptic directions he'd been given in Harvard Square the day before.

"Thanks for the lift. Good luck with the gig in Brattleboro."

He grabbed his gear, pulled on the woolen cap Naomi had knit for him and watched as the car sped away in the twilight, filled with a bunch of musicians. He'd spent the past two hours perched next to a drum set, sharing a joint and never once mentioning that he'd spent the last year in Vietnam. The guys in the van would probably have been more comfortable if he'd been an ex-con just released from the Concord prison than a Special Forces medic.

He checked the map scribbled on a napkin, got his bearings and headed up a hill to his destination. As he got closer he smelled the wood smoke and heard the rustle of wind chimes and the ba-a-ing of goats. As he rounded the bend in the narrow lane he saw first a barn and then a farmhouse, its windows warm with lamplight. In one of them a peace sign banner obscured the view into the house.

He knocked on the door. Inside he heard murmured voices and the music of a sitar. He knocked again, more emphatic the second time. The door was opened by a girl with masses of curly hair.

She appraised him cautiously and looked behind him to see if he was alone. As he had in the VW with the band, he'd erased any signs of his military past. His tiger fatigues, his dog tags, the photos he'd taken, any remnant of his time in Dak To had been stuffed into a duffle bag and thrown into the back of his father's pickup for a trip to the dump. His hair, however, hadn't grown out yet and was still closely cropped. It was one of the reasons he'd decided to grow a beard.

The girl, apparently satisfied that he wasn't accompanied by a squad of police in riot gear, finally spoke.

"Can I help you?"

"I met Matt Levin in Cambridge. He told me I might be able to find a place to stay at the farm. My name is Jo Monroe."

"Hi, Jo Monroe. I'm Arwen. You'll need to meet Nathan and the rest of the house before you're accepted, but you're certainly welcome to spend the night in the barn. We don't turn folks away in the middle of the night. Come on in."

She held the door open and waved him into a dimly lit hall.

"Have you eaten?"

"Not since I had coffee with Matt last night."

"Come with me to the kitchen. Angela and Leila are cleaning up, but I'm pretty sure they can find you some leftovers. We grow most of our food here."

The large farmhouse kitchen was dominated by a wood cook stove still emanating heat. Two women were at the sink, their backs to him and Arwen. Jo smelled fresh-baked bread and something earthy—turnips, carrots, onions and garlic. The kind of food Naomi cooked. His stomach rumbled.

"Hey, Angela and Leila, this is Jo. Can we offer him some stew?"

One of the women put down her dish rag and extended her hand.

"Welcome, Jo. I'm Leila. Are you a vegetarian or meat eater?"

"I eat meat. But I'll take whatever is available. Thanks."

She lifted the lid on a cast iron pot sitting on the back of the stove.

"I've got some venison stew here. Will that suffice?"

"More than suffice. Thanks."

He accepted the bowl of stew and sat at the long wooden table that flanked one wall of the kitchen.

"How many people live here at the commune?"

"There are fourteen of us. Eight guys, five women and one baby. So, how do you know Matt?"

Jo realized that he was going to be grilled if he expected to be allowed to stay for more than the one night Arwen had offered him. Matt was a journalist writing about the communes that were starting to pop up in rural areas, not just here in Western Mass, but all over the country. Matt had warned him the commune residents were wary. Their reasons for establishing a community were often political and they weren't well-loved by either the local or national authorities. "Respect their vigilance. You'll need to earn their trust." It had sounded to Jo like his experience with the Montagnard villagers. But he was willing to give it a shot. Neither Boston nor Chappy had been a choice for him. After a week at Cove Meadow, he knew he couldn't stay. Patrick had offered him a room again in Jamaica Plain, but what would he have done there? Gone back to Loretta's grilling burgers and melted cheese sandwiches? He felt more a misfit than when he'd first left the island three years before. Running into Matt had seemed like a lifeline.

"Matt and I grew up together on Martha's Vineyard. I ran into him in Harvard Square at a Tom Paxton performance at Club 47."

"What made the topic of our commune come up?"

"We hadn't seen each other since we graduated from high school and we were just shooting the shit, catching up. He told me he was writing a piece for the *Boston Phoenix* newspaper. When he described this place, it spoke to me."

"Why? What are you looking for?" Angela's question was thrown at him in a way that felt like a confrontation.

How did he answer a question like that? How could he articulate what he was looking for to these strangers when he couldn't identify it for himself? Maybe this wasn't such a good idea after all. He'd thought that getting away from the city, where even a backfiring truck made him break out in a cold sweat, would give him a chance to find some peace. He didn't know how to explain his need for peace without revealing his military past. And everything he'd encountered in the States since his return had warned him against calling attention to himself in that way.

In answer to Angela's question, he shrugged. "I guess I'm looking for a peaceful life on the land. I'm not good in the city. If that's not enough of a reason for you, I'll move on in the morning. If one of you will show me where I can bed down in the barn, I'll get out of your way here."

"I'll show you. Follow me." Arwen led him out the back door while Angela and Leila watched them and then went back to scrubbing pots.

Arwen lit a lantern on the back porch and held it high to illuminate the path in the snow that led to the barn. Jo helped her slide the door open and the two of them slipped inside. He heard the rustle of animals stirring in the straw, smelled the pungent odor of ripe manure.

"What kind of animals do you keep?"

"We have one milk cow, some goats and some chickens. You'll have a natural alarm clock in the morning from the rooster. You can spread your bed roll up in the hayloft. Here, I'll show you."

Together they climbed a wooden ladder up to the loft and she pointed the lantern toward a corner where a pile of hay bales offered the semblance of a bed. He'd slept on worse in Vietnam.

"Thanks. This is great. I appreciate the hospitality. I won't overstay my welcome and will be out of here as soon as the rooster announces the sunrise."

"You don't have to adhere to Angela's politics to stay on. She thinks of herself as the gatekeeper, but we're really more open than she let on in the kitchen. Besides, it's not her decision. We vote."

"Look, I can understand you want someone with compatible ideas if you're going to live together communally. But I don't want to have to bare my soul to strangers in order to secure a roof over my head. I've got skills I can offer. I'm willing to work hard. I'm not an undercover agent for the FBI nor am I a convicted murderer. That ought to be enough for you all to decide if you want me."

He unrolled his sleeping bag as he spoke, shaking it out with a snap that caused loose blades of hay to flutter up in the shaft of light cast by the lantern.

"What kind of skills?"

He looked at her. She seemed genuinely interested rather than skeptical, as Angela had been in the kitchen.

"Hunting. Fishing. I can butcher game and filet and salt fish. I can cook." He stopped there, at the safe skills, the ones that simply identified him as someone who had grown up on the land. He didn't add that he was both a sharpshooter and an experienced battlefield medic. This was a commune with roots in a philosophy of peace, according to Matt. It was one of the reasons Jo had sought it out. He was looking for a refuge from the war that still raged in his dreams at night.

Arwen extended her hand. "That's good enough for me. I'm happy to support you tomorrow if you want to meet with the whole commune."

Jo shook her hand. "Thanks. I'll sleep on it. I don't want to upset the equilibrium here if Angela doesn't think I measure up. I've spent enough of my life in places where I didn't fit in or wasn't wanted."

"Where will you go if you don't stay here?"

"I'll figure it out. Look, it's pretty cold out here so I don't want to keep you any longer. I'm just going to crawl into my sleeping bag and zone out. It's been a long day."

"Do you want to share a joint before you sleep?" She reached into the pocket of her jacket. "We grow it here on the farm. It's one of the reasons we're so cautious when strangers show up." She lit up and passed him the joint. "You *have* smoked before, haven't you?"

He took the tightly rolled cigarette from her gloved fingers, thinking as he did so, *if you only knew what I've smoked before and where.*

He inhaled deeply. It was only the second joint he'd had since returning from Vietnam. He was too well-known on the island to inquire about a source without attracting attention and there was no way in Boston he could have kept a stash in the home of a cop. He'd smoked with Matt the night before in Harvard Square, but Matt hadn't mentioned that the commune had a home-grown supply. Maybe sticking around the next morning for the inquisition might be worth it.

"Hey, I'm freezing. Can I climb into the sleeping bag with you until we finish the joint?"

He was already feeling mellow after only a few hits and gladly unzipped the bag so she could join him.

"God, you're shivering," he said and put his arm around her to draw her closer for warmth. She smelled of patchouli and sweat and dope.

"So what brought you here?" It was his turn to ask questions.

"I worked on an alternative newspaper in the city with Nathan—that's Angela's boyfriend and the founder of the commune. I dropped out of Sarah Lawrence and my parents were none too pleased. They called me a beatnik and an anarchist and cut off both contact and my allowance. We were all living together in an apartment in the East Village, running off the newspaper on a mimeo machine and distributing it on the college campuses in the city—NYU, Columbia, even Fordham. Then Nathan went out to California to visit his cousin and found out about this community called Tolstoy Village, based on the ideas of Leo Tolstoy. He came back all fired up about being on the vanguard of cultural change. He somehow found out about this farm and convinced the woman who had inherited it to sign it over to him. We dismantled the mimeo machine and moved it and us up here last March, in time to plant a garden. There were only eight of us then, but our reputation is growing. It must be, if you found us."

Jo was listening, but her voice kept drifting, lulling him. They had finished the joint. That much he knew, because he was acutely aware that they'd had a glowing joint in a hayloft and he deliberately extinguished it by splashing some water on it from his canteen. He was lying back in the hay, Arwen's head on his chest as she murmured on about the history of the commune. She hadn't really said much about why *she* had joined, other than already being a part of Nathan's circle. Eventually, they fell asleep.

He woke in the early hours of the morning, disoriented and sweating, coming out of a nightmare. He must have spoken out loud, because Arwen stirred immediately.

"Are you OK?"

It took him a few seconds to grasp why he had a woman in his arms. She had lifted herself up on one elbow and was wiping the beads of sweat from his brow with the edge of her flannel shirt. It was a gesture of such tenderness that he sobbed.

She pulled him toward her and rocked him.

"Hey, I'm here. You're not alone with whatever is haunting you."

He held onto her, burying himself into her warmth. At some point she took his hand and placed it on her breast. The last time he'd been with a woman had been in

Dak To, banishing the horrors of war in booze and sex for a few hours. Arwen slid her hands under his shirt, the shock of skin against skin sending a message to his brain that was all too easy to comprehend. This time he was fueled by marijuana instead of bourbon, and let it carry him into forgetfulness with this willing woman whom he did not know. Although he'd gotten high a hundred times in Vietnam, he'd never had sex at the same time. It was a punch in the face. A wave of pleasure that swallowed him up and then tossed him up and over a crest, carrying him breathlessly, helplessly, back to earth. He gasped, his heart pounding so hard he heard it.

"Pretty spectacular, isn't it?" Arwen grinned at him as he recovered. He was speechless for a few moments.

"Oh, man. I've never . . . where does that stuff come from? Does it really grow here?"

"Mm-hm. Doesn't it make you want to stay?"

"Is that what this was about—seducing me with sex and drugs so I'd hunt and fish for you?" He grinned right back at her.

"Something like that. I liked you as soon as you walked in the door. I want you to stay."

"I have to ask you a question. Did your parents really name you Arwen?"

"What, you don't think a couple of uptight WASPs from Greenwich, Connecticut, have read *Lord of the Rings*? Right you are. I took the name when I realized they didn't want me as their daughter. And no, I'm not going to tell you what they *did* name me. I'm Arwen, plain and simple."

He rolled over on top of her again, taking it more slowly the second time, responding to her words rather than her touch and the drugs.

They finally slept until the rooster woke them as she had predicted. He would have preferred to remain in the loft, languid and warm, but Arwen scrambled out of the bag after pulling her clothes on.

"It's my morning to milk. The cow will be groaning in a few minutes and banging against her stall."

"Can I help?"

"Sure. Ever mucked out a stall or chopped through ice in a trough?"

"I think I can handle it."

The work warmed him and he admired the deft skill with which Arwen handled the cow.

"For a city girl, you seem to know your way around a barn."

"Oh, my grandparents had a farm in upstate New York. I was sleeping in haylofts a long time before last night."

They left the barn as the sun was clearing the ridge beyond the farmhouse. Jo took in his surroundings in daylight. The warmth and light that had been so welcoming the night before after his long trek were now replaced by the reality of hundred-year-old structures. Some of the windows in the house were patched with plastic sheeting instead of glass. The porch listed. Some of the shutters were missing. A well-trod path to the outhouse seemed to have a trail of yellow snow along the way, making him think some of the guys had simply not bothered to wait, until a couple of dogs came bounding around the corner and one of them lifted its leg.

He and Arwen stomped their way to the back door with two pails of steaming milk. Inside the kitchen someone had revived the fire, but the room was empty.

Arwen plunked the buckets on a counter and pulled a bin out of a cupboard.

"Oatmeal," she explained. "Can you grab that pot hanging from the hook?"

There was no running water, only a pump at the chipped enameled sink. Once again, Arwen worked with fluid, practiced motions as she had in the barn—priming the pump, carting the pot to the stove, feeding the fire to get the heat up to boil the water.

"Where is everyone?"

"We don't all live in the house. There are a couple of trailers and cabins scattered around the property. But we all eat together and in winter everyone gathers in the house during the day for warmth. They wander in slowly. Not everyone's a morning person like I am. Also, winter's a slower time. Not so much work to do."

"Is there coffee? I'm not great till I've some caffeine."

"Sorry. It's not one of those things we can afford regularly. I can make you some herbal tea, though. At least it will be hot."

By the time the oatmeal was cooked, people had begun to arrive from within the house and beyond. Arwen introduced Jo.

"He's a childhood friend of Matt Levin, the guy who was here in October to write about us. Jo is looking for a purposeful life."

Most of them accepted his presence with mild curiosity, even warmth. But when Angela and Nathan entered the kitchen, the mood shifted.

"You're still here. I thought you had decided we weren't what you were seeking."

Jo stiffened. Despite the haven and excitement Arwen had offered him the night before, he wasn't sure he could tolerate Angela's antagonism toward him. He was weighing his choices, ready to turn and go, when Arwen stepped between him and Angela.

"He's seeking peace, a refuge from a violent world. And he's not a slacker, a parasite who's only here to suck at the commune's tit without giving anything back. He can hunt and fish. And he mucked out the barn without complaining."

"Well, I guess he's also good in bed for you to be defending him so strongly."

"Give it a rest, Angela." Jo was surprised it was Nathan who spoke. "Let him speak for himself."

All eyes and ears were turned toward him.

"Arwen spoke only what I told her last night. I'm looking for a place of refuge. I grew up on the land, so I can offer you someone who knows what hard work is. But I don't want to be a source of tension. That's no refuge if I'm not wanted here. All I ask is that you give me a chance to prove myself—name the amount of time you're willing to give me as a trial. If you don't want me after that, I'll go."

Everyone was silent. Even though Arwen had told him the commune voted on decisions, it was clear to him they were all waiting for Nathan to speak. Even Angela, who had been silenced by Nathan's comment, kept her mouth shut. Her face was twisted in a scowl, but she didn't say a word. Jo didn't know what about him set her off, but he wasn't going to waste time figuring it out. Finally, Nathan broke the stillness that had settled on the room.

"Fair enough. If the majority of the commune is in agreement, we'll give you a week." He looked around the room. Arwen shot her hand up defiantly. One by one, others followed, except Angela, who stalked out slamming the door.

Later in the day, Jo poked around in the shed, searching for anything he could use to fashion rabbit snares. He came back with a coil of wire, a rusty pair of pliers and some scrap wood. He worked in the kitchen, which apparently was the gathering place in the house.

"Not everyone's a meat eater you know. Some of us think it's cruel to kill an animal for food." A woman nursing a baby challenged him.

Jo continued bending the wire in his hand.

"My ancestors taught us to take from the earth only what we need to survive. We don't kill for sport."

"Your ancestors?"

"The Wampanoag."

"You're an Indian?"

Jo nodded.

"Are you a shaman?"

He turned from her without a word. Is that what they were looking for? Someone to lead them spiritually? He hadn't picked up that vibe in the short time he'd been here, other than the rather casual acceptance of grass. The unmistakable aroma hung in the air, wafting gently on the drafts creeping in through the loosely fitted windows. He wondered how industrious anyone was after day-long hits on a joint. He supposed it kept the peace.

When he was finished with the three snares and pegs he gathered them up and headed off to track rabbits so he could set the traps along likely trails. As he left, he heard the whine of a log-splitter behind the barn and the smell of diesel fuel. Well, even though they didn't have electricity or indoor plumbing, they apparently had *some* twentieth-century tools.

By the time he returned, the shadows of the maple trees at the edge of the high meadow had lengthened. The splitter was still churning its way through wood and he decided to see if he could help. It was still only day one of his "trial period" and he figured making himself useful couldn't hurt.

As he rounded the side of the barn he heard the piercing sound of metal against metal, followed by a scream. The scene that Jo came upon was one of chaos. One of the men, Simon, was on the ground lying in a quickly spreading stain of blood, and two others were cowering behind the woodpile. The splitter was flying apart, sending splinters of wood and bits of metal randomly out into the yard like shrapnel.

Jo retreated around the corner of the barn and flattened himself against the wall with his eyes tightly shut. He broke out in a sweat and his heart was pounding as he slid to the ground, his trembling legs unable to keep him upright. The whine of the disintegrating splitter echoed in his brain like an incoming missile and his instincts screamed at him to take cover. And then he remembered Simon, sprawled and bleeding in the snow. Something happened to Jo in that moment of recognition, and he pushed back the memories he'd been running away from since he'd left Vietnam. One thing he apparently could not forget was his responsibility for the lives of his comrades.

Jo pulled himself out of his fear and ran to the back of the splitter, where he hit the kill switch, stopping the motor. Then he knelt by Simon, who appeared to be in shock. Jo had none of his medic supplies, none of the tools that had been at hand throughout his tour of duty. But he had his training, his experience and his confidence in himself. He moved swiftly and assuredly, locating Simon's wounds, stanching the blood, calmly checking with the others to determine if they were also hurt or if they could help. He gave them orders to fetch blankets and towels, alert Nathan and get someone ready to transport Simon to a hospital. Within minutes, he'd transformed the catastrophic accident into the possibility that Simon might survive.

With the muscle of the other men, they lifted Simon onto a board and maneuvered him into the farm's van. Nathan drove and Jo rode in back, keeping tabs on Simon's vital signs and making sure the pressure on the wound was holding.

Nathan careened into the hospital's parking lot and ran to the emergency room to alert them and secure help. The farm had no phone; they had had no way to call for an ambulance or let the hospital know they were on their way with a severely injured man. Jo, covered in blood and without his jacket because he had wrapped it around Simon, followed the gurney into the hospital.

The physician on call moved as swiftly as Jo had earlier and raced with Simon to surgery. Nathan and Jo were left in the hall, the adrenaline finally draining as responsibility was lifted from their shoulders.

Nathan went and got them both Cokes from a vending machine.

"How did you know what to do?"

Jo thought about lying, about making up some story about taking a first aid course, but decided he'd rather tell the truth and be banished from the commune than remain by pretending he was someone other than who he was.

"I had a year of training as a combat medic and then served a year in Vietnam. I've dealt with a lot worse than what happened to Simon today."

Nathan studied him with awe.

"You saved his life."

"It's what I do."

"Man, I don't know how you ended up on our doorstep, but you've just earned yourself a place at the farm. If anybody has a problem with the fact that you're ex-army, they can pack their bags."

They stayed, exhausted, until the surgeon came out to tell them Simon was going to make it. "He lost a lot of blood, but whoever treated him on the scene knew what he was doing. He wouldn't have made it without that care."

Nathan put his arm around Jo.

"Let's go home."

When they got to the farm the entire commune was waiting in the kitchen. It was Nathan who announced that Simon had survived. Then he turned to Jo.

"If anyone doesn't know it already, Jo saved Simon's life. I'm declaring his trial period over. He's one of us."

It was Arwen who started the applause.

1964
Boston and Northampton

Chapter 29

"A hunger for the apple on the bough"
Izzy

September could not arrive soon enough. Ever since the letter from Smith College had arrived in April, she had begun marking off the days on the calendar.

It was the interview in Boston, at the Parker House, that had so enflamed her. She'd traveled alone to the city for the first time, grateful to her grandmother for convincing her parents to let her go alone.

"If she cannot navigate a day in Boston, how will she ever cope on her own in college? Besides, I'm sure the powers that be at Smith are not looking for cosseted girls whose parents have them on a leash. Let her go."

And so she had. Izzy had worn a suit, one of her mother's, that had needed only a little taking in, hoping that it made her look older than her nearly sixteen years. She worried that Smith might think she was too young, but bolstered herself with the thought that she had skipped two grades because she was smart. From everything she had read, Smith was looking for smart.

When she arrived at the Parker House she first found the ladies' room, repinned the wisps of hair that had come undone from her French twist in the windy walk from the MTA station and ran her wrists under the cold water faucet to cool both her overheated body temperature and her nervous energy. She crossed the lobby to the bank of house phones, dialed the number she'd been given and announced her arrival. Following instructions, she took the elevator to the fifth floor and when the doors opened was greeted by a formidable woman, also in a suit and wearing very sensible shoes.

"Isabella? Welcome. I'm Dr. Paddy Goggin, professor of anthropology. Come with me."

Izzy assumed she'd have a few minutes to gather her thoughts as they traversed the long, carpeted corridor. But she was mistaken. Professor Goggin began bombarding her, first with observations and then with questions.

"It's an extraordinary time for young women, don't you think? Opportunities flourishing for thinking women to extend the boundaries of what is acceptable—for work, for behavior. Such a role model in Margaret Mead. Have you read her latest research on child rearing and culture? A pioneer. What kind of role do you envision for yourself? How do you think Smith can help prepare you to reach it? What are you reading now? What's the book that has meant the most to you or changed you? How do you want to change the world?"

They finally reached Professor Goggin's room and Izzy settled herself in a chair, accepted the offered cup of tea, took a deep breath and began to address the litany of probing questions the anthropologist had thrown at her.

She was fascinated and intimidated by the woman, but determined not to undermine herself with doubt. She felt challenged in ways none of her teachers had ever pushed her to think and was surprised by the effervescence she felt in rising to the professor's provocative inquiries. She was always conscious of the edge to the questions. Dr. Goggin wasn't merely curious about Izzy's intellectual life. This was an exam, with consequences.

The hour ended when the phone rang and the professor looked at her watch.

"Good heavens, that's my next interview. We've gone so deep in our conversation that I've completely lost track of time. That's a good sign." Her smile extended to her eyes, crinkling with warmth and humor. She held out her hand.

"You're a remarkable young woman, my dear. You'll be hearing from us."

Izzy gathered her things and left, bursting with excitement on the ride down in the elevator. Not once had the professor questioned her about her polio. She hadn't asked how Izzy would manage physically or how the experience of polio had affected her. She hadn't implied that growing up on Chappy might have been limiting. She cared only about what Izzy could do with her brain.

If she had been able to, Izzy would have leaped for joy. She felt as liberated intellectually as she had felt when finally unshackled from her braces after her surgery.

The wait for the letter to arrive in April was excruciating. She acknowledged that she was somewhat unbearable to be around in the house, but couldn't contain her impatience or anxiety. Every afternoon after school she had emptied the mailbox, digging out the bills and catalogs and the occasional letter from Josiah to search for what she hoped would be a thick envelope postmarked Northampton, Mass. She grumbled about the length of time it took for mail to arrive from the mainland.

The letter from UMass arrived first, a thin acceptance congratulating her. Her parents didn't understand why she wasn't thrilled. Her first college acceptance. She definitely had a place. She smiled at their innocence. They'd never put themselves through the gauntlet she'd endured: SATs, applications, essays and interviews. They hadn't experienced the encounter with Professor Goggin that had left her with the conviction that Smith was the perfect school for her.

When the letter finally did arrive with the news not only of her acceptance but also a full scholarship, she didn't wait to get back to the house, but sat in the grass by the side of the lane and savored every word.

Five months later she was standing on the steps of her dorm, saying goodbye to her parents. Nine years before she'd been a petrified seven-year-old frantically grasping for her mother's hand as she was sent off to quarantine. Now, she was impatient for them to be on their way. She was giddy with exhaustion from the early morning ferry ride, the five-hour drive from the Cape to Northampton (who knew it could take so much time to traverse such a small state?), lugging boxes and a trunk up the narrow staircase and the unpacking of those boxes to establish her new home. She could feel her leg start to twitch the way it sometimes did when she was overtired. She grabbed the porch banister to steady herself. The last thing she wanted was for her parents to see and start to fret. For all she knew, her father might scoop her up in his arms and carry her to her room, or worse yet, the infirmary, humiliating her on her first day. She pressed herself against the railing and checked her watch.

"You guys better get going or you'll miss the last ferry and be forced to spend the night with Cousin Sadie." She hoped her teasing was enough of a prod to get her father to turn the ignition key. Her mother made a fake grimace at Sadie's name, then blew her a kiss. Izzy blew back, keeping one hand tightly on the banister.

When they were finally out of sight she slid down to the landing to take the weight off her leg. She didn't need this. Not when she had to get across campus for dinner. She sat, her hands wrapped around her rogue leg and her head resting on her thigh.

"Hey, are you OK?" The voice came from the walkway below the porch. Izzy lifted her head and peered through the slats. A tall, dark-haired girl with skin the color of an oak leaf in the fall approached her.

"You look a little pale. Did your folks just leave?"

Izzy bristled that she was being taken for a homesick freshman.

"I've just got a cramp in my leg, that's all. It'll pass."

"OK. If you need anything, I'm Grace Curtis. I'm the Resident Advisor for Haven House across the way. Welcome to Smith."

"Thanks. I'm Isabella Monroe. My family calls me Izzy."

"Where are you from?"

"Chappaquiddick Island."

"Chappy! No kidding? I was born on Chappy, but my family moved to Providence when I was a baby. I've never been back, but my grandmother loves to tell stories. She wants to be buried there."

"The only cemetery on Chappy is the Wampanoag Burial Ground."

"I know. We're Wampanoag."

"You are? This is too weird. So am I. My dad is the sachem of the Chappaquiddick Wampanoag. Why hasn't your family ever come to Pow-Wow?"

Grace shrugged. "Except for my grandmother, no one else feels a strong connection. I hardly know what it means to be Wampanoag. It's only since being here that I've even thought of myself as Native American. If you haven't noticed, there aren't many of us with brown skin on campus. There's a Cape Verdean girl from Onset and a few black girls from Boston and New York."

Izzy felt strong enough to stand and pulled herself up.

"Thanks for the welcome."

"Any time. See you at dinner."

Izzy turned to go inside and realized her leg was still shaking. She grabbed for the door handle, muttering "crap" as her leg refused to cooperate.

Before she knew it, Grace was bounding up the steps and grabbed her under the arm.

"I've got you. Did you twist your ankle or something? Can I help you up to your room?"

Reluctantly, Izzy put her arm around Grace's shoulder and allowed her to support her into the house. The staircase looked far more formidable than earlier in the day.

"I guess I overdid it with the unpacking."

"Not unusual. Are you one of those freshmen who've been chomping at the bit to begin college life ever since you got your letter?"

Sheepishly, Izzy answered, "You've nailed me. I'm so excited to be here that my leg just won't stop dancing a jig."

They made it to Izzy's room and she collapsed on the bed.

"Do you want me to take a look at your leg?"

"It's OK. I know what the problem is. I'll just rest it until dinner. Thanks for the help."

"No problem. Is this your family?" She pointed to a photo Izzy had coaxed everyone to pose for at the Pow-Wow in July. Even Jo was in it. Izzy nodded.

"Is this your brother? He's cute."

Izzy made a face. "If you ever meet him, please don't tell him or he'll be unbearable."

"Is there a chance I might meet him?"

"Probably. He doesn't live far. Are you serious?"

"One of the things you'll learn really quickly is there aren't many men in the vicinity. We have to go across the river to UMass and Amherst if we want male companionship. Girls with eligible brothers are a favored species."

"I'll keep that in mind, although I know too much about my brother to inflict him on somebody I like." She grinned. "Thanks again for the help up the stairs. I feel really stupid for pushing myself beyond my limit."

"You'll find that a common trait at Smith—pushing ourselves beyond our limits. You'd think we didn't believe in limits at all. Take care."

She closed the door quietly and Izzy flopped back on the freshly made bed. It smelled of the lavender Naomi had tucked between the folds when Izzy was packing up the linens. The scent soothed her and helped her relax. She hoped the trembling would subside in time for dinner. She didn't want to have to drag out the cane her mother had insisted she pack in the trunk. "Just in case," she'd said.

How odd, she thought, *that the first person I meet is another Wampanoag.* And then she drifted off to sleep.

It was nearly dark when she was awakened by a knock on the door. It was Grace.

"Hey, I saw that you didn't make it to dinner. Is your leg still bothering you?"

Izzy stretched and checked; the twitching had stopped. "No, it's fine. I fell asleep and that seems to have done the trick."

"That's good. Look, I figured you'd be famished, so I made you a sandwich. I hope you like ham and cheese."

"Wow! Thanks. What are you trying to do, butter me up so I'll be sure to introduce you to my brother?"

"You're too quick. You must be a Smith girl." She grinned. "Look, I've got to run—house meeting. By the way, yours should be starting soon, so eat up and get downstairs. See you soon."

Izzy gave herself a couple of weeks to settle in before she contacted Josiah. She sent him a letter with her house and phone number and asked him to let her know the next time he was in Northampton. She kept the tone light, but the fact was, she was unexpectedly homesick. Even with Grace acting like a surrogate big sister, Izzy hadn't yet found her footing both literally and figuratively. Her leg acted up whenever she was stressed, which was regularly, and she had finally resorted to using her cane. And Grace's observation about the paucity of brown skin on campus reverberated with her in every class, where she felt she was the Native American representative, expected to instruct and enlighten her classmates. She'd never felt like that on the Vineyard, where so many classmates had at least some Wampanoag blood that nobody stuck out. At Smith, Izzy was aware that she stuck out. People were confused by her honey-colored hair and her light brown skin, and she was tired of explaining her heritage. She never heard anyone asking the white girls about their heritage.

So she was excited when the girl on bells one Saturday afternoon announced that Izzy had a visitor. She peeked over the railing into the front hall and saw Josiah, looking like the beatnik farmer he'd become—his beard full, his hair tied back with a bandana, dressed in a flannel shirt, faded blue jeans and metal-tipped work boots. She whooped and came down the stairs as fast as she could— which wasn't very—and threw herself into his arms.

"Jo! You came!"

He twirled her around. "Hey, Bird, of course I came. I can read between the lines. Can you come out with me for a cup of coffee?"

"Can I ever!"

They walked down the hill to Main Street and slipped into a small café.

"What's with your leg?"

"Nothing."

"Bird, this is Jo you're talking to. Don't mess with me."

"It craps out on me when I get tired or stressed, which unfortunately is rather often. After breezing through twelve years of school in ten, I have finally found my intellectual match in Smith. It's fucking hard."

"Well, I can see college life has added to your vocabulary."

"Sorry. I'm getting my ass kicked scholastically. Do you know how many valedictorians and salutatorians there are in my class? Apparently we are the leading edge of the baby boom and there are so many of us we are grappling for the top position like a pack of wolves."

"I have no doubt you will emerge as the alpha wolf, Sis."

"Thanks for the vote of confidence. How's life on the farm?"

"Let's just say we're doing our own grappling. New folks arriving, old folks leaving, shifting politics. Not sure it's what I signed on for."

"Will you stay?"

"Don't know yet."

"Do me a favor? Stick around in Western Mass until I'm on firmer ground academically. It really gives me a boost to see you."

"I told you last New Year's that I'd be here for you. I'll stop by every week if that's what you need."

"Well, I'm not that pathetic yet, but every two or three weeks would be good. Have you been in touch with Mom and Dad?"

"Not much. How about you? Do they know you're having a rough time?"

"God, no! The last thing I need is for them to come rescue me. Parents' Weekend is coming in October. That's soon enough. Hey, would you come then, too? You could be my buffer—even if it's just for dinner. Please?"

"You ask a lot of your big brother . . . But, yeah, of course I'll come."

They walked slowly back to campus and Izzy took him to Paradise Pond, where they sat watching the sunset. It was there that Grace found them.

"Hey, Izzy! I saw you signed up for biology help and I wanted you to know that our schedules match, so I'm your tutor. I can start tomorrow afternoon. Does that work for you?"

"Sure, Grace. Thanks. Hey, this is my famous brother, the beatnik farmer Josiah. Jo, this is Grace Curtis. She was born on Chappy but her family moved away before the Monroes could trap her into being our playmate."

"Hi, Jo."

"Grace. Are you in Izzy's class?"

"No, I'm a couple years ahead of her, but I ran into her the first day of the term and made a nuisance of myself until she threw up her arms in defeat."

"Actually, Jo, Grace has been my guiding light, helping me to navigate the treacherous shoals of freshman year."

"Which you're actually managing pretty well."

"What is this, a conspiracy to bolster Izzy's self-confidence? Both you and Jo seem to have some imaginary Izzy in mind."

"I think we both see you pretty clearly, Izzy. You've got good instincts. Trust them. Hey, nice to meet you, Jo. I've got to run. See you tomorrow, Iz."

Jo walked Izzy back to her house and gave her a bear hug on the steps. "I'll be back in a couple of weeks. Love you, Bird."

"Love you back."

Chapter 30

"Moments of glad grace"
Josiah

Jo was halfway down the hill when he heard his name being called. He turned and saw Grace running after him.

"Hey, I'm glad I caught you. Just wanted to touch base with you about Izzy. I feel like her big sister and it's great to know she has a big brother looking out for her."

"Is anything wrong?"

"Just the usual freshman freak out when they come to grips with how hard it suddenly is after they've sailed through school before. Izzy puts a lot of pressure on herself and I'm trying to encourage her to lighten up a little. Did she tell you about her leg?"

"She didn't have to. I could see it in her gait. She had polio as a kid and she's only been walking without crutches for a couple of years. She told me she has it under control, but I think she's afraid if she goes to the infirmary she risks the big guns being pulled in. In her mind, that could lead to who knows what—another operation, a leave of absence or dropping out of school. I know my sister, she's stubborn."

"If you want, I can keep a closer watch on her. She's a great girl, and I think she trusts me."

"Thanks. She is a great girl. I've always worried about her. It would give me a real peace of mind to know you were looking out for her."

"Happy to. I'm glad we met."

"Me, too. I'll stop by in a couple of weeks. Hope to see you then."

"Sure thing. Happy farming."

She turned to go and Jo stood and watched her climb the hill until she disappeared into the campus. There was an ease to her and a quiet strength that gave him confidence in her ability to watch over Izzy. She wasn't like any of the girls at the farm. She was grounded. And even though she'd left Chappy and hadn't grown up imbued with Wampanoag traditions, he recognized something in her that reminded him of Naomi. Maybe one didn't need herbs and teas and poultices to be a healer, because that is what struck him about Grace. She was a healer.

It intrigued him that he was so taken by her Wampanoag blood. He, who'd spent the last several years looking outside the tribe for his identity, just as Cousin Sadie had threatened so long ago at the Pow-Wow. But now this girl had walked into his life and he felt like he'd been smacked upside the head with his own shattered drum.

1965
Northampton and Chappaquiddick

Chapter 31

"And he had known at last some tenderness"
Josiah

It was March when Josiah got a letter from Izzy, who had climbed out of her freshman panic and begun to flourish, especially with her writing.

"Hey, Jo, I've invited Grace to come out to Chappy during spring break. Can you spare a few days from your mimeo machine and spring planting to help me show her around?"

He'd seen Grace now and then when he'd come to town to spend time with Izzy. Occasionally she'd joined them for coffee or dinner. And when he'd managed to score a block of tickets to a Joan Baez concert in exchange for a bag of the farm's marijuana crop, he'd held one for her. But every time he'd seen her they'd been surrounded by others—usually Izzy, but also the posse from the farm the night of the concert. As compelling as he found her, he hadn't pursued her, hadn't attempted to get to know her beyond their mutual caring as Izzy's protectors. He wasn't sure what was holding him back.

He'd adapted easily to the relaxed sexual attitudes at the farm, where monogamy was perceived as a bourgeois constraint, and changing partners or having more than one partner at a time was an accepted part of daily life. Even Arwen, who had introduced him to the idea of "going with the flow," had moved on to someone else. He couldn't imagine Grace choosing a community like the farm. He wasn't sure he'd choose it now himself. But he had stumbled upon it and it had chosen him, and now he was bound up in its complicated culture. As the world beyond the farm had become more turbulent—the civil rights movement in the South, the widening of the war in Vietnam—the farm had taken the disruptions as a loud and clear signal to increase their engagement in the struggle. More militant protestors had joined the commune, and the group was now putting out a weekly newspaper for activists around the country instead of sporadic broadsheets. Jo, as the resident Vietnam vet, reluctantly found himself alternatively vilified or revered as the expert on the escalating conflict and the simmering antiwar movement.

A few days after Izzy's letter arrived, Jo had an altercation with Andy, a guy who had recently arrived at the farm, one of the leaders of a West Coast commune. He started spouting a bunch of crap about "ideological purity" and no room for people with a foot in each camp. He was speaking directly to Jo.

"I know you were in Special Forces, Monroe. How many Vietnamese peasants did you kill? How much covert dirty work did you do for the CIA? Who are you spying for now?"

Jo tried to leave, figuring the more he listened to the jerk, the more likely he'd resort to fists rather than words. But the guy pulled him back roughly and that was enough to release the tightly wound springs that contained his anger.

Jo hadn't forgotten how to fight, and apparently Andy had never learned. Jo flattened him pretty quickly, left him with a bloody nose and walked out to the meadow to cool off with a joint.

Nathan found him.

"Maybe this would be a good time to take your sister up on her invitation to go back to the island."

"What? Do you believe that bullshit about me spying? Are you kicking me out?"

"I trust you. But Andy has planted a seed of doubt that's now spreading its roots out into the group, especially the newer members who don't know you like I do. We're a community that advocates nonviolence. I'm just asking you to take a break for a couple of weeks, let things settle down while I cool everyone off."

Jo stood. "Can you give me a lift to Northampton?"

He packed up all his stuff, not sure if he would, or even wanted to come back.

When he arrived in Northampton, instead of going to Izzy, he went to Grace's dorm first and spoke to someone in the lobby.

"She's at the library. She usually hangs out in the science stacks with the other chemistry majors. You want to leave your stuff here?"

He found her in a study carrel.

"Hey."

"Hey. What brings you here?"

"An earlier than expected arrival for our trip to Chappy."

"So you've decided to come with us?"

"Yeah. Look, are you deep into studying, or do you have time to go for a walk with me?"

"The books can wait. You look like crap. But I suppose you're going to tell me the other guy looks worse."

"That obvious? But yeah, he's probably got a broken nose and all I've got is a sore fist."

"You want to talk about it?"

"That's why I came to find you."

"Does Izzy know you're here?"

"Not yet. I wanted to talk with you first."

"OK. Let's go for that walk."

He started haltingly. He wasn't sure how much she knew about his past, but knew he couldn't talk about what happened on the farm without bringing up the war.

"Did you know I was a medic in Vietnam?"

"Uh-huh. Izzy told me. She's enormously proud of you. But she worries that you don't talk about it. Why now? Why to me?"

"Until today, I thought I didn't need to talk about it. But my reaction to a provocation about my past made me realize that probably hasn't been the best decision. I chose you because you listen. And I trust you."

She stopped on the path and looked at him.

"Thank you."

"Don't thank me until you hear what I have to say."

"I don't care how hard it's going to be. All I ask is that you don't lie to me."

"Agreed."

And for the next two hours he described for her the harsh words that had precipitated his anger; the crushing brutality of his life on patrol in Vietnam; the decisions he'd had to make—save a life, take a life; the distrust and ambiguity and violence that had rendered him numb. When he finished, he was wrung out and jittery.

"I could use a joint."

"I can't offer you that, but I can give you this."

She stepped closer to him, put her arms around him and held him.

He stood rigid for a moment, stunned by her acceptance, and then wrapped his arms tightly around her pliant, giving body. He buried his face in her neck.

They didn't go back to the library. They didn't tell Izzy Jo was in town. Instead, Grace found a place for them to crash for the night.

"My friend Jill has an extra room in her apartment. Her roommate dropped out a month ago and she hasn't found a replacement. I called her. She said we can stay there tonight."

"We?"

"I don't want you to be alone. No, that's just an excuse. I want to be with you. It will be pretty primitive. I don't know if there's even a bed. But Jill said I can use the kitchen if I leave her some leftovers for when she gets back from a play rehearsal later. I'll cook you a hot meal, we can talk some more. OK with you?"

They picked up his bag and bed roll at Grace's house and she signed out for an overnight.

"They still treat us like children, but it's better if I play by the rules. This way no one will think I'm missing if there's a fire or something."

They cruised through the market, Grace assessing vegetables with all her senses.

"Is there anything you can't abide to eat? I'd hate to try to seduce you with my culinary skills and have you wind up retching or going into anaphylactic shock."

"So you plan on seducing me?"

"I've planned on seducing you since I met you last fall. No, I take that back. Since I saw your face in the family portrait Izzy keeps next to her bed."

"Why have I not realized this until now?"

"Because you are an idiot?"

"And even after all I told you today . . ."

"Especially after all you told me today. You trusted me. You let down the barrier that you've kept between yourself and the world and let me in. Now I'm going to let you in."

They walked in silence to Jill's apartment, laden with grocery bags, the bedroll and his duffle bag. Laden also with the weight of their revelations.

Grace retrieved the key from a hook under the porch and opened the door. They deposited the food on the counter and then looked at each other.

"I think dinner can wait," he said.

She smiled and took him by the hand down the hall.

Making love to Grace was another revelation. The sex at the farm had been sheer physical gratification, fueled by pot and freedom. Up until this night with Grace, he'd reveled in the lack of commitment, in the enjoyment of pleasure for pleasure's sake.

This was something at once far more complex and blessedly simple. A profound joy. A sense of well-being at the touch of this incredible woman. A delight in his ability to give her pleasure. All without the enhancement of his drug of choice. At the start, he had pulled a joint out of his pocket, ready to light up and share with her—his usual ritual at the farm. But she had closed her fingers over his hand.

"We don't need that. I don't want the haze of dope between us when we connect for the first time. I want you, raw and naked, not wrapped in the cotton wool of obfuscating brain chemistry. Come to me just as you did this afternoon on our walk. Come *with* me."

And he did.

What he felt as she rose to meet him was a connection that surpassed the physical act of being inside her. He felt like a wanderer whose stumbling journey has finally brought him to the place he had been seeking. In Grace he found his home.

When he woke the next morning he realized he hadn't had a nightmare and he hadn't had a joint. Grace was in the kitchen chopping and stirring. She turned her head and grinned.

"The meal I never cooked you last night."

"Where's your friend?"

"She had an early morning class. And I've got an appointment with my advisor in about an hour, so eat up."

She offered him a spoonful.

"M-m-m. You're a good cook."

"Thanks. It's one of my little pleasures. A respite from the academic grind. I think that's why Jill lets me come here—so I can cook for her."

"Do you come often?

"Do I detect a glimmer of curiosity about whether I've brought other men here?"

Jo started to sputter a protest about it being none of his business, but Grace held up her hand.

"It's OK. After what happened last night it *is* your business. The answer is no. You're the first."

She turned away. "And I hope the last."

He put his arms around her from behind. "I hope so, too," he whispered in her ear.

Later in the day they gathered up Izzy and climbed a bus together to start the multi-leg journey to Chappy.

Tobias and Mae were both waiting for them on the dock as the late ferry steamed into Oak Bluffs.

He hadn't seen them since Christmas, and Mae looked thinner and more haggard. But the joy and warmth of her welcome softened her features and eased his concern. She seemed genuinely delighted to meet Grace.

"I've heard so much about you from Izzy. I hope you consider this a homecoming."

The strain that often accompanied his visits home was less apparent. He had felt that both Mae and Tobias were more guarded with him since his return from Vietnam, as if they didn't want to upset him and drive him away again. It made him uncomfortable to wield that kind of power over them. He had questioned himself as he got older and farther away from the angry boy who had stalked away from the Burial Ground nearly four years earlier. Why had he been such a jerk? He wasn't sure why they seemed more relaxed this time, and maybe it was simply Grace's presence that deflected what would normally be far too much attention focused on him. Whatever it was, he accepted it.

He and Grace climbed into the back of the truck with the suitcases. Izzy, ever perceptive, had picked up on a change in the dynamic between Grace and Josiah, despite their efforts throughout the long journey to keep their intimacy undiscovered.

"I'm going to ride up front with Mom and Dad. You two have been communicating silently all day about something, so have it out by yourselves in the back of the truck. But I swear, Josiah, Grace is my guest and I want you to be nice to her."

Once they were underway, Jo clasped Grace's hand out of sight of Izzy and his parents.

"She sounded really pissed. She's no fool."

Grace bit her lip. "I hope she's not hurt that we are together. I never want her to feel shut out or cut off from my friendship."

"Neither do I. You're the best thing that's happened to her since she got accepted to Smith. I just don't know how she's going to react. It makes me want to keep our relationship quiet while we're here."

Grace looked at him with a mixture of disbelief and caution.

"I think that would be a mistake. If she's already sensed something is going on, how can we possibly hide it from her when we're under the same roof for a whole week? And when she does figure it out, think about how hurt she's going to be if she thinks we are keeping secrets from her. Besides, even if we aren't going to be sharing a bed, do you honestly think we can disguise our feelings for each other? I know I can't. I have zero ability to mask my emotions. I guarantee that not just Izzy, but every member of your family will be able to read my face like a book."

"And just what are those emotions?"

"Wonder, delight, disbelief that an amazing man is sitting beside me right now under a miraculously beautiful and mysterious sky, holding my hand with incredible tenderness and passion, and reminding me of what he gave me yesterday."

"Speaking of yesterday . . . I haven't had a chance to tell you how extraordinary it was. You are unlike any woman I've ever known."

"I felt the same way."

"It was scary, actually."

"In what way?"

"I've never lost myself so completely in someone else and yet emerged believing that you had found me. Thank you."

"Thank you, Jo. I don't know how much farther it is to your house and, therefore, how much time we have. But I think you better kiss me soon."

And he did.

As they pulled into the driveway, Grace held him back for a moment.

"We're agreed, it's best to tell Izzy, right?"

"Agreed. But let's wait till tomorrow. We can take a walk to the beach and let her scream or jump for joy out of earshot of my parents."

"Sounds like a plan. I guess we better climb down or they'll be sending a search party."

Jo and Grace were carefully blank when sleeping arrangements were described by Mae.

"Izzy, we've put the camp bed in your room for Grace. We thought you girls wouldn't mind some togetherness, and it seemed more hospitable than giving Grace the couch, or throwing Jo out of his room."

"Thanks, Mom. I think we're all pretty beat. At least I am. We can catch up in the morning if it's OK with you. Come on Grace, I'll show you our luxury accommodations. G'night, everyone."

The next morning, after the requisite blueberry pancakes, Jo proposed the walk and the three of them left for the beach.

Izzy babbled along the way and Jo hung behind, watching Grace's bent head listening intently to his sister and Izzy's exuberance in pointing out everything she loved about Chappy.

When they reached the water all three of them kicked off their shoes and rolled up their jeans. It was late March and the water was ridiculously cold, but they let the gentle foaming rivulets dance over their toes. After a few minutes Grace pulled back and collapsed on the sand laughing and made a sand angel.

Jo hadn't seen her this loose ever, but understood it was the Chappy magic simply working its way through her body and spirit, unknotting and unraveling a semester of hard studying and intense responsibility. It didn't take long for Izzy to join her, flat on her back. Grace grabbed Izzy's hand and swept it across the sand with her as they expanded their angels' wings. Izzy laughed, her trilling, bubbling sounds caught by the wind and carried out to sea.

"Thank you for inviting me, Izzy. I had no idea what an effect this place would have on me. I want to thank you for something else as well."

They were still on their backs, facing each other. Izzy's eyes opened wider, curious but seemingly unaware of what was coming.

"Thank you for bringing Jo into my life."

Izzy's eyes darted to Jo, sitting a short distance behind them.

"Jo?" She sat up abruptly. "What exactly do you mean, 'into your life'? Hasn't he been around for a while, hanging out with us?"

"I mean more than hanging out. Something changed between us on Thursday. Something happened to bring us closer."

"Thursday? I thought Jo arrived from the farm yesterday. You mean you two were together without me? Jo came to you and not me?"

"Maybe I could join this conversation instead of being discussed in the third person? I went to see Grace when I first got to Northampton because I needed to talk something out."

"And you couldn't talk to me?"

"Not this time, Bird. I turned to Grace because I'd seen her in action with you and I trusted her to be straight with me. I trust you, too! But I didn't want to burden you with my crap when you still had an exam to get through."

"Can you 'burden' me now that my exam is over, or do you and Grace have some big secret now between you?"

"No secrets, Izzy. That's why we're talking with you now," Grace interjected.

Jo moved closer.

"I've been asked to leave the farm. I punched a new guy in the face who had accused me of war crimes and spying for the CIA. I was a mess when I got to town. Grace helped me."

He took Grace's hand.

"When Jo unburdened himself to me, something clicked inside me. You know what an adolescent crush I've had on him since I saw his photo that first day of school. Well, I took the plunge and acted on that crush. And, what do you know, it was mutual!"

"So does this mean you guys are a couple?"

Grace and Jo nodded.

"Um, where does that leave me? The nerdy little sister pestering you to take her along to the movies? Have I lost my best friend to my brother?"

"Absolutely not! You know me better than that. I'm not one of those girls who abandons her friends as soon as a guy enters the picture."

"What about you, Jo? Do I have to arm wrestle you to get time with Grace? Because if I do, you know who will win. I have very well-developed upper body strength. I may have crap for legs, but my arms have taken me far."

Jo could hear that Izzy was doing her best to put a positive spin on what she'd just been told. His brave kid sister.

"I'm not taking Grace away from you, Izzy. If anything, it's going to mean my spending even more time in Northampton."

"Oh, my God! The farm! What will you do now?"

Jo listened in amazements as Izzy turned from her own loss to his.

"I'll figure it out."

"Will you tell Mom and Dad, or should I just pretend I don't know? Speaking of Mom and Dad, are you going to reveal your, um 'changed' relationship?"

"We hadn't really talked about that yet. We were more concerned about being honest with you. No secrets among us, OK?"

"I thought something was going on between you yesterday. I'd never seen so many soulful looks before. Hey, look. I'm a big college girl now, even if I'm barely seventeen. I'm happy for you, really. My best friend and my brother make each other ga-ga. It's a lot better than having you hate each other and being caught in the middle. See how philosophical I can be?"

"You're the best, Bird. I promise, no abandonment."

"You will hear from me if either of you hurts the other. I love you both too much."

They spent the week immersing Grace in Chappy's wildness and isolation, from the moors and beaches of

Cape Poge to the sacred history of the Wampanoag Burial Ground at North Neck. But they did not go to Innisfree.

Jo hadn't been back to the Burial Ground since the night he broke his drum. But he knew it was a place he had to take Grace. Not only because of her grandmother's wish to be buried there, but also because of its place in his own confused history.

They went without Izzy, who had old friends to see in Edgartown and who waved them off, telling them she'd had enough chaperoning for the day. They took bikes from the shed and pedaled first past the old Keaney cottage, barely recognizable after forty years of battering by nor'easters and overgrown with poison ivy and cedar seedlings that had taken root in the mossy roof.

"My mother grew up in that cottage," he told Grace as they stopped by the ramshackle gate leaning nearly horizontal over what had once been a well-tended garden.

"Does it sadden her to see it so abandoned?"

"I don't know if she comes anymore. After she sold Innisfree she told me it was time to look forward, not back. My Uncle Patrick has a photo of the whole family in front of the house when it was in its prime. They all looked so happy."

"Do you think you will look back at Innisfree as a place of happiness?"

"I don't honestly know. The loss of it left me with such a bitter taste it's hard for me to think of it except with pain."

"Will you take me there some day?"

"Not now. Maybe next time. Let's push on to the Burial Ground."

They left their bikes on the path and walked up through the boulders that marked the older graves. Jo led her to his grandfather's headstone.

"You're named for him. Did you know your grandfather?"

"He died before I was born. I think my mother was pregnant with me at the time, though. So I was here for his funeral. He was the sachem."

He moved away from the grave and cut short the discussion about his grandfather. He didn't want her to ask whether he had any desire to be sachem himself.

They wandered to the promontory away from the graves and sat on the grass overlooking the water.

"When I needed to be by myself, this is where I came."

"Do they talk to you?"

"My ancestors? Not loud enough for me to hear. I sometimes think it's not me they are speaking to."

"I can understand why my grandmother wants to be buried here."

She leaned her head on his shoulder and he circled her with his arm. The wind lifted her curly hair and the limbs of the tree above them rustled. Tiny buds on the tips of the branches were almost ready to pop.

He breathed in the sea air, its tang awakening a memory he had pushed away.

"Let me tell you about the last time I was here," he said. "It will explain a lot about who you've gotten yourself mixed up with."

Telling Grace about that night, reliving the confusion and anger and despair, brought him one step closer to finding the answer he was seeking about who he was.

When he finished, she traced the structure of his face with her thumb as if she were anointing him with sacred oil or war paint.

"I see a man who embodies the strength of both his mother's and his father's people. The way a newborn baby's skull has a soft spot that needs time to fuse, your identity will emerge even stronger because of your struggle." She kissed him, gently at first and gradually building as pent-up desire finally caught up with them after several days of lying in separate beds on opposite sides of a thin wall.

They made love under the tree, his coat spread out beneath them and the lowering sun igniting their skin with the deepening hues of a maritime sunset.

On their last night they sat on the dock at Cove Meadow, their legs dangling over the still water of the pond. The Milky Way encircled them overhead, a broad brush stroke of shimmering light.

Grace leaned her head back. "It's amazing how close to the sky—to the whole universe—I feel out here. Nothing gets in the way. Every sense seems more acute. I feel the wind stroke my cheek; hear the mouse skitter through the grass; taste the sea in the clam you shucked for me; smell the layers of ancient silt laid down in the marsh; see you on your native soil. How can you bear to be away from this?" She threw her arms wide to encompass the circle of land and water and sky.

"I loved it as a child. But then it became alien to me. Not the place. But the community. The expectations, the labels. At Innisfree I was immune to them. It was my safe haven. When we lost it, I lost my sense of belonging. That's another 'sense' this place heightens."

"What will you do now that you've left the farm? Will you stay here?"

"Unless the magic of the island has affected you so much you're going to drop out of Smith and stay, I don't plan to stick around."

"Does that mean you want to be near me?"

"Haven't I made that clear in the past week? Look, I know things have happened really quickly between us, but we also knew each other for half a year before everything changed. I don't want you to disappear into the library. I want to be with you."

"You'll come back to Western Mass?"

"Yes."

"What will you do?"

"Don't know yet. I'm sure I can pick up some odd jobs. I'm good with my hands. I fix mimeo machines in addition to writing articles that get printed on them. I'll land on my feet. I have so far."

"Is that all you want, to land on your feet, drifting from one job to another, from one bag of dope to the next?"

"Whoa! Do you have a problem with how I get through the day?"

"Jo, I know it's way too early to say this, but I love you. I love your gentleness and generosity. I love your complexity and your intensity. I love how you make me feel—not only when we make love, but also when we're just sitting around being. You've made me see myself as something more. Someone loved. So no, I don't have a problem with you. I just have questions. Because I see you as someone with so much to give."

Jo was stunned. What he had expected to hear was a laundry list of his faults, not a recitation of why he was loved. But in the midst of that recitation was that one expectation—that he could be more. More what?

He buried his head in his hands, trying to find the words to respond. But before he could answer, he felt her stir next to him.

"Well, I guess I've made a fool of myself." She was up and striding quickly off the dock and up to the house.

"Grace!"

But she didn't turn around, and he didn't go after her.

He stayed on the dock. In his pocket was his last joint. He held it in his hand and studied it, hearing in his head not Grace's words of love, but her comment about his drifting. He looked at his life since leaving the island and saw it less as drifting and more as careening, lurching from one misguided attempt to seek peace with himself to another. Had he lost again?

He lit the joint.

Well into the haze, he heard footsteps and looked up. Please let it be Grace. But it wasn't. It was Mae.

She sat next to him and reached for the joint. He thought she wanted to take it away from him, but instead, she took a long toke and then handed it back.

"Let me tell you a story," she began. And proceeded to recount her descent into despair when she found herself pregnant with Ned's baby and succumbed to the forces of fear and shame that led her to run away. But then she continued, with her slow climb out of the hole she had dug for herself.

"What saved me is loving your father," she said. "Do you love Grace?"

She waited for his answer.

"Yes," he whispered.

"Jo, I know there are costs to loving. You have to be willing to be vulnerable and cut through the crap that prevents you from speaking the truth about who you are. Only you can decide if the cost is worth it. But I will tell you one thing. She loves you."

Mae got up and walked slowly back to the house.

Jo threw what remained of the joint into the pond.

When he returned to the house he could see Izzy's light was out. As desperately as he wanted to talk to

Grace, he knew words alone would not repair the damage he'd one with his silence. The pain in her voice when she left the dock, thinking he didn't love her, reverberated throughout the night. He didn't sleep much, and when he finally did crash, it was into another nightmare. Whatever peace this week with Grace had won him, he had obliterated with his stupidity.

In the morning, his mother knocked on his door.

"May I come in?"

He mumbled an assent from the twisted sheets of his bed.

She sat on the edge of the mattress.

"Izzy and Grace are getting ready to leave. Are you going with them?"

He pushed himself up, groggy and sweat-drenched.

"You had a bad night."

"Yeah. Nothing like my own pig-headedness to destroy my best chance at happiness."

"I don't think the damage is irreparable."

"But I don't know how to fix it. And I know I can't go with them today."

"You'll figure it out, Jo, if you love her. Don't give up on yourself. She hasn't."

"How do you know?"

"I saw enough this week to believe she's willing to wait for you."

"She sure didn't wait last night."

"You of all people should understand how she might run away from a painful encounter before she's thought it out."

"I hear you."

"Now, do you think you can rouse yourself enough to say goodbye? And don't protest. Not saying goodbye is a big mistake." She left without another word.

He listened to his mother and cleaned himself up with a fresh t-shirt and jeans, splashed some cold water on his face and found everyone in the kitchen packing up the food Mae had put together for their journey.

Izzy was the first to see him.

"Rip Van Winkle awakens. Mom says you're going to stay a few more days. Can you drive us to the boat?"

It was clear to him from Izzy's casual greeting that Grace hadn't shared anything with her of their conversation. Knowing that calmed him in a way he hadn't expected. What had happened last night was for them alone to sort out. They didn't need other voices pulling them apart or pushing them together. He saw it as a peace offering. Grace didn't say a word, but she was watching him.

"Sure, I'll drive you. Happy to."

The ride to OB was filled with Izzy's chatter. Grace had maneuvered so that Izzy was sitting between them, eliminating any opportunity for any physical contact. Grace spent most of the drive focused on the landscape outside the window.

He had no intention of just dropping them off and found a parking spot near the ticket office. While they bought their tickets, he hoisted their bags out of the back of the truck and then accompanied them to the pier to wait for the arrival of the boat.

As if she were reading his mind, Izzy suddenly darted away from them to talk to one of the steamship freight handlers. He looked like someone she went to school with. Her departure left Grace and Jo alone.

They both started to talk at once. He stopped, let Grace go first.

"I'm sorry about last night. Too much, too soon. I put you in a really awkward position with my . . ."

"Grace, stop. I'm the one who should be apologizing. I didn't say anything last night because I was overwhelmed and I couldn't find the words. I'm the idiot. The words are 'I love you.' I do. But I know the words are not enough. Somehow I have to figure out how to show you that I mean them."

"Is that why you're not coming back? You don't have to prove anything to me."

"I have to prove something to myself. You were right, I'm drifting. Hell, I'm completely rudderless. Can you wait for me?"

She moved toward him and embraced him, and he held her as they rocked back and forth.

"I take that as a yes," he murmured.

He stood on the dock until the ferry was a speck.

That night at supper his parents asked him if he was planning to return to the farm.

He considered lying to them. He was nearly twenty-two, a war veteran, no longer dependent on them. But his moments of honesty with Grace were reshaping him.

"I was asked to leave the farm for a while after a difference of opinion with someone. I've decided it's a good time to make a clean break. I'm not going back. The leadership is evolving and the new people are deeply suspicious of someone like me. You know how I feel about finding a place where I belong. I no longer belong at the farm."

"I can't say I'm unhappy about your decision. In truth, I'm relieved, Jo," Tobias said. "I've always had the sense that, for all their talk about community, they weren't prepared to accept someone who didn't act or think exactly as they did. I can understand why you didn't feel you belonged. You're your own man."

"What will you do now?" Mae asked.

"Stop drifting. You are both so focused, especially you, Mom, in the way you found your way back and built the Boat House. How do I do that?"

"What do you want out of life, Jo?"

"I know I want Grace. When I'm with her, I'm a better man. She sees parts of me that I'd forgotten, good parts. I've found peace with her. Do you know I didn't have any nightmares since I've been with her—until last night, when I thought I'd lost her."

"We've seen the effect she's had on you, even in the short time you've been here. What's in the way, what could push her away?"

"She sees me as having more to give than my current choices seem to be leading me. I don't blame her, if I take a hard look at myself."

"I think Dad and I agree with her there. You've got such strengths, Jo. You're smart, you're compassionate, and you're a fighter— in the best sense of the word. Despite the unorthodox way the farm was going about it, I know their ideas about social justice are what appealed to you. You're a good man, Jo. Grace knows it. We know it. I hope you know it."

"Thanks, Mom. It's starting to sink in."

The next morning he rode his bike to the high school in Oak Bluffs and asked to see his old math teacher, Catherine Doner.

"Mrs. Doner has a free period at 10:30. If you can wait, I'll let her know you're here."

Math had been his best subject, and he remembered Mrs. Doner exhorting him to consider applying to college. For so many reasons—his anger, his confusion about who he was, the lack of financial resources in the family—he dismissed the idea. He didn't know how she would react to his return, but he figured he had to start somewhere and he respected her opinion.

"Josiah Monroe! When they told me in the office you were here, I couldn't believe it! Tell me everything."

And he did. He found Catherine Doner, someone he could still talk to.

"So the question now is, what do I do with the rest of my life?"

"Well, here's what's changed and here's what's stayed the same in your circumstances. You're still a bright young man. You've proven that, with your success as a medic and even your alternative journalism. What's different is that now you have both the GI Bill to support your education and four years of challenging life experience to demonstrate your resilience and your ability to tackle something difficult. Do you want to follow up on your medic training by going to med school?"

He shook his head emphatically.

"Then consider a field like engineering. You've got the brains, and I think you'd like it as well as be good at it."

"Where do I begin?"

"Let's take a walk to the guidance office. I'm sure Mr. O'Neill has a wall full of catalogs that can get you started."

He spent hours combing through course descriptions, academic requirements, and financial aid criteria. Mrs. Doner invited him to lunch with some of the other teachers, all of whom knew him and wanted to know what he'd been doing.

He left the school with a plan.

It took him a few weeks of soul-searching and doubt-inducing work to pull it all together. But when he was finished, he made the decision to hand-deliver his application to the University of Massachusetts with a stopover in Northampton.

Mrs. Doner reviewed his essay and supplied him with practice exams for the SAT. She wrote one of his recommendations. She did everything to support him except stand at his shoulder while he typed the application.

"You were one of my best students, Jo. It broke my heart in senior year when you decided not to go to college. You've made up for it so many times over with this decision. Good luck!"

Jo got off the bus in Northampton with the manila envelope tightly clasped in his hand. He sat in the living room of Grace's dorm, enduring curious stares until she appeared in the doorway. The look on her face of joy mingled with curiosity filled him up.

He rose and handed her the envelope.

"What's this?"

"My rudder."

She carefully removed the sheaf of papers and a smile broke out, animating her face.

"May I read it?"

"That's why I gave it to you."

She sat on the couch next to him and read the essay. When she turned to him with tears in her eyes, he knew he had done the right thing.

1969
Amherst and Boston

Chapter 32

"The darkness drops again"
Josiah

Josiah started his engineering degree at UMass as Grace began her senior year at Smith. He found an apartment halfway between Amherst and Northampton and bought a used VW capable of getting him across the river without breaking down more than once a month.

The day Grace graduated, he asked her to marry him. She said yes.

While he finished his degree, Grace enrolled in the nursing program at UMass and they graduated together.

Mae, Tobias, Naomi, and Izzy came to celebrate with them. Izzy was in her first year of grad school at Harvard studying for a doctorate in English, and she was happy to skip a day of classes to drive from Cambridge to Amherst to congratulate her brother and sister-in-law.

After dinner they all went down to South Hadley for a sunset river cruise, teasing Tobias that even on a day off he wanted to be on the water. The three elders were sitting below enjoying the scenery and their whisky while Izzy, Jo, and Grace leaned against the railing on the upper deck and caught up with one another.

But it was Mae who was the major topic of conversation.

"Mom had pneumonia early this spring," Izzy said. "Dad's worried she's not completely recovered."

"She doesn't look well. Maybe I can encourage her to see someone in Boston. I'll offer to go with her." Grace kept her suspicions to herself, but she was concerned.

Chapter 33

"The labyrinth of her days"
Mae

Mae demurred and didn't want a fuss made, but Tobias was insistent and she finally agreed to see a specialist at Mass General.

Grace and Tobias were with her when the pulmonologist reported back on the results of her tests.

"I'm sorry. The cancer is back. But the good news is that treatment options have improved in the past twenty years."

He spent the next twenty minutes outlining what those options were, and then made a recommendation.

"In your case, the treatment with the best chance of success for you is a bone marrow transplant."

Mae took a deep breath. "I can't say that this is a surprise. But even anticipating that the news would be bad, I need some time to come to grips with all this. I'm not ready to make a decision today."

She and Tobias returned to Chappy. They sat on the deck of the ferry in the open air, Mae with her eyes closed and leaning back in Tobias' arms to absorb the warmth of the sun and the strength of her husband. Later that night he held her again while they both sobbed.

"Please forgive me, Tobias. I know I sound selfish. I'm scared. Everyone sees me as a fighter and, until recently, so did I. But when I look back, it was always for somebody else, someone I loved, that I fought for—you, Jo, Izzy. I don't know if I have anything left to fight for myself."

"I know you don't see it right now, but even when things were at their lowest point between us and Jo, you didn't give up. You held out hope and you offered him what he needed to come back. This is another low point for us, Mae. There's no denying that. But if it's love you need to fuel your will to fight this time, take it—from me, from the kids, from Maureen. Any one of us will open a vein for you. Not just to give you our blood and our bone marrow, but to give you our strength and our spirit. There is no one this family needs more than you. If not for yourself, fight for us."

Mae burrowed into his embrace. "I never ran away from adversity before, and God knows, I'm not ready to leave you. I wish I didn't have to put you all through this."

"And we wish you didn't have to be sick. But you are, and we will be with you. Whatever you have to face, we'll face together."

The next day, she called Mass General and agreed to the transplant. Later in the day, Tobias called Jo and Maureen and let them know Mae's decision.

"She needs a donor with a tissue match. They start with blood relatives. Are you willing to be tested?"

Jo practically leaped through the phone with his answer. "I'm on it, Dad. I'll be there tomorrow."

Maureen was equally willing. "I'll contact Danny and Patrick as well, Tobias. I don't think they'll hesitate. I'll pray about how to approach Kathleen. I don't want to deny Mae the help if Kathleen is a match, and I also don't want to deny Kathleen the opportunity to atone."

Izzy was crushed that she wasn't a candidate to be a donor, but Mae lessened her frustration.

"I will rely on you to give me regular infusions of literature when I'm spending hours waiting, as you know all too well I will be doing. Can you bear to sit with me in a hospital again?"

"Oh, Mama, how can you ask? At least it's not Children's. I'm going to get right on a reading list for us."

Maureen's prayers resulted in Kathleen's willingness to be tested, but she was not a match. When she learned she could not be the heroine, she slipped away again. Maureen, Patrick and Danny were also not matches.

"Makes you wonder a bit, doesn't it?" Mae said to Maureen when the results were in. "Do you think it's possible Ma had a lover?"

"Ma as Mary Magdalene instead of Saint Catriona? I'd rather not go there at this stage in our lives. You're my sister, plain and simple."

Chapter 34

"Courage equal to desire"
Josiah

But Jo was a match.

He hung up the phone after the call from the hospital and found Grace, folding laundry in the bedroom.

"Who was that on the phone?"

"Mass General. I'm a match."

She put down the towel in her hand and crossed the room. "How do you feel?"

"The strangest sensation. A kind of euphoria."

He held out his hands and studied them.

"I can give my mother back her life with what's inside me."

Grace pulled him to sit on the edge of the bed.

"I've been doing a lot of studying about the transplant process. Although it's incredibly intense at the beginning, getting her body ready to receive your cells and assuring that they regenerate, what follows is a long rehabilitation period. She's going to need a lot of care at home. I've been thinking about whether we could do it. Your grandmother is too frail; your dad needs to work."

"You mean, go back to Chappy?"

"Yes. I could probably find part-time work at the hospital or a nursing home and still be able to help your mom. What do you think?"

"I think you're amazing. And also on the same wavelength. I was thinking about it myself, even began looking into jobs on the island. If you're willing, I say we go for it. I feel I owe my mom a lot. I thought my coming home would at least lift her spirits. But now, with the transplant . . ."

"There's something more, Jo. You're not just giving life to your mother."

"What do you mean?"

Grace took the hands he'd been studying with awe and placed them on her belly.

"You've put life in here as well."

A month later the family gathered at Maureen's convent, where Mae and Tobias had been staying during her days of testing and waiting. The next day, Mae would begin the first part of her treatment, destroying her own bone marrow before she received Josiah's.

Izzy came over from Cambridge and Grace and Jo traveled from Amherst. Patrick arrived with the usual bottle of whisky and Danny, on assignment in Germany, sent a telegram. Maureen was hosting a meal that was both a celebration and a benediction.

When they were all seated at the table, Jo stood and cleared his throat to make a toast.

"To my mother, who gave me life and fought for me, both through the courts and later waiting out my own mistakes. She must have known that sooner or later she'd get payback."

Mae smiled and waved away his teasing. Jo continued.

"Grace and I have something else to say tonight." Grace stood and joined him.

"First, we've decided to return to Chappy. Ever since Izzy invited her a few years ago, Grace has been longing to set down roots there. She shares my love of the island and, as you all know, when I met Grace I stopped my wandering. Where she is, is where I want to be. It seems like a good time for me to take the road home."

He stopped and savored the expression on his mother's face. Despite her illness and the anxiety about the risks facing her after tomorrow, her face was illuminated not only by Maureen's candles, but by joy.

"There's more." Everyone around the table stirred as Grace clasped his hand.

"We're bringing someone else with us, who won't arrive until December. Our child will be born on Chappy."

Mae squeezed Tobias' hand; Izzy whooped; Patrick raised his glass; and Maureen whispered "God bless."

1970
Cove Meadow
Chappaquiddick Island

Epilogue

Josiah's blood cells exploded with life inside Mae's body. After months of monitoring and medication, the nourishment of Grace's cooking and nursing, the distractions of Izzy's stories, the steadfastness of Tobias' love and the simple presence of her son, she flourished, defying cancer once again.

When her grandson was born at Christmas, she held Caleb at the window and showed him the Milky Way.

In March, on a hazy, gray day as the ground began to thaw, Jo packed Caleb into a Snugli and paced the land adjacent to his parents' house at Cove Meadow. In a few weeks, they would break ground for his young family's home.

"Your granddad and grandma bought this land for us before they knew we would return. Even though it's not the land I grew up on, it's Wampanoag land, Caleb. Our ancestors lived here hundreds of years ago. They grazed their sheep here and harvested their hay and set their boats in the water from its shore.

"We will try to do the same," he said. But he looked with longing across the water at the familiar contours of Innisfree emerging as the mist lifted. Despite Cove Meadow's place now as the center of the Monroe family, for Josiah it was Innisfree that would always remain the family's heart.

Discussion Questions

1. Although Josiah's decision to leave home is precipitated by the sale of Innisfree, it is the "missing piece" of his history rather than missing the land that drives his journey. Do you think the conflict he feels between his Irish and Wampanoag heritages is understandable? Was Sadie right when she warned Tobias that Josiah would chose the dominant white culture? Does the outside world view Josiah as a white man?

2. Although *The Uneven Road* is essentially the tale of Josiah's search not only for the Keaneys but for his identity, the story is told from the point of view of each member of the Monroe family. Why do you think the author chose to use multiple points of view? Did that work for you?

3. What impact do you think the turbulence of the 1960s—the Vietnam War, cultural changes, political activism—had on Josiah's journey to manhood?

4. One of the themes recurring in both Book One and Book Two is the strength and support provided by women's friendships. What does Lydia bring to the bond between her and Mae? Why is the friendship so fraught for both of them—not only because of the incident with Tobias but also because of Innisfree?

5. Do you think Mae was justified not only in keeping her distance from her family in Boston but also banishing any mention of them to her children? How did that choice affect not only her, but her siblings and her children? What would you have done?

Acknowledgments

My primary thanks for this book go to my readers, who wrote to me emphatically asking me not to skip a generation as I originally intended, but to continue Mae and Tobias' story in Book Two. Because of their enthusiasm, I put aside my well-laid plans, picked up my pen and wove a new episode in the lives of the Monroes. The story of their grandchildren will make its appearance in Book Three.

As the story moved into the 1960s, I was on accustomed terrain—Boston, Northampton and the farm country of Western Massachusetts are as familiar to me as the beaches and woods of Cape Poge. But I did not serve in the armed forces during the Vietnam War and I am therefore indebted to former Green Beret, Lt. Col. Bill Boyd USA (ret), for sharing with me his memories, his scrapbooks and his experiences in the early years of the war. Any errors in my depiction of Josiah's tour of duty at Dak To are mine alone.

My thanks also to Daisy Miller, my first reader, whose hard questions and insightful reactions helped me to hone the tale to its essentials; to Mary-Theresa Hussey, who edited *The Uneven Road* with keen perception and historical accuracy; and to Julie Winberg, who proofread the manuscript with a sharp eye, an ear for the right word and a love of the clearly written sentence.

My final thanks to my husband, Stephan Platzer, whose photos grace the covers of the First Light books and who once again listened every night to the next chapter. It was a very special kind of pillow talk.

Sources of the Chapter Titles

Each of the chapter titles in *The Uneven Road* is a line from a Yeats poem. The source poem is listed below the chapter title.

Chapter 1 "On the grey sand beside the shallow stream"
       Ego Dominus Tuus
Chapter 2 "I have walked and prayed for this young child"
       A Prayer for My Daughter
Chapter 3 "The key is turned on our uncertainty"
       The Stare's Nest by My Window
Chapter 4 "Walking with slow steps"
       The Sad Shepherd
Chapter 5 "You tread on my dreams"
       He Wishes for the Cloths of Heaven
Chapter 6 "The cold wet winds ever blowing"
       The Pity of Love
Chapter 7 "A fire was in my head"
       The Song of Wandering Aengus
Chapter 8 "A frenzied drum"
       A Prayer for My Daughter
Chapter 9 "I have nothing but the embittered sun"
       Lines Written in Dejection
Chapter 10 "I only ask what way my journey lies"
       Cuchulain's Fight With the Sea
Chapter 11 "Love is the crooked thing"
       Brown Penny
Chapter 12 "Dance upon the level shore"
       Who Goes With Fergus?
Chapter 13 "A prayer for my daughter"
       A Prayer for My Daughter
Chapter 14 "Someone called me by my name"
       The Song of Wandering Aengus
Chapter 15 "All disheveled wandering stars"
       Who Goes With Fergus?
Chapter 16 "These are the clouds"
       These Are the Clouds

Chapter 17 "My wall is loosening"
        The Stare's Nest by My Window
Chapter 18 "Here we will moor our lonely ship"
        The Indian to His Love
Chapter 19 "While day its burden on to evening bore"
        Cuchulain's Fight with the Sea
Chapter 20 "A grey gull lost its fear and flew"
        On a Political Prisoner
Chapter 21 "Together in that hour of gentleness"
        Ephemera
Chapter 22 "And the cries of unknown perishing armies beat about my ears"
        The Valley of the Black Pig
Chapter 23 "Gaze no more in the bitter glass"
        The Two Trees
Chapter 24 "She carries in the candles"
        To An Isle in the Water
Chapter 25 "Go gather by the humming sea"
        The Song of the Happy Shepherd
Chapter 26 "Let us try again"
        Solomon and the Witch
Chapter 27 "Now all the truth is out"
        To a Friend Whose Work Has Come to Nothing
Chapter 28 "Once more the storm is howling"
        A Prayer for My Daughter
Chapter 29 "A hunger for the apple on the bough"
        Ego Dominus Tuus
Chapter 30 "Moments of glad grace"
        When You Are Old
Chapter 31 "And he had known at last some tenderness"
        The Man Who Dreamed of Faeryland
Chapter 32 "The darkness drops again"
        The Second Coming
Chapter 33 "The labyrinth of her days"
        Against Unworthy Praise
Chapter 34 "Courage equal to desire"
        No Second Troy
Epilogue

Read an excerpt from Book Three of *First Light*

The Deep Heart's Core

Linda Cardillo

Chapter One

"The islanders have a saying: 'Some come here to heal; others to hide.' I don't think you need a hiding place, as far as I know, but come home to Innisfree and heal, sweetheart."

Elizabeth Innocenti read the words in her grandmother's elegant, spare hand. She had pulled the familiar, cream-colored envelope with the American postage stamp from the stack of mail that sat unread on her desk. She knew by the calendar that it had been nearly a year since her husband, Antonio, had succumbed to the neurodegenerative disease that had first robbed him of his mobility and finally his life. But for Elizabeth, it could have been an hour for the sharp pain that still knifed through her when she woke every morning to the emptiness in her bed, the sheets on his side tight and flat, the pillow without his scent.

She was a widow at thirty-seven, alone now with her child and her in-laws, whose loss of their only son reverberated without consolation throughout the villa in the hills above Florence where they lived together. When her mother-in-law, Adriana Innocenti, wasn't keening in grief, her wails cast out like a forlorn shepherdess seeking an echo, Adriana's deep-set eyes, rimmed in the blue-black smudge of insomnia, stared accusingly at Elizabeth for being alive.

She had always struggled to find acceptance in Adriana's eyes. She had first come to Italy to create the independent project that her progressive New England college required of its students to complete their degrees. A passionate student of history and media arts, she was determined to follow in the footsteps of her idol, Ken Burns, and become a documentary film maker.

She had never anticipated that she would fall in love—with Italy or with Antonio. She had arrived in Florence with a longing for something different and unknown, and so had been open to whatever it offered—quiet afternoons in a Uffizi gallery mesmerized by DaVinci's *Annunciation* or a brilliant morning in the Piazza del Duomo contemplating Ghiberti's bronze doors on the Baptistery. She ate batter-fried zucchini flowers and spaghetti à la carbonara for the first time. She attended parties given by boys in silk shirts who drove Ferraris and lived in palazzos on the Altra'arno.

She met Antonio in the Laurentian Library, where they were both doing research—he for his thesis as a law student and she for the film she was planning that explored the effects of Savonarola's reign on the lives of Florentine women. Antonio, serious and contemplative, had seemed to be immersed in the ancient texts stacked around him on the table they shared without conversation for more than two weeks. A nod or an occasional "Buon giorno" was the extent of his acknowledgment of her existence. And then, one Thursday afternoon, as the discreet bell calling the monks of San Lorenzo to vespers reminded library patrons that it was time to take their leave, he unexpectedly invited her for a coffee.

That first coffee led to another, and then—when he understood why she was in Florence—he took her through the Museo dell'Antica Casa Fiorentina so that she could explore how the women of Savonarola's time had lived.

"You need more than books to understand Florentine life," he told her.

A few weeks later he offered to take her to the *Palio* in Sienna. Like all of Italy to Elizabeth, the *Palio* was both thrilling and incomprehensible—a furious horse race in the city's sloping central piazza; intense and bitter rivalries among neighborhoods vying for the championship; a riot of color as bands and flag throwers in medieval costume marched through the narrow streets and emerged into the open piazza to the roar of the crowds packed around the perimeter. Antonio held onto her in the throng, protecting her from the surge and push. They were surrounded by emotion and passion and intensity to a degree Elizabeth had never experienced before, and she absorbed it through her skin, her ears, her eyes and, finally, when the race was won, through Antonio's kiss. The energy of the crowd and the heightened moment of victory punctuated by trumpets and the triumphant toss of the colors in an arc over them thrust her into an embrace of Italy from which she did not emerge until Antonio's death.

His love for her had been inexplicable to his mother. Despite Elizabeth's willingness to let go of all that tied her to America—family, language, even her New England sense of place and home—she had never been able to win Adriana's respect as her son's wife.

Elizabeth clutched her grandmother's note and went out to the garden of the villa where she and Antonio had spent their married life. La Torre di Bellosguardo was where Antonio had been born and raised. After Elizabeth and Antonio had married, his parents had converted the cinquecento villa into two apartments and insisted that they live there. She walked past the potted lemon trees on the terrace and down the stone steps to the sloping lawn that overlooked the city. The sun glinted on the terra cotta roof of the Duomo. She had lived in Florence for fifteen years, fourteen of them as Antonio's wife. She had borne their son, Matteo, a boy of thirteen who was thoroughly Italian, despite summer visits and alternating Christmases with his American grandparents and extended family. She had been a good wife to Antonio—his confidante and advisor, his lover, his advocate and nurse as his disease had progressed and now, the bereaved mourner at his graveside.

Adriana and Elizabeth could not comfort one another, could not acknowledge that the other's grief compared to her own.

Elizabeth reread her grandmother's letter as the sun slipped behind the hills. In it, Lydia Hammond offered her granddaughter the summer place that she and her late husband had bought decades before on the isolated barrier beach of Cape Poge on Chappaquiddick Island off the coast of Martha's Vineyard—a place that had once sheltered three generations of Hammond children from the day after school let out in June until Labor Day. It was Mae Keaney, the original owner, who had called the place Innisfree, after the poem by Yeats, when it had been her home and a café for fishermen on the bay that she ran for her livelihood. Elizabeth's grandparents kept the name, since that was how the islanders referred to the peninsula. As they had expanded the compound, they kept the connection to Yeats and continued to name additions after his poems. Lydia had called the girls' sleeping cottage "The Linnet," and decorated it with Audubon prints of finches and yellow curtains dotted with birds perched on delicate branches. The boys' cottage had been dubbed "Byzantium," and was filled with sailing gear. Even the tub room, where hours had been spent preening, had the name "The Peacock."

When she was in high school, Elizabeth stumbled upon "The Lake Isle of Innisfree," the poem that had been Mae Keaney's inspiration, and she calligraphied it for her grandparents as a Christmas gift. Lydia had framed it and hung it prominently in the living room of the main house. Enclosed in Lydia's letter was a photocopy of the poem.

> *I will arise and go now, and go to Innisfree,*
> *And a small cabin build there, of clay and wattles made...*
>
> *I will arise and go now, for always night and day*
> *I hear lake water lapping with low sounds by the shore;*
> *While I stand on the roadway, or on the pavements grey,*
> *I hear it in the deep heart's core.*

Elizabeth heard it as well, and decided to go home.

Despite Adriana's antipathy toward her daughter-in-law, Elizabeth's announcement at dinner that she had decided to accept her grandmother's invitation was met not only with disapproval but protest. Not because Elizabeth was leaving, but because, of course, she was taking Matteo with her.

Adriana put down her fork—like everything else in the villa, ancient, heavy with memory and tradition.

"How can you do this to us? Take away the only thing we have left, the only joy that eases my aching heart!"

"Mama, it's only for the summer—the way we used to do before Antonio became ill. You remember that my grandmother has a cottage by the sea. It will be good for Matteo to get away from the city for a few weeks."

She did not add, good for him to get away from his nonna's unbearable sorrow; good for him to be an American child for a while, with cousins to play with and Fourth of July fireworks and baseball games to attend. She also said nothing of her own pain. That this house, Italy, held too many memories for her, too many places where she turned a corner and was brought up sharply by a vividly remembered scene—a caress, a long look across the room, a smile of gratitude and longing.

"If you must go, why can't you go alone? We can take Matteo to the sea, if you think that's so important."

Adriana sniffed, indicating that she considered it unnecessary. She herself would sit in her black dress all summer, locked in her room turning the pages of Antonio's childhood photo albums.

Elizabeth was weary. She had no desire to inflict more pain on her mother-in-law. But she also knew she needed the comfort and healing her grandmother had so wisely recognized. She would not find it in the villa.

She deferred that night from arguing with Adriana. But she wrote to her grandmother to let her know she and Matteo would come in June and quietly began making plans to fly to Boston as soon as school was out.

The struggle with Adriana continued. Elizabeth tried to keep the conversations away from the dinner table after the first night. Matteo was grieving in his own way and the last thing Elizabeth wanted was for him to feel torn between his mother and his nonna. Adriana's suffocating reliance on Matteo as her only hope would only deepen the boy's grief, and Elizabeth knew it was not only for herself that they needed to get away.

When Antonio had been alive—a phrase still unfamiliar and strange to her—she had always backed away from direct confrontation with her mother-in-law. It simply wasn't her nature, and she saw no point in putting Antonio in the position of having to choose. But with her son, it was different. She had no doubt that Adriana loved Matteo. But she knew in her heart that, if ever she was to have a reason to defy Adriana, Matteo was it.

The afternoon after she had booked their flights she found Adriana sitting in the loggia feeding bits of orange to her parrot. Her hair was pulled back into a severe bun, accentuating her high cheekbones. She had once been a fashion model, frequently on the cover of Italian *Vogue*, and even into her sixties, she remained slender and striking, with a dramatic beauty. But since Antonio's death, she had barely eaten and Elizabeth was now struck by how skeletal her face appeared. Unaware that she was being watched, Adriana's fragility was exposed. Elizabeth was stunned by how old she appeared, how vulnerable, and for a few moments her resolve waivered.

I should stay, she thought, knowing that she wouldn't leave Matteo.

And then Adriana saw her and the vulnerability hardened, sheathing her in armor. She cooed to the parrot, wiped her hands and raised her eyebrows that Elizabeth would be seeking her out.

"You've been out?"

"The marketing, some errands. I wanted to talk before Matteo gets home from school."

"Oh, Lisa, you're not going to bring up this idea again of going to America this summer!"

Antonio's family had always called her by the Italian form of her name, Elisabetta. Adriana addressed her by the diminutive, Lisa. To diminish me, Elizabeth had thought. She had never had a nickname in her family—not Liz or Beth or Betsy.

"I'm sorry, Mama. It's not an 'idea.' It's already in motion. I bought the tickets today."

"You would do this, knowing how much it hurts me!"

"Not to hurt you, Mama. But to help Matteo and me. Please understand. The pain is too fresh, the memories in this house too raw. Everywhere I turn I see Antonio's face and am reminded that he is no longer here."

"You want to run away from the memories and forget him! He's not even cold in his grave!"

"No, Mama. Not to forget. Only to find a way to continue living without him."

"You have no idea what it means to bury a child. You cannot fathom a mother's loss."

"I think I can imagine it. I am a mother. Matteo's only a boy, a boy who has lost his father, who needs his mother more than anything right now."

"Then stay here with him."

Adriana's face was taut with both anger and pleading. She was distraught, she was outraged. It was easier for Elizabeth to hold her ground against the anger, and she focused on the demand in her mother-in-law's tone. Adriana didn't want her pity, Elizabeth knew.

"No, Mama. If I am going to be strong enough for Matteo, I need to heal. We need to go."

And she left the loggia, retreating to the thick-walled room with the arched ceiling and deep-set windows that had sheltered her and Antonio throughout their marriage. She ran her fingers along the top of the dark paneling that climbed nearly six feet up the stucco walls. It was rimmed with intricately carved stone pine trees, each one linked to the next by its widespread branches. On their wedding night, Antonio had whispered to her a fantastical tale of the powers of the tree, harboring dreams and wishes within its foliage like magical fruit. It was a story told to him by his grandmother when he'd been a boy unable to sleep.

"We sleep in a bower, protected by the circle of trees. Nothing can harm us within these walls."

But the trees hadn't protected Antonio and no longer offered her the solace of sleep. Her hand snagged on a sharp branch and a splinter dug deep into her ring finger, drawing blood.

She pulled it out and sucked away the beads of red, then curled up on the window seat and wept.

Watch for *The Deep Heart's Core*,
Book Three of First Light

Coming in late 2016

Linda Cardillo is the award-winning author of the critically acclaimed novels *Dancing on Sunday Afternoons, Across the Table* and *The Boat House Café*, as well as novellas and children's fiction.

Linda's First Light series includes Book One, the 2014 novel, *The Boat House Café*, and the current Book Two, *The Uneven Road*. Book Three, *In the Deep Heart's Core*, will be available in late 2016. She is also at work on a trilogy set in 16th century Italy focused on a dynamic group of literary women. The first book in the series, *The Poet*, is based on the life of the poet Vittoria Colonna, the only woman Michelangelo ever loved.

In an earlier life Linda worked as an editor of college textbooks before earning an MBA at Harvard Business School at a time when women made up only 15% of the class. Armed with her Harvard degree, she managed the circulation of *Inc.* magazine during its successful start-up, founded a catering business and then built a career as the author of several works of nonfiction, from articles in *The New York Times* to books on marketing and corporate policy. She later went on to teach creative writing before her debut novel, *Dancing on Sunday Afternoons*, launched Harlequin's Everlasting Love series.

With Ann DeFee, Linda is the co-founder of Bellastoria Press (www.bellastoriapress.com), an independent publisher of books about women with grit and gifts, who not only survive but flourish; and wildly imaginative and colorful children's picture books. Bellastoria Press books have been called everything from lyrical and sparkling to quirky and laugh-out-loud. Readers will find stories told from the heart, with an eye for vivid detail, an ear for snappy dialog and a funny bone that gets exercised regularly.

Linda loves to cook and is happiest when the twelve chairs around her dining room table are filled with people enjoying her food. She speaks four languages, some better than others. She plays the piano every night—sometimes by herself and sometimes in an improvisational duet with her younger son. She does *The New York Times* Sunday crossword puzzle in ink, a practice she learned from her mother. From her mother she also absorbed a love of opera, especially those of Puccini and Verdi, whose music filled her home when she was a child. She once climbed Mt. Kenya and has very curly hair.

Visit Linda's website at www.lindacardillo.com; follow her on Facebook at Linda Cardillo, Author; or write to her at linda@lindacardillo.com.

33714414R00227

Made in the USA
Middletown, DE
24 July 2016